For John

THE KILLSWITCH

Best Wishes,

IAN PARSON

Ian Parson

Copyright (C) 2022 Ian Parson

Layout design and Copyright (C) 2022 by Next Chapter

Published 2022 by Next Chapter

Edited by Charity Rabbiosi

Cover art by CoverMint

This book is a work of fiction. Names, characters, places, and incidents are the product of the author's imagination or are used fictitiously. Any resemblance to actual events, locales, or persons, living or dead, is purely coincidental.

All rights reserved. No part of this book may be reproduced or transmitted in any form or by any means, electronic or mechanical, including photocopying, recording, or by any information storage and retrieval system, without the author's permission.

In memory of Simon 'Sibs' Sibley 1965 – 2022

Dedicated to punks, hackers & ornithologists everywhere

1

1970

Aiden Fitzpatrick was five years old. He strolled along a tree-lined path with a book tucked under his arm. Aiden loved books. He'd spent the afternoon beneath his favourite oak, rolling new words around in his mouth, pretending he knew how to pronounce them and what they meant. He lived just up the hill.

"Where you goin'?"

He looked up at a boy about the same age as him on a bend in the path. The kid wore a Spiderman T-shirt. Aiden smiled. He liked Spiderman and was always up for new friends.

"Where you goin'?" the stranger repeated.

"'Ome," Aiden told him.

"You can't come this way."

"I always go this way."

In the 70s, it was not unusual for small children to make their own way within their locality. Nobody gave it too much thought.

In response to Aiden's statement of fact, the boy held up a stone. He drew back his arm as though about to throw.

"Nobody passes this way!" he declared.

Aiden dropped his book and picked up a stone of his own.

"I am," he said defiantly and launched his missile.

They threw simultaneously. It was impossible to say who actually started it. It didn't really matter. Aiden dived under a shrub on his side of the path and hastily gathered some stones about him.

The other lad ducked behind a tree. It was a good spot. He had the sweep of the path covered. He popped out intermittently, launching missiles. His aim was nothing for Aiden to worry about. But he clearly had a large supply of ammo within easy reach.

The kid had prepared for this at leisure. He'd been waiting for an opponent. It was nothing personal, anyone would do. He just liked stone fights. He was that age. It was the seventies.

He needs the practice, Aiden mused.

He took to firing sparingly, allowing his opponent to run down his superior reserves.

The boys merrily set to, each using their own tactic. They were rather enjoying themselves until they heard a shout.

"Oi!"

It was the park keeper holding his hat in place and jogging towards them. He didn't look best pleased, and to five-year-olds he was big.

"Leg it!" the unknown kid shouted, and Aiden followed him through the rhododendrons, out of the park, and up the main road.

After a few minutes they fell in behind a stationery car. The parkie was no longer chasing them. Once they'd left the boundary of his responsibility he didn't care.

"You're not a bad shot," the kid told Aiden.

"Thanks," Aiden replied. "You need practice."

The kid smiled. "Do you live round 'ere?"
Aiden pointed up the hill. "Up there."
"I'm Stevie."
"Aiden."
They beamed at each other and that was it. They might never meet again, but if they did, they were already buddies.

2

A few weeks later, and it was Aiden's first day at school. He heard the alarm go off in his mum's bedroom.

"Aiden!" she shouted across the landing. "Get up!"

"I am up."

He'd already eaten a bowl of rice Krispies and drunk a glass of milk. Now he was browsing a comic.

"Don't leave a mess in that kitchen!" his mother shouted.

He ignored her and glanced at the clock. Eight-thirty. The school started at nine. It was only a five-minute walk. He carried on reading.

At a quarter to the hour his mum poked her head around the kitchen door. She stood there in her dressing gown with her hair ruffled. She seemed more subdued than normal. "You better not be late."

He glanced at the clock again. "I won't."

She hovered in the doorway, and he couldn't concentrate on his comic.

"I might as well go," he announced, sliding back his chair.

His mum tried to give him a kiss on the cheek. It was

clumsy, awkward. Neither of them were used to shows of affection.

"See ya," he said, squeezing past her.

"Don't take no shit," she called after his tiny departing form. "And learn something."

At the school gates, hordes of parents and children buzzed around. The noise was deafening. Aiden slowed his walk as he approached. He glanced suspiciously at all the kissing and cuddling. He skulked to a parked car and leaned on the front wing. All the other kids had somebody to see them off. He felt like a misfit. Not that he wanted his mother present; she would only find a way to embarrass him. But it would have been nice to have somebody.

"Aiden!" He heard his name being called and was stupidly grateful. "Are you startin' today?"

It was Stevie, his stone-throwing pal. Things were looking up.

"Yeah."

"Me too."

They beamed at each other.

"Mum, this is Aiden, my friend from the park."

"Hello, Aiden."

He looked up at an impressively tidy woman. Her hair and makeup were immaculate and her coat well cared for. She wore it with the collar turned up—

Like a movie star, Aiden thought.

"Hello," he mumbled.

"So, you boys are friends? That's nice. Stay close and they'll let you sit together."

They both liked the sound of that. Then a bell clanked above the general hubbub.

"Hold hands, quick," Stevie's mother whispered. "Say you're together."

They did as she suggested. They clung tightly to each other as the group of new recruits shuffled towards the gate.

Very soon, they were standing before an ancient-looking man. Aiden looked up at tufts of hair protruding from his nostrils. Stevie noted the coating of dandruff halfway down his shoulders.

"Names?" he barked.

"Aiden Fitzpatrick."

He ticked his sheet of paper.

"Stevie Williams."

He ticked again.

"Go through," he instructed.

A young woman hovered behind the door.

"Go through and find a chair," she said.

They did.

The room filled up with noisy five-year-olds until the woman finally closed the door behind herself.

"Good morning, children, my name is Miss Anderson."

An expectant hush fell over the room.

"The seat you are now in will be your place for the rest of the school term."

The boys beamed at each other. It felt like a victory.

"We're going to stay best friends forever." Aiden whispered

3

A few years passed. Aiden was eight now.

"Are you awake yet?" His mother's voice blew across the landing.

"Yeah," he called back.

He'd been awake for ages, lying on his bed, reading how the Victorians had built the London tube network. It blew his mind that this had actually been made to work, and that it still worked over a hundred years later.

He rolled a new phrase around his mouth.

"Metropolitan Line." He said it aloud purely because he liked the sound of it. He was improving his vocabulary at an alarming rate.

"Metropolitan Line," he whispered softly.

"Get me a cup o' tea," his mother shouted from her bedroom.

Aiden went to the kitchen.

As he waited for the kettle to boil, he threw an empty wine bottle into the bin.

"'Ere." He plonked a mug of sweet tea on the floor beside her bed.

"I threw the empty away," he said. She smiled sarcastically.

"I 'eard you chuckin' glass around." There was a *don't judge me* air about her.

"I'm goin' to Stevie's," he announced and turned on his heel.

"They don't want you round there this time o' the morning!"

He ignored her.

The streets were filled with people heading to their daily tasks. Aiden was suspicious of them all. He used the quieter back lanes. He never approached Stevie's house from the front door. Besides, you never knew what you might find in the lanes. Once he'd come across a pile of books in perfect condition.

From the cobbles, he looked up to Stevie's kitchen window. He could see his mum wrapped in a dressing gown, fussing over the stove.

She saw him and waved him up.

He climbed the back wall using the same hand and foot holds he always used. He slid across the roof of the outside toilet and lowered himself into the yard. He skipped to the door and flicked the latch.

He could hear old Mr. Stanray coughing from the downstairs flat. He hurried up the stairs to where his pal was waiting for him.

"Alright?"

"Alright?"

They smirked at each other.

"Wanna go down the train yard before school?" Stevie asked.

"Yeah alright."

"I wanna check the nest."

Aiden smiled at his little buddy. "Yeah," he said. "Course you do."

"We're going down the yard, mum," Stevie shouted.

"Not on an empty stomach. Come on, come on, get in here."

She ushered them to the little table that took up half the kitchen.

"'Ow's your mum?" she asked pleasantly as she fried bacon

whilst spreading margarine and red sauce onto slices of day-old white bread.

"Alright."

Stevie watched a sparrow on the wall outside. "'Urry up, mum."

"Alright, keep your hair on." She raised an eyebrow at Aiden. He smiled at her.

"We wanna go down the yard."

"'Ave you got time?"

There was no response.

"Stevie?"

He glanced towards her, then back at the sparrow. A small flock had joined it.

"What? Yeah?" he said.

"I don't want Mr. Scott phoning me up an' telling me you was late for class."

"We won't be." Aiden immediately jumped to his friend's assistance.

"There's a blackbird nest in the old carriages," Stevie said.

"I know, dear," his mother smiled. "You 'ave mentioned it once or twice."

She winked at Aiden, and he smiled back. They were sharing a moment about Stevie's ornithological obsession, but there was more to it than that.

Aiden was feeling something to do with sex because her dressing gown was gaping around the cleavage.

"The chicks 'ave hatched. I don't want to miss them fledging," Stevie said.

"I know, dear," she winked again. "But you mustn't be late for school."

"I know," he agreed.

Stevie was as obsessed by birds as Aiden was by books.

They would walk for miles on the back of the flimsiest rumour trying to spot some feathered delight.

Stevie would climb up trees or rummage in bushes. Aiden had peace to read.

Through roaming they developed an excellent knowledge of the city. Knew which areas you risked a beating, and where the kids were friendly.

Inevitably they were forced to defend themselves from time to time. Aiden taught Stevie to launch a rock with unerring accuracy. Stevie added it to his arsenal and nurtured his growing reputation as a fighter.

In the 70s, towns and cities throughout the land were still littered with bombsites. Thirty years after the war had ended, there were still many shortages. Rocks and stones were not among them. Children regularly left trails of broken bottles in their wake. It was the seventies. Little boys smashed glass. Nobody cared.

4

Stevie's father Tommy owned a lorry which he used for removals. He also had a yard and a warehouse to store furniture. He was a no-nonsense, fun-loving guy. He treated the boys better than anyone Aiden knew.

On Wednesday nights he took them to the big sports centre. They swam up and down the pool under the strict eye of the coaches. Afterwards Tommy would give them five pence each to buy sweets. That was the highlight of the evening.

Invariably, Aiden would be allowed to sleep over. Tommy let them stay up late and watch the sport with him. He had a real gift for sarcasm. He criticised footballers and snooker players, even the boxers.

He talked as though he genuinely believed he could do better. Aiden found him hilarious. Stevie found him embarrassing.

At weekends Stevie's parents held parties after the pubs closed. These culminated in Irish singsongs. Sometimes the male patrons got argumentative and Stevie's mum made them take it outside where arguments turned to fisticuffs.

The boys would press their little noses against the glass, betting each other as to which fighter would end up victorious. Stevie would moan and whinge for ages if he ever fell asleep and missed a fight.

5

The boys were ten years old. They were climbing on the warehouse opposite the house. Stevie was a natural. He flew across the brickwork. Aiden was more careful. He concentrated harder but was equally happy up near the roof. At first, they didn't notice Stevie's sister Beverley come out. She slammed the gate, which got their attention. She was wearing outrageously high platform shoes. Her blue jeans had a tartan strip down the outside of each leg, making sure everyone knew she loved the *Bay City Rollers*.

She had on a bright yellow blouse with ruffled cuffs and a multicoloured, stripy woollen tank top with a huge badge of the Rollers in the middle.

Her hair at the back was long and feathered. Her fringe lined up perfectly with her eyebrows.

She thought she looked the absolute business. Aiden agreed silently but wholeheartedly.

His vantage position offered a tantalising glimpse of white bra strap running across her shoulder.

"What are you losers doing?" she demanded to know.

"We ain't losers," Stevie shot back.

He was dangerously high. Right where the drainpipe connected to the guttering. Practically on the roof. Fortunately, Health and Safety laws didn't exist yet. So it was all good.

"What's the matter? Won't no girls play with you?" she called up sarcastically.

"We can play with girls if we want," Stevie protested.

"We got plenty o' girls to play with," Aiden piped up. He had moved onto a narrow little windowsill. It looked as precarious as it was.

She sniggered. "I would 'ave thought you'd be playin' down the church, little Stevie."

She called him *little Stevie* to wind him up. It never used to bother him when he was little. But now that he was double figures, he disliked the moniker intensely.

"I don't go church!" he spat out contemptuously.

"I thought you liked birds?"

"Uh?"

She moved, and Aiden stared at her bra strap again. For some reason it unnerved him.

"I said, I thought you liked birds."

"So?" her brother muttered defiantly.

"So there's some bird nesting on the spire. A kestrel I think."

"I know that."

"Yeah, sure." She folded her arms, somehow taunting Aiden. "I know about all the birds around here."

"Yeah, the feathered kind maybe."

"We know about girls."

Aiden joined in. "Yeah, we know plenty."

She shook her head, and her breasts wobbled. Aiden nearly fell off his window ledge.

"Aw, bless," she uttered sarcastically before throwing her cigarette butt on the ground and heading back to the house.

"Let's go down the church," Stevie called as soon as she was gone. "If we sit quiet, they'll come."

They climbed down and marched off without a care in the world.

6

Two more years passed.

A male blackbird sat on a thick bramble. He'd chosen the highest point in the dense jumble of thorns.

His feathers were shiny. His beak bright yellow and his eyes sparkled. He was king of all he surveyed.

He let forth a burst of complex song. Then pecked half-heartedly at a berry by his feet.

Not quite ripe but it was wise to keep tabs on such things.

The thicket he perched on ran down to a disused railway yard. Old rusty tracks crisscrossed oil-stained, litter-strewn ground. Abandoned carriages slowly rusted.

Not many years ago, the noise down here was deafening. Men shouted, cranes turned, and heavy machinery rattled and clanked. Now it was the calming drone of bees, the gentle buzz of insects, the melodic harmonies of birdsong that filled the air. No trains had passed this way for a long time.

Nature as always had reclaimed the territory.

A female blackbird scooped in and perched on top of a carriage. She called to her mate.

She was dull. Her feathers were ruffled and unkempt, as though she'd no time to preen. As though she'd been busy caring for demanding offspring.

In reply the male let forth another complex tune.

It was designed to reassure her, whilst warding off potential competitors for his mate, his territory, his soon to be ripe berries.

Beneath the disused carriage, Stevie closely followed every nuance of the exchange.

To him, these were majestic creatures living in a parallel world. A world that, if he was patient, offered tantalising glimpses of itself through the behaviour of its inhabitants.

Stevie Williams may be just twelve years old, but he has an incredibly mature understanding of the natural world.

Humans he didn't get. Everyone kept telling him he was lucky to be born here. How could that be right? Imagine living in a country with parrots for example. Surely they were the lucky ones, whoever they were.

Stevie knew the birdwatching made him a misfit. He told himself it didn't matter.

But still he wanted to belong, to feel acceptance. In the animal kingdom, he found what human society denied him. Creatures didn't judge.

He moved slightly, and the blackbird took off, screaming a warning as it flew.

Stevie didn't want to cause undue alarm. He dragged himself backwards and the calls grew less frantic. He found Aiden leaning against a carriage.

"Hey."

"Hey." He closed his book. "Did you see 'em?"

Stevie nodded. "Didn't you hear 'em?"

"I was readin'."

"You must 'ave heard them?"

"I was readin'."

"Come on. Let's go."

They walked along the tracks until they were beneath a huge bridge. Traffic buzzed on the road above them. A giant billboard that hadn't been there yesterday blocked their path.

"Land acquired for development by 'The Trust'. What's that?" Stevie asked.

"Development! They're going to develop."

Stevie looked at him blankly.

"They're goin' to build down 'ere," his literary friend told him.

"Oh." Stevie pondered for a moment. "That's bullshit. Why does everythin' 'ave to change?" He kicked a can in frustration.

"They call it progress."

"Fuck progress. Where's the wildlife meant to go?"

"There's nothin' we can do," Aiden reminded him.

"It's bullshit," Stevie muttered angrily. "If I was king I wouldn't allow it. I'd have a big switch, and when they change things I don't like, I could just flick the switch and change it back again."

Aiden joined in the game. "Yeah and if it was a good day, I'd flick the switch and have the day all over again."

"Yeah," Stevie agreed. "An' if a day is shit, we can flick the switch and move onto the next one."

Both boys had passed the 11-plus. They were smart kids capable of great things. They'd been at grammar school for a year now.

Unfortunately, Aiden had read books that contradicted things the school taught. He began to suspect they were being conned. Groomed into accepting an official narrative. He wanted to learn, but his questions in class were not appreciated. He was actually being advised to read less. Read less! Like he was supposed to embrace ignorance. It was bullshit.

"Sir, if there are five thousand religions being practiced on Earth. How do we know ours is the right one?"

"Stop showing off, boy, and don't be ridiculous," had come the answer.

He sat quietly fuming at the back of the class. It had been a genuine question.

I don't belong here. I'm not like these people.

Meanwhile Stevie was being made to feel like an outsider because he preferred football to rugby and because he liked birdwatching.

"This is a rugby school," they insisted. "Football is for plebs and birdwatching is not a career. At best it's a genteel past time for spinsters."

He was told to leave childish things behind and focus on passing exams.

And they had the nerve to call it an education. It was absurd.

Stevie read the small print and cursed again.

"Private property," he fumed. "No trespassing! Fuck that."

He yanked the sign from the ground and threw it into the brambles.

Aiden knew his pal was just letting off steam. He wasn't really angry about some development.

It was change, it was school. It was the annoying realisation they were different. That boys like them weren't supposed to be into literature and ornithology. It was everything. It was life.

"It'll all work out." He instinctively tried to reassure his pal.

"They want me to stop boxing, too," Stevie whined.

"It's shit," Aiden sympathised.

"People are shit," Stevie replied darkly. "I wanna learn to knock the stupid smiles off their faces."

"You can already do that."

"I wanna learn to hit harder."

"Well, don't hit me."

"I'd never do that."

"Good, 'cos I'd have to hit you with a rock to make it fair."

Stevie smiled. They both knew he'd never do that either. "You comin' back to mine?"

Aiden nodded gratefully and they started to run. Small children again, the gathering storm clouds temporarily forgotten.

7

The Trust was started by a group of ruthless investment bankers. They claimed to be in it for the money but what they really craved was power. They believed the rumours. Tim Berners Lee's *Global Information Highway* would prove to be a real game changer. A real kingmaker.

They held extremely high opinions of themselves and extremely low opinions of everyone else. They believed theirs was a God-given right to all the best things life could offer. The suffering of others they considered a price worth paying.

Their first acquisition was a factory in the North. The place was allowed to fall into decline. The staff were tricked out of redundancy pay. Assets were stripped out and sold off. Using substandard materials, the land was redeveloped.

They repeated the trick again and again, destroying lives every time, but the profits rolled in.

Once they'd built up the necessary finances, they branched into commodities. If you lacked morals this was practically a license to print money. They targeted third world countries and tied naive villagers into long-term contracts for raw materials.

Once they controlled supply, the price and the profits rose exponentially. This money was invested in the next phase of the Trust's expansion.

Processed food was the new game in town.

Contracts were won to supply prisons, schools, and hospitals.

Advertisers were paid small fortunes to entice ordinary people away from the stove and towards the microwave. The Trust employed teams of scientists who worked out the precise combination of sugar and salt to make a product irresistible.

In a few short years, the Trust controlled 70% of what was eaten in the country. Public Health was not a deciding factor in how they ran the operation. Profit margins were all that mattered.

Next they moved into the hospital bed market. Competitors were swallowed up at a phenomenal rate.

In a short space of time, nobody else was large enough to fulfil contracts for health providers. They ruffled a few feathers along the way and there were court cases. But it all worked out in their favour.

Newspaper owners who stuck with them through the lengthy period of litigation were suitably rewarded afterwards. It became a symbiotic relationship.

Within a decade of conception, the Trust were the largest company in the FTSE 100 and still growing fast.

Greedy new members came aboard.

These included politicians more influenced by money than morality. Whose loyalty was to the bottom line not the constituents. Such men were going to be invaluable in the days ahead. The current laws were written for analogue. The dawning era would be digital. New legislation was going to be needed. Having policy makers on the board of directors would ensure these laws went whichever way the Trust hoped.

Taking advantage of cutting-edge technology would allow them to bypass the current outdated political system.

They realised that one day computers would be commonplace.

In head office, a young man addressed the board. He had only been at the Trust for a year. Now here he was in the most executive of boardrooms, trying to explain computers to, in his opinion, a group of doddery old men.

"So, in the future, all business interaction will be conducted through a network of computers. Machines capable of talking to each other and doing the sums in a fraction of the time it would take a human."

Blank faces stared back at him. So he continued.

"And information will be stored within the computer. People will be able to access their files from anywhere in the world."

"There'll be no paperwork?" someone asked doubtfully.

"That's right."

"Seems unlikely."

Somebody else tutted at the back of the room.

The young man ignored it and began to wrap things up. "And that concludes the presentation for today, gentlemen. Are there any questions?"

"How do we control this?"

"Nobody will have overall control."

"That's preposterous, why would we allow such a thing? Let's outlaw it." He glanced down at his notes. "This, Global Information Highway, nip it in the bud so to speak. I don't like it. It's subversive. I want it outlawed."

"Unfortunately, the technology has already been developed, sir. The scientists in question have acquired the necessary patents and bequeathed their work to the human race in perpetuity and for free. This is happening whether we like it or not, and control has been relinquished, forever."

"I don't like it. People have newspapers and television for information. It's a perfectly good system where the content is easily controlled. Why can't they be satisfied with that?"

"People like the idea of being able to communicate directly."

"But we will know what they are saying to each other? At least assure me of that."

The young man tried a different tack. "As I was saying just now, sir. There was recently a landmark case. The judges have allowed encryption."

"Encryption." He spat the word from his mouth as though he'd never come across it before and didn't like the taste of it.

The young man wanted to scream. He'd explained all this not five minutes ago. Fortunately for him someone else stepped in.

"Naturally, we are appealing the court's decision. Trying to make encryption illegal for the masses, sir. If we can't stop this thing, we can at least stop people messaging each other privately, for free."

"That's preposterous. It would allow our enemies to join forces with no effort whatsoever. Any reasonable judge should be able to see that's dangerous."

"If the judicial system find against us again, I propose we employ this young man's two-pronged assault."

"The old boy smiled a little at the suggestion.

"Run it by us again," he said.

The young man smiled nervously, and wiped sweat from his forehead. He wasn't going to get away so soon after all.

"As I say, currently no laws exist around the new technology. For example, it would be simple to discredit anyone we choose. And they would have no legal recourse."

"Were we to lose the appeal for example, it wouldn't take much to portray the judiciary as 'enemies of the people' whilst publicly throwing doubt on their narrative every step of the way."

"Question their narrative?"

"Yes, sir, with all guns blazing."

The chairman smiled. "Kindly elaborate once more."

"If they claim the moon is made of moon rock, we flood this world wide web with documents, photographs, letters, anything. All claiming it is cheese, or granite, or even soap, it doesn't matter. What matters is reaching a point where confusion reigns. Doubt is cast far and wide and the facts get lost in the miasma."

"World Wide Web?'

"It's what they are now calling the Global Highway, sir."

"And we can use this World Wide Web to spread false messaging?"

"We can, sir."

"Is anyone likely to cause a nuisance?"

"There are a handful of fanatics, sir. Kids really. They managed to win the encryption case despite no financial backing. They blindsided us on this, but we know who they are now. We do not anticipate any surprises in future."

"Fanatics, you say?"

"Yes, sir."

"Fanatics make me nervous. They never know when they are beaten."

"They are only fanatical about computers, sir. We are not talking hardened revolutionaries here. They see themselves as moral crusaders, that's all. They got so obsessed with the public's right to privacy they started a campaign. It was unexpected and the public took their side."

"They must be shut down." The chairman smiled unpleasantly. "Let this be their last taste of victory."

"Yes, sir."

"And I want you to find a way to close down this World Wide Web. One day we might have to."

"Yes, sir."

"It would be marvellous to achieve full automation though. Imagine if we could manage without workers."

"Yes sir."

8

At the dawn of the digital age, *encryption* meant nothing to the vast majority of the public.

Thank God for one student who understood it perfectly. His name was Robert Jenkins or RobBob to his friends, and he was outraged the government wanted legal authority to read his emails. He realised this was just the beginning— that digital communication was an excellent alternative to chopping down all the trees. He failed to see how electronic mail was any different from the postal service we all know and love. The continuation of privacy or encryption was imperative.

These new-fangled computers might actually do some good. But only if the common man was allowed encryption. Who was going to communicate anything meaningful if they thought the authorities were reading it over their shoulder?

One of the oldest enshrined laws in history *The right to privacy* was under attack.

RobBob was a true pioneer. He was in at the very beginning. He understood the world of computers was about to explode, and society would never be the same again. He also realised no rules had yet been written. How could they be? The equipment had barely been invented. Until governments caught up, this was as lawless as the old Wild West.

People were going to make mistakes. They needed privacy.

He joined forces with a handful of geeks. They took on the best lawyers at the government's disposal and won.

RobBob had no idea his opponents weren't really the government. Nor that his victory had cost the Trust billions of dollars. He was just an idealistic student who didn't want people reading his emails. He didn't know how the world worked.

Shortly after the court case, the police pulled him as he left his dealer's house.

Two years for possession of narcotics and a further six months for intention to supply illicit drugs. It was an eighth of hash for God's sake. He'd said he was going to share a joint with his girlfriend. No wonder he felt bitter. No wonder he took it personally. As he languished in prison, he reflected on his naivety.

He realised now what they'd meant when they warned him about making enemies in high places. *Now* he realised, with two years staring at four brick walls to look forward to.

At the time, he hadn't listened. He'd simply trusted that he was doing the 'right' thing and it would all work out for the best. He learnt the hard way. Next time, he wouldn't be so stupid.

RobBob was intelligent. He needed stimulation. So for two years he sat in his cell, reading about revolution, learning about crime, and festering. He wasn't being rehabilitated he was being self-radicalised.

Meanwhile, it was fair to say activists were rubbing their hands together in glee at the prospect of long-range secret communication. At last something to even up the struggle a bit.

9

Two years passed.

Aiden and Stevie were up before the headmaster again.

"You have been specifically told not to venture to the far end of the playing fields during lunch recess," the headmaster reminded them.

"There's sparrows nesting down the bottom bank," Stevie explained, gesturing towards the neglected shrubs beyond the rugby pitch.

"You're blaming the fauna for making you misbehave?"

Stevie shrugged. "I'm just telling you why we was down there."

"You are an insolent child, are you not?"

Stevie shrugged again and rolled his eyes for good measure.

"Do you even know what insolent means?"

He shrugged again.

"I do." Aiden offered.

"Was I talking to you boy?"

"I thought you was talking to both of us."

"I was addressing Mr. Williams, but now I'm addressing you. Why are you constantly up before me?"

Aiden looked him right in the eye. "I dunno."

"We prefer being outside, sir," Stevie explained.

"Are you a soldier?" the headmaster asked.

"No, sir," Aiden answered solemnly.

"No chance," Stevie muttered.

The headmaster shot him a sideways look.

"A professional rugby player perhaps?"

"I hate rugby," Stevie mumbled.

"Stupid game," said Aiden.

"Get out!"

They slowly walked in the direction of the classroom. Knowing they were expected to rejoin their fellow pupils but dragging their heels.

"I hate it here," Aiden muttered.

"Me too," Stevie agreed. "Jimmy Johnson said their woodwork teacher's a right laugh."

"I know, an' we get Christian Brothers from the 18th century. They never tell us the truth about nothin'."

"Why are we going back?" Stevie asked.

Aiden stopped and looked at his pal. "I dunno."

"Let's bunk off," Stevie suggested.

"Yeah," Aiden agreed in a heartbeat.

They were inquisitive-minded, intelligent young men. They'd been promised learning, knowledge, and bright minds to pick. They loved those things; the very prospect had made them giddy with excitement. But they'd been lied to, let down, misinformed.

Nobody wanted to feed their insatiable curiosity. They just wanted to fill their heads with outdated nonsense.

And just like that, they were making a choice that would affect them forever.

They strolled in silence through the empty school corridors; climbed the perimeter wall and headed for the city centre.

They removed their school ties, put their collars up, and felt deliciously naughty.

The top end of town was crowded with housewives and young mothers pushing prams. Despite their half-baked attempt at disguising themselves, they attracted enough curious looks to feel conspicuous. They kept moving to the bottom of town.

Stevie poked Aiden in the side.

"Look," he whispered, nodding ahead. And there was an element to his tone that Aiden had never noticed before. It was somewhere between awe and confusion.

He had spotted some youngsters. Not schoolkids but close to their own age.

They were perched in a colourful row on a low wall outside a record shop. They had a giant ghetto blaster belting out the fastest tune either boy had ever heard.

"Punks," Stevie whispered.

"Yeah," Aiden agreed.

They settled self-consciously on the same wall, albeit maintaining a wary distance.

They observed the uncouth, loud, scruffy, music lovers and were deeply impressed.

These people did not give a fuck.

Neither of them had ever heard anything like it. This was not music you'd ever hear on Radio 1 or the tunes that came out of Beverley's room.

This was new, loud, obnoxious, interesting. It spoke to them the way it spoke to misfits and disillusioned teenagers the length and breadth of the land. They identified immediately and nothing would ever be the same again.

Aiden was tapping his foot.

"You like this?" Suddenly right in his face, asking a question, and demanding an answer was a girl.

He nodded.

Her friend came alongside her. She was wearing a black

leather jacket covered in studs. Her hair was jet black with flame red tips. The boys were well impressed.

"He likes The Clash."

"Do you?" the second girl asked, slightly aggressively he felt.

"Yeah." he assumed that was the band he and the whole street were being forced to listen to.

"Turn that rubbish off!" screamed a young hipster walking past with his pals.

"Yeah, its crap," added another.

The punks ignored them. The hecklers moved along. The music stayed.

Aiden was amazed. How did that not end in violence? It went against everything life had taught him so far. He was even more impressed now.

"Dickheads," one of the punk girls muttered.

"Yeah," Stevie agreed enthusiastically.

She smiled at him. "So," she thrust her chin forward, "why aren't you at school?"

Stevie shrugged and went bright red.

"Why'd you think we should be at school?"

"Aw, ain't he cute." She patted his crimson cheek.

"Yeah," her friend agreed.

"Can I keep him?"

"Course you can."

"What's your name?" she purred.

Stevie was way out of his depth. This girl was toying with him the way a cat does a mouse. "Stevie."

"An' who's this?" She nodded her head towards Aiden.

"Aiden."

"What's your name?" Stevie asked.

"Easy tiger." She giggled.

It was the sexiest thing he had ever heard.

She looked them both up and down as though making a decision.

"I'm Nikki," she said, "and this is Karen."

"Nikki with an i," she added for clarity.

"Two i's then?" Aiden said, slightly pedantically he realised, but he couldn't help himself.

"Yeah," she smiled at him. It was a kind smile.

Nikki with an 'i' wrapped an arm around Stevie's neck and messed up his hair.

"Nikki two i's, that's me."

Both girls laughed so the boys joined in. Nervously, enthusiastically, with a hint of wonderment and way, way out of their comfort zones.

Karen sat down alongside Aiden.

"So you like punk?"

"Yeah, what I've heard so far," he said— meaning what they were listening to right now.

"What else do you like?"

"I like readin'."

"Readin'?"

"Yeah."

"Me too."

Meanwhile Nikki plonked herself down next to Stevie. She was so close she was almost on his lap. He'd never been this close to a girl before. She threaded her hand into the crook of his arm. "Do you like readin' too?"

"Not really."

"Me neither," she confessed. "I'm more of a do'er. You know, a hands-on kind of girl."

Stevie wasn't sure what that meant, but he thought she was flirting with him. He couldn't believe his luck. Just slipping her hand into the crook of his arm had brought the old captain to attention, so nothing else really mattered.

He sneaked a glance at her. She was smiling knowingly. She squeezed his hand.

"So what do you do?" she asked. "You know, when you're not reading?"

"I like birds." He regretted it as soon as the words were out.

"Oh, yeah?" She squeezed his hand harder and laughed.

He was on the verge of being mortified.

"I bet you do." She poked him playfully in the ribs.

My god, if this is what I'm missing when I'm at school I'm never going back. "The feathered kind," he added.

"Yeah of course, budgies and robins an' that." She squeezed his hand again. She might as well have been squeezing his cock the effect it was having on him. "Not the other kind?" she asked quietly.

"Yeah, course!"

"You're going red."

"I'm not."

He looked along the wall. Nobody was paying them a blind bit of attention. His dick felt like it was going to burst through his trousers.

"I like your necklace." It was all he could think of.

She smiled and wrapped her arms around the back of his head. "I like you."

Karen was jabbering away at Aiden. He nodded here and there but didn't understand half the words she was saying.

They were sitting in a row, facing a record shop. Literally staring at the giant display window. They couldn't help but notice when a member of staff appeared behind the glass.

"What's he doing?" Nikki wondered aloud.

"He's taking down a poster," Stevie pointed out.

Nikki squeezed his hand hard. "We can see that!"

They watched the employee unroll a giant poster and in no hurry whatsoever, tape it to the window.

The poster contained all the usual information—

Tickets available here.

18+ only.

The name of the venue, the time the doors opened, the date (Aiden worked out instantly it was a Saturday) and across the centre in large neon green type, most importantly of all, the name of the band, The Clash.

"Wow," muttered Nikki. "They're coming here?"

In the late 70s/early 80s, music actually mattered. It had outgrown its innocent teenybopper beginnings and was not yet all about the money.

Technological developments produced cutting edge recording and amplification techniques. The sound quality was unlike anything that had gone before.

Record companies were making so much money they were prepared to give musicians time to refine their art.

Mix in the squat, dole culture where wannabe rock stars could bounce off each other, and some meaningful tunes were being hammered out. New stuff, experimental stuff, stuff your parents hated, stuff that actually dictated your direction in life.

Bands like The Clash were creating a new future. A whole generation of deprived kids were being told not to settle for the crumbs on offer.

Up and down the land, thousands were determined to help themselves to a slice of the actual pie. Take ownership of their shit, mundane, boring life and change it. This seismic shift occurred on an industrial scale, and it terrified the establishment.

However these were violent times. It was risky to stand out from the crowd.

If you were a punk in a Teddy boy club or a mod in a biker bar you were in big trouble.

Aiden always tried to avoid casual violence. Stevie on the other hand had loved a good fight since the very first time they met.

He'd been a promising boxer but never got on with the discipline required for the ring.

Street brawls on the other hand required no rules.

If he thought it was going to kick off, he didn't bother with questions or warnings. He only had one modus operandi. Punch first, catch them with another as they fell then he and Aiden would be running away before anyone could retaliate.

Kids in the 70s knew no better. Violence was not only tolerated it was seen as manly.

Besides if the occasional punch in the mouth was the price to be paid for membership to the punk tribe it was worth it.

They were young. Life on the edge was exciting. They didn't stop to consider the possibility of falling off.

On the way home from first contact with Nikki, Stevie couldn't hide his glee.

"Did you see her?" he asked for the umpteenth time.

Aiden smiled. He usually only saw his pal excited when he'd just beaten the shit out of someone.

"Yeah."

"That is one sexy girl."

"Yeah I know."

"I'm going on about her too much aren't I?"

"It's OK."

"Karen seems nice as well."

"Yeah."

"What's the matter? You don't fancy her? Maybe you should find a girl like Nikki. Did you see her legs?"

"Yeah."

"I'm gonna marry that girl."

10

Stevie turned up for class a few days before the gig with blood red hair. He thought wearing it down flat made it acceptable for school, presumed the staff would appreciate that he hadn't sprayed it up into full Mohican.

They didn't see it that way at all. He was sent to the headmaster to explain himself.

"What difference does it make? I can still read and write whatever my hair looks like."

The head was really struggling. The actual offence was bad enough, but this gutter urchin genuinely seemed to not care about the reputation of the school.

"There is no excuse, no excuse for what you have done today."

"Well," Stevie seemed not to have heard, "my excuse is that I'm going to a gig this weekend and last night was the only time my girlfriend could do my hair."

"What?"

Stevie completely ignored the obvious fury in the face of the respected gentleman facing him across the desk.

"Last night was the only time it was convenient…"

"I heard you, boy. Your inability to comprehend the gravity of the situation leaves me with no choice. You are suspended forthwith."

Stevie turned on his heel and made for the door.

He was about to turn the handle when he heard the head's voice behind him.

"I haven't given you permission to leave."

Stevie wasn't best pleased himself. He just wanted to get out of there.

He turned to face the headmaster.

"Haven't we finished?" he asked.

"I have never in all my years met a young man as insolent and..."

Stevie cut him off again. "Oh. This is a complaint? Put it down on a form then and send it to the complaints department!"

And he left the office, slamming the door as he did so.

11

It was the day of the gig. Punks began to gather around the venue from early in the morning.

They preened up and down the pavement, judging their peers without mercy. They approved or disapproved of things they wore, things they said, and most of all their hair.

This was an age when styling products consisted of shampoo, conditioner, hairspray and Brylcreem. If you wanted something out of the norm you had to be creative. You had to steal ideas off other people.

You couldn't look online or in custom magazines. Those things hadn't been invented yet. There was *Sounds* and *NME* and that was it. Neither contained handy fashion tips for budding punk rockers. If they had, no self-respecting rebel would ever dream of taking such advice.

You had to create your own look and you had to be seen with it before somebody else got there first.

Nikki spent hours deciding what to wear. She and Stevie were at the venue long before it was due to open its doors. This was their town, and she was the queen of the scene. She hadn't put in all that effort to turn up at the last minute. As far as she was concerned, she was part of the show.

Stevie was in love. He just wanted her to be happy. He'd agree to wear whatever she asked. He knew it meant a lot to her, and he wanted to be supportive.

Today Stevie was wearing skin-tight tartan bondage trousers covered in zips. His neon pink T-shirt had an anti-vivisection image emblazoned across the front. One sleeve and the front were ripped open then repaired with bright red cotton, signifying dead animals. He looked a mess. He looked amazing. He wanted someone he knew to see him. He didn't have to wait long.

Here came Aiden. He too had made an effort. Ripped his jeans and spiked up his hair a bit but they were in different leagues. If this was a competition there could only be one winner.

"You look great," Aiden conceded.

"Cheers. I know."

There was a dog lead attached to a collar around Stevie's neck. He flicked the lead, drawing attention to it as though he wanted Aiden to comment.

"What's with the lead?"

"Here watch this."

Nikki was holding the other end of it and paying close attention.

"Ready?" Stevie addressed her.

She nodded, then said at the top of her lungs, "I got a dog; he's big and strong. He barks a lot; his teeth are long."

She actually had a good voice. It rose confidently above the general din of the crowd. People turned and stared. This was a show. This was entertaining.

It was Stevie's turn to take the stage. "Bark, Bark, Bark."

And he was off, barking at those in the queue whilst Nikki kept a tight hold. Him appearing to strain at the leash. Her pretending it was a struggle to keep control. It was pure living theatre.

After a few minutes Stevie was all barked out. He took a bow and Nikki curtsied.

"Ladies and gentlemen, the next performance will be when we want it to be," she announced to no one in particular.

Aiden started clapping and the crowd broke into impromptu applause and catcalls. Nikki and Stevie tried to appear unfazed.

At this point a guy approached them. Menace filled the space around him as though it were a physical entity. His T-shirt was little more than a faded rag held together with safety pins. Front and back it bore the logo of an obscure German anarchist band. His head was shiny bald except for a bright red Mohawk. It had been hair sprayed within an inch of its life and stuck out from his forehead to his neck half a metre into the air. He wore thick black eyeliner that added to the air of danger. His ears were full of metal. His grubby, skin-tight black jeans were tucked into military style boots that ran halfway up his legs.

It was like in the movies when you meet the vampire, and you know you should run away or you're going to die.

The stranger looked Stevie up and down and said, "You're a singer?"

"Yeah."

"You in a band?"

"Not yet."

"I'm looking for a singer for my band."

"Oh?" said Stevie, trying desperately to stay cool.

"You interested?"

"Sure."

"You know the pub down Harmond Street, the Falcon?"

"Yeah."

"We're having a band meeting in the upstairs room. Tomorrow evening nine o'clock."

"I'll be there."

The stranger nodded approval.

"Maybe see you inside?"

"Yeah," Stevie replied as the stranger walked to the front of the queue with three or four mates in tow. Aiden watched him exchange a few words with the doormen who let him in.

"He looks dodgy," Aiden muttered. "Who was that?"

"That's RobBob," Nikki replied. "And if by 'dodgy' you mean a nutter, then yeah, I suppose so."

She started laughing and twisting her fingers in and out of Stevie's. He was playing finger tennis and laughing along with her like the lovesick puppy he was.

"Whadda you mean?" Aiden wanted to know.

"Oh it's just rumours. I'm sure none of it's true," she replied.

Aiden shot a concerned glance towards his pal. "You ain't gonna go, are you?"

"What?"

"Tomorrow, to meet that guy?"

"It's a band meeting," Stevie replied as though that explained everything.

"The Falcon? You know what it's like round there."

"It's not a date. It's a band meeting." He smirked at Nikki to confirm he'd just made a joke. She always praised his lame ass jokes.

"Nice one, babe."

"Yeah, him and some other nutters," Aiden replied. "Sounds dodgy as fuck to me."

Stevie smiled at his mate. "Yeah, but a band."

Aiden shook his head and smiled back. It was pointless trying to make him see sense.

"So you're going?"

"Yeah. Course. He can't be that bad."

Aiden turned to Nikki.

"What's he like Nik?"

"He's fine, really," she said, sounding amused.

"See?"

To Stevie, that was the end of the matter. If he spent his whole life avoiding everyone considered 'bad' he'd never have any friends.

"I'm in a band," he beamed. "I'm a singer in a band."

"Not yet," Aiden cautioned.

"Yeah you are babe," Nikki confirmed.

Aiden wanted his mate to have his moment. "Yeah, yeah you are," he said.

"Hallo, Excuse me?"

She turned around to see a young girl with a camera hanging around her neck. You didn't see many cameras in those days.

"You look amazing," the girl said. "I wondered if I could take your picture?"

Nikki recognised an opportunity when one came along. "Sure."

"Could you stand there in front of the sign?"

Nikki did so, and the girl snapped off a few shots.

"Do you want to be in as well?" she asked Stevie who jumped willingly into the frame and wrapped his arms around Nikki.

"I love your accent," Nikki said.

"Thanks."

"Where are you from?"

"Germany, Berlin."

That is so cool, thought Aiden.

He had obviously clocked her camera but had also noticed her shiny hair, her huge eyes, her long shapely legs, and now she's from Berlin? She was the most exotic creature he had ever seen.

"I'm Nikki."

'Mia,' she replied.

That is such a beautiful name, he thought.
"I'm Aiden," he announced.
She turned towards him and smiled. "Nice to meet you, Aiden."
Their eyes locked, and he was in love.

12

Everyone was nursing hangovers. The day was nearly over when Stevie crawled from Nikki's bed and made his way warily to the band meeting.

The Falcon was a rough, backstreet boozer on the wrong side of town. He knew the area from his childhood. He and Aiden had survived a few stone fights with the local kids back in the day. But he ignored the warning bells in his head. His desire to be the singer in a band was far stronger than any concerns about hostile natives.

You gotta start somewhere, he told himself.

He walked into the pub, and just like in an old Western movie, the place went quiet. All eyes turned to him. He approached the bar and, heart pounding, said as nonchalantly as he could, "I'm here for the band meeting?"

The barman sniffed. His elbows remained firmly planted on the wooden counter. He looked at Stevie and with an expression that remained completely neutral said, "Door round the side, boy."

"Cheers." He tried to appear older with his monosyllabic reply.

The barman nodded.

Stevie avoided eye contact with anyone else and made it out unscathed. Not that he was ever in any danger. They all knew about the band.

This community liked outsiders. Punks were kindred spirits and a new customer base for the pub, the shop, the local dealers. If they caused no trouble they'd be welcome round here.

Stevie found the rickety old door easily enough and banged on it a few times. There was no answer. Not wanting to hang around, he pushed the latch down and the door opened.

"Hello?" he called.

There was no response, so he entered and climbed the stairs. At the top, the very least he hoped to see was a drum kit and a microphone on a stand.

But there was none of that. Just three scruffy punk rockers sitting on hard-backed, wooden chairs.

Stevie was conscious that all eyes were on him.

"Ah, here he is."

RobBob made a sweeping hand gesture. "Take a seat."

There was one empty chair. Stevie took it.

RobBob stood and pointed dramatically at him. "This is our front man," he announced. "Meet Stevie."

He pointed at the next guy. "Paulie," and Paulie half waved.

"And that's Jay."

Jay nodded a greeting.

That was the introductions over with.

"Right," RobBob began, "we are now a band."

He looked around. "We need a name. Any suggestions?"

There was much shuffling of feet before Stevie spoke up.

"The Dogs," he suggested.

He could already see Nikki dragging him round the stage on a lead.

"Why 'dogs'?"

He told them.

"She could do that anyway."

"It needs more," Jay proposed. "The 'something' dogs maybe."

"White Riot?" Paulie suggested.

"Nah," RobBob dismissed the suggestion.

"I love being in a band," Stevie said dreamily, and for the first time the tough guy images they had all been concentrating hard on portraying slipped and just briefly they looked like four excited little boys.

"I love being in the Nasty Dogs," Jay said, his tone suggesting it was a proposition as a band name.

"Nah," came three voices in unison and the tough guy images were safely back in place.

"We don't need a name right now," RobBob declared. "What we do need right now is equipment."

The others nodded agreement. RobBob continued. "Paulie here's got access to a van. Sometimes it's available, sometimes not. But it's here now, right?"

Paulie nodded confirmation.

RobBob carried on. "So we can use it to get some equipment sorted out."

"Now? Nothing's open now," Stevie noted.

He was ignored.

"Right, Paulie?"

Paulie nodded again.

RobBob smiled and it wasn't an expression you would necessarily associate with joy.

"So the next question is: who's gonna play what? Well, I'll tell ya. Paulie is on guitar, Jay on bass, me on drums, and Stevie as I say, our front man"

Nobody objected.

"Any questions?"

Stevie tried again. "Where we gonna get equipment from? At this time of night?"

It was way past 5pm, it was the seventies, and all retail outlets were closed.

Jay made a sort of mocking, snorting noise and shook his head. Paulie sniggered a bit. Stevie didn't ask again.

"Right," RobBob said. "This is where it gets real. Being in a band takes commitment. So if anyone ain't willing to take the Snarling Dogs…" There was a pause to allow objections to the band name but none came, "…seriously they should leave now."

All eyes turned towards Stevie.

"Why are you lookin' at me? I'm committed!"

RobBob smiled that joyless smile. The word *good* slipped from the corner of his mouth.

They were just four misfits in a dingy old room. But they were united, all in it together. They were the Snarling Dogs, prepared to take on all comers in the interests of 'the band'.

Besides what else were they going to do? None of them had a job, nor any prospects of getting one. Misfits went to the back of the queue and the queue was really long. They were kind of forced to make do. Nobody else was going to provide for them.

This was how Punk evolved. Young outcasts with the attitude required to do their own thing and to hell with what other people said.

"Right," RobBob declared. "One of these each."

He threw a small, soft black object to each of them before rising from his chair and heading to the door. "Let's go start a band," he said.

"Yeah," agreed Paulie.

"Fuckin' A," said Jay.

Stevie looked down at what he was holding. It was a beanie hat with holes cut out for the eyes. He followed the others downstairs.

. . .

Twenty minutes later they were sitting in the van on a suburban side street. It was dark, and there was nobody about. Stevie was already breathing heavily. The balaclava covering his face was hot.

They all had them on, pulled down so only the eyes were visible.

"Don't forget," RobBob said as he climbed out the passenger side. "In an' out. And keep it running," he muttered to Paulie as he gently closed his door. He lifted the rear handle, and Stevie and Jay climbed quietly out. They left the back doors wide open.

"This way," RobBob hissed.

The three dark figures walked in single file up an alley towards a row of garages.

RobBob stopped at the first one.

He pulled a crowbar from inside his jacket and as quick as a flash it was hooked under the tiny gap at the base of the big metal door. He leant down on the other end of his bar and pushed. He created a big enough gap for them to get their hands in.

He laid the crowbar gently on the ground and they lined up along the door.

"On the count of three, pull," RobBob whispered.

"Won't it be noisy?" Stevie whispered back.

"One, Two, Three."

They pulled in unison. Immediately the grating sound of metal on concrete echoed off the walls around them. All attempts at stealth were abandoned.

"Be quick," RobBob muttered.

There was enough light coming through the mangled door for Stevie to see the garage was set up as a rehearsal space. Everything they needed was right here in front of him.

As he stared, Jay was already picking up the drum kit. In one motion he turned and headed back to the van.

"Move it," he hissed.

Stevie wanted a microphone. There it was, sitting in its stand. He didn't bother unplugging it from the amplifier. He just grabbed it and laid it across the amp. Operating on adrenaline and youthful exuberance, he picked up the whole lot. He turned on his heel and started running.

In less than two minutes they were all safely back in the van. Paulie calmly pulled away from the scene of the crime.

Once round the first corner, the van filled with relieved laughter.

"Whose stuff was that?" Stevie asked eventually.

"Some dickheads," Jay replied.

"NF," RobBob muttered.

"National Front?"

"Yeah."

"We hate those twats," Paulie interjected. He glanced at Stevie. Practically asking if he agreed with his stare.

"Me too. My girlfriend's half black. She gets loads of stick. I fuckin' hate it."

Paulie smiled. That was the correct answer.

"You know her," RobBob told him. "Nikki."

"She's hot." Jay nodded approvingly, and Stevie smiled.

"Yeah, I know."

Paulie looked at him in the rear-view mirror. "How did you end up with a babe like her?"

RobBob caught his eye and nodded approvingly. He'd passed tonight's test with flying colours.

"She chose me," he answered.

"You're gonna love being in our band," Jay muttered. It didn't matter that the words bore the ring of a warning. Stevie already loved being in the band.

"Yeah," he said, "I know."

They made it back to the Falcon without incident. Paulie pulled up quietly at the side door and turned the headlights off.

THE KILLSWITCH

They unloaded the gear in silence. It was late by the time they had finished.

"Right," RobBob said as he locked the door at the bottom of the stairs. "Tomorrow. Two o'clock. Don't be late."

The next day at two o'clock, Stevie was supposed to be sitting in a Geography lesson. But he wasn't. He was in the upstairs room of the Falcon shouting, "One, two, One, two…" into a microphone. Turning dials, saying, *yeah* a lot, followed by many more *one, twos*…

RobBob hammered away at the drum kit as the other two tried their hardest to get something musical out of their instruments.

Let's try a Clash song. How about Tommy Gun?"

"Yeah."

You had to admire their enthusiasm, but after a couple of hours the realisation this was not as simple as they had assumed it would be hung heavily in the room.

"I thought you could play, Paulie."

"I thought you could sing."

"Let's take a break," suggested RobBob, mainly to release the tension.

So they took a break. Jay and RobBob regaled them with stories from the punk movement so far.

Young, disenfranchised people had become a force to be reckoned with.

"Nobody is only what they first appear to be. We've all got something going on."

RobBob and Jay had been all over. Their travels had even taken them to Belfast.

The stories from there fascinated Stevie. He'd seen the *troubles* on the news but knew nothing about the subject. Although his catholic background meant he felt some sympathy with the 'wrong side', it was confusing. He was an ill-informed child who instinctively recognised the unfairness being perpetrated.

Despite the strong catholic, indeed Irish bias at school, it was not something that appeared on the curriculum. Like all awkward topics it seemed to him they shied away, the subject was closed.

Here people spoke their minds without hesitation. It was exhilarating.

"It's fuckin' mental over there," Rob was saying. "There are all these roadblocks everywhere. But there's this club. It's a tiny little shithole but it's fuckin' brilliant. It's the only place in the whole of Belfast, Northern Ireland probably, where nobody gives a shit what religion you are. An' the speed they got over there, fuckin' 'ell." He finished his statement with a sort of drum roll, then another, and another.

Stevie screamed into his mic, Paulie plucked away furiously at his G string and Jay slapped the bass for all he was worth. They kept at it for a good fifteen minutes.

Then RobBob picked up where he had left off. "At the airport they got armoured cars. Armoured fuckin' cars, at the airport!"

Stevie spat the words into his mic, "Armoured cars at the airport, might as well live in a fuckin' fort!"

And they were off again, making a hell of a racket.

At the next break, Stevie asked, "What happens if the fascists find out we've got their kit?"

He was curious. If they were expecting trouble, he wanted to be pre-warned.

Jay smirked. "You don't have to worry about them."

There was an elongated silence. RobBob explained, "We warned 'em we wouldn't tolerate an NF band around here," he said. "I'm not havin' the fuckin' Nazis trying to take over our movement. Trying to brainwash young kids and what 'ave you. We told 'em we couldn't allow that."

Obviously there had been some kind of altercation, and the

stolen equipment were spoils of war. The reasoning was a bit light on detail, but it was plenty good enough for Stevie.

"Punk is for everyone," RobBob continued. "Black, white, whatever."

"Too right," Stevie agreed.

These were his people, and he was in, one hundred percent committed to the cause.

13

It was Saturday morning. Aiden and Stevie were sitting in Stevie's kitchen. His mum was preparing them a bacon buttie as they chattered excitedly about bands and singers she had never heard of.

She was biding her time.

She gave them their plates and fetched tomato ketchup from the overhead Formica cupboard. Only once they had started tucking in did she move to the doorway. She leaned against the frame and now she had them cornered as she casually mentioned, "Brother O'Reilly phoned me yesterday."

The chatter stopped. Neither boy looked up.

Her soft comment had landed like a hand grenade on the table before them. Aiden and Stevie exchanged the briefest of looks. She could spot their furtive glances when they were a hundred metres away in the lane below her window. She wasn't about to miss an exchange as guilt-ridden as that one right in front of her eyes.

"What do you suppose he wanted?" she asked.

The sound of chewing was the only reply.

"Steven?"

A singular accusatory raised eyebrow burned into the top of Stevie's head. He didn't need to look up; he knew it would be there. And when she used his full name, it never ended well for him. He shrugged.

"That's it, just a shrug?"

She tutted, sort of. It was a horrible noise, unnerving. She turned to the other boy, her son's lifelong friend and constant companion.

"Aiden, do you want to hazard a guess?"

"No Mrs. Williams."

"No?" She paused dramatically. "Are you sure, because he mentioned you as well."

Aiden was fighting the urge to look to his pal for moral support. He also shrugged and avoided eye contact.

"It's important that you go to school," she said.

"They don't like us," Aiden stated.

"It's shit there. We hate it!" Stevie blurted out, "Why do you think that is?"

"Who knows?"

"You don't think it's to do with this punk thing?"

Why are you always on their side?"

"I'm not."

"You are," Stevie screamed. "Come on," he said, so Aiden pushed his plate aside and obediently followed his pal from the kitchen.

She let them pass. She shook her head as she watched them ascend the stairs and race into Stevie's tiny bedroom.

She finished making a third sandwich and carried it to the front room.

"Here you are, love."

Tommy sat up and smiled at her.

"Thanks, love." He took a bite. "A cup of tea would go lovely with this."

He grinned at her, and she didn't smile back.

"What is it, love?"

"I'm worried about them."

"Why? They're just doin' what all kids do."

"This punk thing. It's different, an' this girl Nikki. Have you seen her?"

"She can't be that bad."

"You ain't seen her. All that eye makeup, an' the hair, bloody 'ell."

Tommy sniggered. "What's 'er figure like?"

His wife was not smiling. "You've gotta talk to those boys."

He took a sip of tea.

"What about?" he asked.

"They are bunking off school and I don't think they're using the time looking at bird's nests."

"What are they doin'?" he asked to fill the silence.

"What do you think?"

"I dunno."

"Exactly!"

That response did not make things any clearer as far as Tommy was concerned.

"Oh," he said by way of a non-inflammatory reply.

"*Oh?* Is that all you've got to say? The headmaster phoned me yesterday, an' all you can say is *oh?*"

"What did he say?"

"He thinks that Punk Rock is to blame."

"Yeah an' they blamed Elvis when we was at school to."

"This is different."

He smirked, thinking she was joking. She didn't smile back.

"You've seen 'em with their spiky hair an' all that. That's what that Nikki looks like, you should see 'er Tom."

He smirked, thinking she was winding him up.

"I dunno why you keep smirking."

"Oh." He tried to make his expression more serious.

"Oh, bloody *oh*. We'll 'ave that put on your 'eadstone."

Tommy smirked again. He couldn't help it. He wiped it from his face and tried a more conciliatory approach.

"Look love, I can't tell 'em not to like certain music," he pointed out, "or certain girls," he added gently. "This ain't Russia. But I'll speak to 'em, see what's what, alright?"

He attempted to poke her playfully in the ribs, but she dodged out of reach. So he winked at her while taking a bite of the sandwich,

"Smashing sandwich, love," he declared between swallows.

"I just want 'em to find nice girls and settle down."

"I know love."

She backed away towards the kitchen.

She wasn't ready to joke about it.

Tommy tried to watch the television, but he was distracted by his wife's concerns. Above all he wanted her to be happy. He took his empty plate down to the kitchen.

"It's just a phase, love. He'll settle down soon enough."

"I'm worried about 'em, Tom."

He nodded. It amazed him how she was so protective of Aiden. I mean, he liked the kid but to her he was as good as blood.

"They'll be fine. Don't worry."

"But this bloody punk rock."

"Its only music love." He wrapped his arms around her waist. "Remember when Elvis hit the scene? Remember the fuss? Your mum thought we was all going to hell."

He was reminiscing, trying to lighten the mood.

She was having none of it.

"Music?" She tutted disapprovingly. "That ain't music."

She started clattering dishes and pans around as she always did when she was thinking about something she didn't want to have to face.

"Anyway," she turned to face him, "this ain't about music.

This is about girls." She turned to look at him. "One girl in particular."

A smirk climbed towards his face. He glanced downwards and hurriedly wiped it away.

"Oh."

"That's why you've got to talk to them. Find out what's goin' on."

"I will, love."

"An' it's time they went to work," she added, "and had a bit less free time."

14

"Who's Nikki?" Tommy lit a cigarette as he asked the question, it was a cool manoeuvre. Definitely the sort of thing a hero in a bête noir would do Aiden thought.

"What?" Stevie looked surprised.

His father smiled. "You 'eard."

"Why do you wanna know?"

"Why don't you wanna tell me?"

Aiden smiled at that. He imagined a hero in a novel would toy with his opponent this way.

"Only, your mother is worried about you, the pair of you."

He always called her *your mother* even though technically she wasn't his mum.

"I dunno why." Stevie thought he sounded like Sid Vicious.

Aiden remained silent.

"When did you last bunk off school?"

Stevie remained silent.

"Now you know why."

"Your mum thinks you pair are losin' the plot. She thinks there are girls behind it."

The boys exchanged a fleeting glance in the darkness. It was nowhere near fleeting enough.

"It's this punk thing innit? I mean look at ya!"

"What do you mean?" Stevie demanded aggressively.

"You was a teddy boy," Aiden noted.

"You're sayin' this is the same?"

"Yeah," said Aiden.

"No," said Stevie.

Tommy laughed, moved closer, and clapped both boys across the shoulders simultaneously. "OK," he said, "tell me about it."

The boys glanced at each other again.

Tommy guessed correctly that his son would be harder to extract information from.

"Aiden?"

Aiden smiled at him. "It's just brilliant. Excitin', you know?" he replied.

Tommy recalled his own youth. It wasn't that long ago. He and his mates had become aware of Rock and Roll at the same time as girls. Oh yes, he knew only too well. Some of the best times of his life.

"Yeah, I think so," Tommy replied, "but what's with all the chains, an' the hair, jeeezzus." He attempted to touch his son's spiky effort. Stevie slapped his hand away.

Aiden shrugged. He wasn't completely sold on the clothing either if he was honest. It made them targets, but the package wasn't complete unless you made an effort in that department.

"How you look is important," Stevie said.

"Yeah, for the girls, I get that."

"No," Stevie was defensive again.

"Oh, it's not that?" Clearly Tommy disbelieved him.

"No, it's not." Stevie was practicing his angry young man.

"No," Aiden said more softly, "we are friends with a couple of girls, Nikki and Karen. But it's not all about sex these days."

Tommy snorted. "OH, right," he mocked. "What's it about then?"

"Music," they replied in unison.

Tommy had a good way with the boys. He was that rare breed back then, a man who treated children as equals. He didn't lecture them as they experimented with fashion or tell them their hobbies and interests were stupid things they'd grow out of. On the contrary, he'd always encouraged his son's love of birdlife, even when his friends and colleagues warned it was a bit sissy. And he wouldn't hear a bad word said about Aiden's fascination with the written word. He knew they were smart and thought both lads showed potential in abundance. All they had to do was settle down and find a nice girl. It had worked for him. It was tried and tested, the way of the world. Punk rock or no punk rock he couldn't imagine any drastic changes to the status quo anytime soon.

He looked towards Aiden, expecting him to expand, to extol the virtues of the other girl.

"So you like Karen, do ya?"

Aiden also claimed, "It ain't like that."

He was also given short shrift.

"Did I ever tell you about the girl I met in Brighton?"

"Yes," the boys replied in unison.

"Well, you're older now. Wanna hear the X-rated version?"

"No!" said Stevie.

"Yes!" said Aiden.

Tommy winked at Aiden. He threw Stevie a smile. "Don't tell your mother!" he hissed.

15

Aiden left father and son at the crossroads and slowly shuffled back home.

He turned the front doorknob and a voice greeted him immediately.

"Ah, there you are." His mother was padding down the stairs. "Where've you been?"

"Nowhere."

She came closer and sniffed him. "You've been drinkin'," she accused.

"So?"

"What do you look like?"

Aiden didn't reply.

She sniffed him again. "And you've been smokin'."

"So?"

Aiden saw a shadow flit across the doorway of the living room behind her. They were not alone. He looked round the door.

A total stranger stood by the electric fire.

The first thing Aiden took in was a soaring eagle belt buckle. It was holding up Wrangler jeans that were flared and filthy across the thighs as though something oily had been on his lap. He wore a brown sweater that had been through the washer so many times it had lost all shape. However, the stains must have been deeply ingrained, and no washing machine could help with that. His boots were black military style, unpolished and laced in a sloppy, haphazard manner.

The man was tall, six foot at least, and his hair was long and unkempt.

Biker, Aiden thought.

"Oh, look. A baby punk," the man said, as Aiden's mum walked in behind him.

"This is my son Aiden. Aiden this is Martin."

Martin blew out a cloud of hashish smoke.

"Alright," he said.

"Give us a drag," Aiden replied.

"Fuck off."

"I'm going to bed." Aiden was already halfway up the stairs.

Why don't you come an' watch TV like a normal boy?" his mother called after him.

Aiden chose not to reply, and when the bedroom door slammed behind him, all the tension left his small body.

"He's just weird," he heard his mother say. "He likes reading books. Thinks he's so bleedin' smart."

He flung the door wide,

"I'm not weird!" he yelled.

"Yeah, you are," his mother replied.

"All punks are weird," added Martin.

"And bikers are thick!" Aiden yelled and slammed the door.

He sat on his bed and the tension returned in droves at the thud of military-style boots coming his way. He forced himself not to look up when the door burst open.

"What did you say?"

Aiden said nothing, but kept his head bowed.

"Watch it, kid."

He remained silent, eyes downcast, and after a few minutes the door was closed, and he was left alone. That rather surprised him. He'd expected a little slap at the very least.

Maybe Maaarrrtin ain't all bad? In his mind he elongated the man's name, mocking him. It made him feel better.

He leaned down and pulled a book from under his bed. He turned to the marked page and carried on reading where he'd left off. Paris back in the golden age. It was fascinating.

The artists of the communes spoke to him. He was like them. People who didn't fit in. The Lost Generation were the punks of their time.

He discovered with shock how the Stock Market Crash of 1929 had brought the roaring twenties to a dramatic close. He read the pages with genuine dismay. What had happened to all the people?

His thirst for knowledge led him to Berlin in the early 1930s.

Before long he had forgotten Paris. This was truly the *Good old days* in all their glory.

He imagined a big switch he could flick that would transport him to those heady times.

He imagined going to Berlin with Mia.

16

Stevie was breathing heavily as he skirted around the rugby pitch. He was keeping to the cover of the huge rhododendron shrubs that grew around the perimeter of the school grounds.

He ignored the pain in his throbbing hands as he climbed the wall. He jumped down onto the pavement and started walking, cursing with anger every step of the way.

In town, Nikki was sitting on the wall as he knew she would be.

"Alright?" she greeted as he approached. Her hair had been transformed into an impossible shade of neon green. It shimmied as she moved.

She was sitting alongside Mia who had clearly benefitted from a Nikki style makeover. She was wearing a biker's jacket covered in studs. Her hair stuck out randomly like Robert Smith from the Cure. The make up around her eyes was outrageously purple. She looked amazing.

"Remember Mia," Nikki said.

"Alright," he muttered as he went to sit the other side of Nikki. Just seeing the love of his life, and he was beginning to feel better.

. . .

Most punks were unemployed. They stayed in bed as long as possible to save money. Once they surfaced from their pits, they'd head to the local meeting point. Usually a record store or somewhere you could lounge about.

How else were they going to find out what was happening? There was no Instagram. Immersing yourself into a subculture like punk required commitment. Ideas and information were shared face to face. To hear the latest news and find out what was new, you needed to get out there. To see and be seen.

The 70s and 80s was a time the youth turned their backs on *expectation*. Against all the odds they rearranged a small part of the world into something they preferred.

Naturally, the older generation went batshit crazy.

It was war. Geriatrics were not giving up their deeply ingrained bias and bigotry without a fight. And those too old to fight would moan, whinge, and whine every single step of the way.

If there was to be a more tolerant world, getting there was going to be tough. The older generation held all the aces.

But punks had youth on their side. And there was squats and dole money. Cash in hand jobs and little back-street pubs. An alternative lifestyle wasn't an easy choice, but it was possible. Surviving on the periphery of civilised society was still viable if you committed.

RobBob had called a meeting.

"They're going to tighten the laws on squatting."

"There should be less restrictions not more."

"Exactly. How do you think bands like the Clash could afford to live while they were learning to play?"

One day there will be only two rules— *be yourself* and *tell the truth*.

"There needs to be a third," Nikki piped up. "Equality for women."

At the time these were new and exciting concepts. Some would argue they still are.

Sixteen-year-olds then as now couldn't help noticing that decent apprenticeships were no longer available. It was all Mcjobs then and Amazon deliveries now. Who wanted that? Where were the pensions, the paid holidays, respect for the workforce?

The rot started right then. When the strength of a country, its youth, were allowed to grow so disillusioned with their prospects they dropped out of education in their thousands. Academically, quietly, girls started to do better than boys. Most didn't notice. Nikki did.

"We are measurably better than men for the first time ever," she proudly informed Mia, who looked stunned.

What she had just heard went against everything she had been taught. Which in a nutshell amounted to one thing: a woman should know her place.

Nikki defiantly questioned everything the world stood for. It was magnificent.

She would quote feminist writers and argue in public with grown men. It was liberating. Mia modelled for her, took photographs of everything, and soaked it up like a sponge.

"Remember," Nikki never tired of saying. "Any time a woman has an original thought, men always think she's stupid. Fuck 'em."

Mia nodded and felt deliciously naughty.

"I'm gonna run my own business. I'm gonna be a designer. Being creative is my calling. They'll try and take advantage of that, like they do with nurses and teachers, anyone who loves what they do, but I won't let 'em."

Mia thought it sounded improbable, but she was nothing if not supportive. "Good for you."

"That's why I want my own bank account."

"Wow is that allowed?"

"Only recently. Can you believe it? It's like the dark ages or something."

Mia loved hanging out with Nikki.

The dingy squat where she rested her head was filthy and the boys there kept getting pissed and trying to shag her.

She'd much rather be learning about women's rights and working on her photography. Very quickly they grew close.

They were discussing Gloria Steinham's new article in Spare Rib. There was a full-page picture of the lady herself.

"That is a great shot," Nikki said. "She looks beautiful but kind of powerful too."

"We could take one of you like that."

"Really, you think so?"

"Course, it's just the lighting."

17

Aiden had a vague idea why he was outside the headmaster's office. But his disinterest was palpable.

After what seemed an eternity, the word *come* finally emanated from behind the door.

He slouched in and saw the head writing at his desk. He didn't look up and more valuable seconds Aiden would never get back dragged past.

When he could bear it no longer, he coughed.

The headmaster still refrained from looking up. He finished writing and placed his pen carefully on his desk. Clasping his fingers together he sat back. Only then did he glare at the boy before him.

"What on earth do you think you look like? That," he motioned at Aiden's attire distastefully, "is not regulation uniform."

He looked him up and down again. "It's not even close," he added.

He opened the drawer.

Aiden rolled his eyes. He knew what was coming.

The headmaster pulled a black leather strap from the drawer and came around the desk.

The strap was twelve inches long, an inch wide and half an inch thick. It trembled, the way a rubber dildo would, as he walked.

"Put out your hands," he said without looking Aiden in the eye.

Aiden did as he was told and without further ado received three lashes on each hand.

He didn't make a sound; he wouldn't give him the satisfaction.

"Tomorrow you will be correctly attired, or you will be suspended from the school premises. Do you understand?"

Now he looked at Aiden's face.

The boy stared at him sullenly.

"Return to your classes."

In the hallway, Aiden was fuming. His hands were stinging. His eyes fixed on some invisible point ahead. His face looked like thunder.

"Fuck this," he muttered under his breath.

18

On Friday night Aiden had stayed at Stevie's. The morning would mark their introduction to the workplace. They were given the obligatory bacon sandwich then Mrs Williams watched them from the kitchen window as they strutted across the back lane. It was a quick skip to the warehouse where they were to report to Al at nine o'clock sharp. She could make sure they were on time; the rest was up to them.

They squeezed past a lorry where two men were loading furniture.

"Is Al about?" asked Stevie.

The elder of the two motioned towards the little office.

"In there."

The only man in the office was sitting at a desk reading a manual when the boys came barging in.

"Fuck me," he said. "What 'ave we got 'ere then?"

"I'm Stevie. This is Aiden. We start work today."

The man seemed not to have heard.

"What the fuck do you look like?"

Aiden felt a little self-conscious.

"We're punks," Stevie stated, unsure if he could be heard over the man's laughter.

"Oh, you're that all right," he managed to say.

The boys stood before him, Aiden feeling a little out of place and Stevie getting wound up.

"Go on then," Al said, once he'd laughed himself out.

"What?"

"Did you not see that bloody great lorry outside?"

"Course."

"Well, it ain't gonna fill itself. Go and 'elp load up."

"Punks," they heard him say once he was alone in his office, and the laughter started up again.

"What's he fuckin' laughing at?" Stevie wanted to know.

Aiden didn't want any trouble on their first day. "He seems alright. Did you see what was on his desk?"

"No, what?"

"Didn't you see it, a computer?"

"I think they're brilliant," Stevie replied as Aiden had known he would. "I hope he lets us have a go?"

"They'll never catch on," Aiden teased him.

"Fuck off!" he replied as they squeezed down the side of the huge removal lorry.

"You pair come 'ere. I'm going to show you how to carry a chair."

They were shown the basics and put to work. When the furniture was safely strapped down Al said to them, "Get in then."

"In the back?"

"I don't want people seeing punks up front in my lorry."

So they rode in the back, and they slid up and down whilst the furniture remained stationery. It wasn't particularly safe, but it was great fun.

They worked until lunchtime then filed into the office where Al handed them each a five-pound note.

"You done good, boys."

"Thanks." Aiden had never owned a five-pound note before. He was beaming.

Stevie shoved his into his pocket without looking at it.

"Is that a computer?" he asked.

"Yeah. Why? Do you know about these things?"

"A bit, yeah." Stevie moved towards it and tapped a key a few times.

"You won't get nothing. It's not connected yet. I've got to read the manual first."

He flapped the aforementioned manual at Stevie until he backed away.

Stevie took no offence. "Same time next week?" he asked.

Al nodded. "Now fuck off the pair of you."

They walked into town.

"This is alright, eh?" Aiden said as they sat on the wall.

"I suppose," Stevie agreed.

"Whaddya mean 'I suppose'? The sun is shining; we got money in our pockets. This is great."

"Do you reckon he'll have that computer connected up next week? I'd love to have a go on it."

"Why? What are you gonna do on a computer?" Aiden laughed and shook his head, "Do you think Mia will be out today?"

"Oh that's more interesting, is it?"

"Yeah."

"I knew you liked her."

"So?"

"She don't say much."

"So?"

As the weeks passed this became their new routine.

Work in the mornings and head into town with money in their pockets in the afternoons.

Aiden normally spent his on second-hand books or magazines.

Stevie wasted his on cigarettes and cider.

19

Nikki was an only child. She and her mum lived on the end of a row of identical pebbledash houses.

Nikki had always been headstrong. Her mother took the attitude that confrontation with her daughter just wasn't worth the grief. Nikki's mother preferred a friendly relationship to living in a constant state of high tension. Things were hard enough as far as she was concerned. The family home should be a refuge in the storm.

And when it came to clothes, music, or boys it was easier to let her daughter do whatever she liked. Make her own mistakes. Life was too short and to hell with what the neighbours thought.

If they wanted someone to blame, they could point their accusatory fingers at the old man. Of course they'd have to find him first.

Nikki was born to stand out from the crowd. She dreamed of being a fashion designer. She'd been attracted to punk by the clothes more than the music. She considered herself a misunderstood woman in a male-dominated world. Someone unwilling to settle for the hand fate dealt her.

She was determined to be true to herself. To do what she wanted, who she wanted, when she wanted and look sensational whilst she did so. She longed to feel safe in an unsafe world.

Being with Stevie gave her that security she craved. He was the best boyfriend she'd ever had.

But for now she was with Mia.

"What was Stevie's friend called again, Aiden?"

"Yeah." Nikki smiled. "You like him?"

Mia smiled back.

20

It was Sunday evening and Stevie was at Nikki's. They were both covered in sweat, lying on the bed smoking cigarettes.
"You should let me pierce your ear," she suggested.
Stevie didn't hesitate. "Yeah alright."
In truth he would have agreed to pretty much anything at that precise moment.
"Do you want a stud, a hoop, or a big cross like Billy Idol?"
Stevie considered the options.
"A big cross," he decided.
Only when he was walking home did he begin to consider the consequences of his actions. He was absolutely madly, head over heels in love with Nikki. He already knew she was the one. He was going to have kids with her and stay together 'til death do them part. When he was with her, all rational thought went completely out of his head.
Only now, walking home alone in the cold, did it dawn on him his parents might not be thrilled with his new accessory. His mum already didn't like his hair.
He approached from the back lane to see the kitchen light

on. That was bad news. Even worse, his dad was sitting at the table nursing a cup of tea.

Stevie crept in anyway. He hovered briefly in the doorway, "Night, Dad," and he was gone.

"Come 'ere a minute."

He reappeared. "Yeah?"

"Come in. Take a seat. I want to talk to you."

Tommy waited for his son to sit and get comfortable.

"Show me your ear."

"What?"

His dad waited, so eventually he had no option but to turn his head.

"Bloody hell!" Tommy forced plenty of sarcasm into his voice. "Who did that to you? Want me to get 'em?"

"No one."

"Well, you didn't do it to yourself. Who was it? Aiden?"

"No."

"Who then?"

"A friend."

Tommy laughed. "Ah, is this friend called Nikki by any chance?"

Stevie couldn't help himself. He had that guilty look on his face, and Tommy laughed again.

In the front room, Stevie's mum turned the volume down on the television and listened. A lot of her friends' husbands would try to thrash some sense into him. But she recalled the treatment her brothers used to get and how it just made them worse.

Deep down she was relieved they had a *don't beat the kids* policy. Even if their youngest was going off the rails a bit.

21

It was early morning and RobBob was half awake. He could hear talking through the paper-thin wall. Jay was in the adjoining room with Emma the posh girl. He could also hear a bin lorry in the back lane.

Separated by a sheet of graffiti-covered plywood was about as far apart as he and Jay got these days. The lifestyle they adhered to kept them together.

They were taking on the establishment in the name of the people.

It was true that most of *the people* were ungrateful, sometimes aggressively so. But it wasn't their fault. They simply didn't know what was good for them. RobBob didn't blame the average citizen. They were exhausted. Worn down by the effort required to keep a family afloat.

They had kids to ferry to football, ballet, or tiddlywinks practice. They took extra shifts. They commuted such vast distances it was dark when they left home and when they returned.

In their sparse moments of free time they could barely manage a few pints down the local where politics was not a welcome subject. The bestselling newspapers in the country were little more than comics. The electorate was purposely kept dumb.

Most struggled through their three score years and ten never once realising they were being played by those above.

Generation after generation, individuals were invited to point accusatory fingers at easily identifiable minority groups below them. The invitation was accepted in vast numbers.

"Yeah, it's their fault. Those Jews/Arabs/Blacks," they parroted. Never once stopping to ask, *'If a recent arrival with no qualifications and a rudimentary grasp of the language can take my job, what does that say about me? About my education?'*

RobBob used to think they just needed the facts explained. It took him a while to realise they were happy in their ignorance. Add the deference groomed into them since birth, and it's no wonder the system continues. Doff your cap to anyone with a posh accent and don't question us peasant.

RobBob was different. He found it impossible to *not get involved* or *not take it personally*.

He did take things personally. And he considered facts and truth to be important things worth fighting for.

Once he started digging, and discovered the reality of the system, he was involved.

He threw himself willingly into battle for the greater good. The public could thank him later. It was just a matter of time until the keepers of truth would be victorious?

Jay was the logistics wizard. RobBob was the enigmatic leader.

Working in conjunction with civil rights groups and union leaders they were getting results.

From the next room, he heard Jay's low tone as he whispered something. Emma giggled in response.

He smiled. Jay had a way with the ladies.

RobBob took solace in these quiet moments when they

THE KILLSWITCH

presented themselves. You never knew how long they would last. This brief bit of peace at the start of the day offered a chance to catch his breath. As soon as he emerged through the front door, people would flock to him. Everybody wanted a piece of him. They would bathe in his fiery glow, take encouragement and strength and the revolution would stay on track.

He glanced at his clothes lying on the floor. Perhaps he should get to the launderette soon. But not today, there was too much to do.

With the parliamentary vote getting ever closer, they had to leaflet the city centre like never before. But as with any grass roots campaign it was hard work. People came, people went. There was never enough money to cover everything, and as always when RobBob was involved, the heavy artillery of the Establishment were pointing directly at them.

The law, the press, the dole office staff— it was a concerted effort. All actively working against misfits like him.

Official files referred to them as *undesirable aliens*.

As such, sleeping too many nights in the same bed was out of the question. Meals consisted of whatever was available, often at unusual hours.

They were constantly looking over their shoulders and changing plans at the last minute. The pressure was immense. Being in the band was a chance to unwind for RobBob. A little bit of time out. As close as he actually got to a *normal life*.

He tried to imagine a normal life. Working on a bin lorry perhaps?

He listened to the men in the lane.

But as he listened his antenna twitched. Something about these particular workers on this particular morning was not as it should be.

There was no banter. In fact there was no communicating at all. The lorry was noisy, but the silence of the crew was louder.

RobBob leapt from bed and peeked through the window. Cops, loads of them in formation behind the lorry.

"Jay!" he called. "It's a raid."

No sooner had he shouted the warning than the front door flew off its hinges.

Shouts of, "Police! Police!" echoed down the hallway and through the house.

RobBob didn't have time to pull on his trousers. Anti-terrorist officers filled his bedroom whilst he was still clutching his dirty old denims.

"Hands on your head," someone shouted and there were so many guns pointed at him, he did so immediately.

He stood in the grotty room, dressed in a tatty old pair of Y-fronts. His brand-new snake tattoo curled up his chest and across his shoulder. His bright red hair hung down over his face. He sighed. They had him. The game was up.

In the next room, he heard Emma object, then the horrible sound of something crashing to the floor. Closely followed by it crunching underfoot and the sound of officers laughing.

Jay's unmistakable baritone objected with profanity attached. He was cut short as though the wind had been knocked from his lungs. RobBob heard officers in the other room laugh again.

He remained passive. It was the only way to avoid unnecessary pain. The cops liked that he wasn't stupid. That he stayed calm.

Inside he was furious. They had worked so hard and now the plans were scuppered.

22

At the police station RobBob refused to tell them anything. He sat in his cell cold and hungry. He'd requested the phone call he was legally entitled to hours ago. He was still waiting.

The police denied him a blanket, food, or a cigarette and they would call the solicitor only when they were good and ready.

First, they wanted to talk to Jay.

"Do you want a cuppa, anything to eat, Jacob?"

"Yeah, I could murder a bacon sandwich."

The lead detective nodded towards his junior colleague. "You heard the man."

He pulled out a packet of cigarettes and Jacob took one.

"No problems?" he asked.

"Nah."

Jacob pulled a lighter from his pocket and lit his cigarette.

"You did really well."

He nodded as he blew out a cloud of cigarette smoke. "Thanks."

As he waited for his commanding officer, Jacob was fed and

watered. This was to be his last mission, his final debrief. He wasn't overly thrilled. He loved being an undercover anarchist.

He was put in a quiet side office to wait for the inevitable questions. When they did come, they were pleasant. Why wouldn't they be? The mission had been a success.

"I expect you're pleased to come out of it unscathed."

"I guess."

"Glad to put it all behind you?"

"Not really. I feel I can offer more."

"Your face is too well known. And when this comes to court…" His voice trailed off. There was no need to add 'people will be trying to kill you.'

Jacob flicked ash on the floor. "I've had an idea," he said.

"Oh really?"

"Yeah. These computers. They're all using them."

"Yes, we've read your reports."

"Maybe you are right, and it's too risky to infiltrate anymore. But this is the new age. Surely we can just see what's on their computers to find out what they are up to? And breaking and entering, well, that's my speciality."

The debrief officer was staring at him as though he was quite mad.

"What do you know about computers?"

"A bit, but I thought I could do a course. How hard can they be?"

"That's not the path set out for you. They've got plans."

"I like to follow my own path."

"Is that right?"

"Yeah, and I think computers is a growth area. Somewhere I can be best utilised."

But he's not really choosing what's best. He's choosing what's best for him. He always does. And to hell with whoever gets let down or left behind.

"You'll have to ask."

Jacob was not ready to leave behind the life of intrigue and subterfuge. He loved it. We're all built a certain way and that's just who he is.

23

The Trust were holding the meeting in the city's very first skyscraper. They had taken residence on the complete top floor. It was the biggest open plan office any of those present had ever seen. It was huge, with panoramic views all around. Desks for hundreds of workers were already in the space. Currently though, the typewriters were silent. The typing pool started on Monday.

Today, only the select few were present. They were crowded into the smaller adjacent room marvelling at modern technology.

A giant computer filled the space. The first office computer any of them had ever seen.

"Wow, isn't it big?"

"And you're telling me that thing does the work of a whole department?"

"It does indeed."

One of the interns took a step forward. "So, where does the paper come out?" he asked, reaching out a hand.

"Don't touch it!"

The command was barked so loudly everyone turned.

They saw a young man nobody recognised. But he was with the chairman so presumably had some authority.

He moved towards the giant machine and brushed an imaginary handprint away from where it had just been touched.

"This is not a toy," he said.

The watching chairman smiled as though indulging a favourite child.

"Gentlemen, allow me to introduce our newest member of staff. This is Jacob, and he will be heading our new computer department."

There were mumblings of welcome.

Jacob smiled, as well he might.

His new department was tasked with hunting down dissidents. To help achieve this aim, special laws had been rushed through parliament. Few people were aware suspected terrorists had no right to secret communication. Using a computer for encrypted communication was akin to digital terrorism. Who's to say you're not an enemy of the State until somebody has looked into you?

This allowed Jacob to send in undercover operatives and access encrypted messages all in the name of national security. Bad citizens were arrested.

Some of the bad citizens were able to repent. Those with a flair for computers were offered a job instead of a prison cell, a position in Jacob's department.

Officially, this den of digital iniquity did not exist. Unofficially, they quickly grew bigger and more powerful and took an ever-larger slice of the budget.

Over time they began referring to themselves as *Leetabix*. It was a play on the hacker language they used and a nod to how funny they were.

24

It was Saturday morning. Nikki and Stevie were strolling through the open-air market. Nikki as always was on the lookout for second hand pieces ripe for adjusting and accessorising.

"I'm gonna get that ball gown and cut it up short," she was saying as they rounded a corner.

She almost plunged headfirst into a guy blocking the path. No harm was done and under normal circumstances the incident wouldn't even be worthy of mention. But the guy was a skinhead and the stall beside him was selling far-right newspapers.

"Oi, you twat. Watch where you're fuckin' going."

"Sorry mate, didn't see ya," Stevie apologised on her behalf as he manoeuvred himself between the lad and Nikki.

"I ain't your fuckin' mate."

Stevie had been a promising boxer. He liked fighting. He'd grown up in a rough area surrounded by hard, street-fighting men. He wasn't about to be intimidated by some mouthy skinhead.

"Fuck off," he barked at the shaven-headed bully.

THE KILLSWITCH

Naturally, the skin halted in his tracks. But two identical-looking thugs smoothly flanked him.

Nikki had already used the minor delaying tactic to good effect and made her escape. Stevie backed slowly away from the skinheads with his fists up in classic boxer style. He moved backwards until he felt the edge of a stall behind him. Then he turned the corner and fled. He would meet Nikki back at the record shop. This was not their first scrape with Neanderthals. It paid to have a plan already in motion.

Later that day, he told the band what had happened. They were not amused.

"We've gotta send a message. Just because RobBob's away it don't mean they can move back on the market. We gotta make sure they realise."

There were nods of agreement and mutterings of how this is the first multicultural market in the whole country. Punks and Rastas alongside Mods and Hippies all selling different products, all being influenced by each other. "We wanna keep it this way."

"If the Mods fuck off, where will we buy our speed?"

"Those Rastas have the best weed."

These sorts of issues were food and drink to RobBob. With him off the scene somebody else would have to come up with something.

"I know what to do," said Stevie.

The others listened.

The following Saturday around midmorning, they headed to the market. It was a warm, sunny day and the shoppers were out in force.

Stevie had instructed them to wear blue jeans, plain black T-shirts, and beanie hats.

"If we all look the same, that's all witnesses will remember."

The National Front had set up their stall just inside the main gate. It was a prime spot where the crowds were thickest. Paulie stopped while they were still off in the distance.

"It's a bit busy, innit?" he said.

"Just stick to the fuckin' plan," Stevie hissed.

There was no more to say. Stevie waited for his pals to get in position, then he crossed the road, and headed towards the skinheads. He had already recognised the mouthy one from the week before. As he drew closer, the kid looked up and recognition was clearly mutual.

"Oi, boys, look who it is."

There were four skinheads at the stall and two more standing nearby, handing out flyers. They all stared menacingly at Stevie as he approached.

"'Allo again," Stevie said.

"What the fuck do you want?"

"Well, I'm not 'ere to buy one of your stupid comics, am I?"

"You'll turn around if you know what's good for you."

"Is that right?"

His crew attacked from behind. The skinheads never stood a chance. Two had been coshed to the ground before anyone knew what was happening. Two more were down before they had a chance to defend themselves, and the remaining two were set upon so mercilessly they probably would have preferred to be felled by one blow they never saw coming. As it was, they went down under sustained attacks from multiple assailants.

Paulie kicked the stall over for good measure.

Moans and groans were coming from the fascists. Proof to Stevie they weren't badly hurt.

"You ain't welcome on this market," he warned.

Sirens could be heard getting closer.

"You better not be 'ere next week." Stevie planted one final kick and they scarpered before the cops arrived.

The following Saturday, band practice involved hanging around the market all day.

The smiles and approving nods from the traders confirmed his suspicion that Snarling Dogs were *the good guys*. They expected no less from the younger stallholders. It was a nice surprise to be acknowledged by the Asian traders as well. People who had only been in the country a decade or two. Who had fled the consequences of hatred and division. They just wanted to raise families and live in peace. The rhetoric those Neanderthals preached went against everything they had been led to believe the country stood for. They didn't want them on the market any more than Stevie did.

The fascists didn't return for a second act.

When RobBob and Jay got nicked, Stevie could have made his excuses and left the band. Nobody would have judged him harshly. This was a very stressful way of life. People came and people went.

But he was sixteen, it was new and exciting. He liked street battles and Nikki loved him all the more for taking on the fascists. Far from leaving, he officially became RobBob's replacement.

Being in the band kept Stevie busy. There were always new members to audition or a gig so far out of town there was no point anyone coming because how would they get back? It was odd these gigs were barely referred to afterwards. But there it was.

Nikki soon realised the phrase, *We've got a gig tonight*, carried ominous undertones.

She heard about the ruckus at the market, picked up other rumours here and there, and she wasn't blind. For musicians they didn't half pick up a lot of injuries.

Overall though, she approved of her boyfriend's extracurricular activities. Sometimes you can't wait. Change must be forced.

So Stevie kept up the band practice, never once stopping to think about his future. Why should he? He was young and this was just a stop gap. There was plenty of time to decide what he wanted to do with his life.

He didn't realise that whilst you're deciding, day-to-day events become your life. One morning you wake up, and you're in it up to your neck. This thing is you now. He didn't realise that because he was young and reckless.

25

Often strangers turned up at band practice. They needed a quiet word or had some information to impart. This evening it was a friend of RobBob. Just out of nick. He was starting a print shop not too far away and had come to offer his services. It was encouraging that RobBob was still sending valuable new recruits. That he was still up for the fight.

Before social media and mobile phones there were limited ways for those on the fringes of society to safely communicate.

Face to face was always best. Failing that, flyers, fanzines, and newssheets handed out in public were a good way to spread the word. But for that you needed access to a printer willing to produce often inflammatory stuff for you.

Before the guy left, Stevie handed him some artwork.

A few days later he went to collect the printed flyers and there on the desk was a computer.

"Wow you've got one."

"Yeah. It's great?"

"What does it do?"

"Take your flyer for example." He held up a cassette. "All the information is stored on here now. You don't have to do the artwork ever again."

"What if we want to change it?"

"No problem, that's the beauty. I'm telling you, computers are the future."

Stevie smiled.

26

Aiden had given up working on the lorry. It wasn't the same without his mate. He actually preferred lying in bed on Saturday mornings reading but that didn't pay. Until he combined it with selling hash for his mum's boyfriend.

All he had to do was stay home and the customers came to him. It was the sort of job that allowed him to read to his heart's content.

So as Stevie built his new life around Nikki and the band, so Aiden embarked on a new chapter in his.

It was odd how quickly they sort of fell out of each other's orbit.

Aiden would still go to the record shop, but he'd always just miss his mate.

Things could have been far worse. At least he had Mia.

"Tell me about where you're from?" he said as an excuse to hear her adorable accent. She wasn't much of a conversationalist. But he rather liked that. She was more the observant type. Preferred to let her camera do the talking. He liked that as well. It made her interesting.

"Berlin?" She shrugged. "It's OK."

"I'm gonna get a passport and travel the world. I'd love to go there."

She smiled. He would have to do better than that if he wanted her to speak again.

"Tell me about it."

"It is cold in winter."

They were sitting on a wall, so he said, "There's a big wall around it, isn't there?"

"The wall is around the western part."

"Oh, fascinating."

She nodded and smiled. He felt calm and happy.

He was only shaken when Nikki screamed alongside him.

"Stevie!"

"Alright, Nik."

Stevie had turned up looking like a rock star. He was wearing wraparound shades. His hair was neon blue, and his T-shirt had more holes than a sieve.

Mia nudged Aiden. "It's your friend from the Clash gig."

"Yeah."

"Do you think I can take his picture?"

"He loves having his picture taken. He's in a band."

She snapped a couple off. Stevie noticed and posed for her. She took a few more.

"Alright, mate, who's this?"

"This is Mia. Mia, this is Stevie."

"I want copies," he said.

"Of course," she replied.

"She could take some at your next gig," Aiden suggested.

"Great idea."

Stevie lifted his top.

"Look. Like it?"

He had a skull and crossbones freshly tattooed over his heart.

Mia photographed it.

"It's wicked, mate."

"Cheers, mate."

The rest of the crew had been trailing Stevie. They'd caught up now and were dominating the area. Paulie was the only one Aiden recognised.

"I gotta go. If I don't see you before, see you at the next gig?"

"Sure."

Stevie turned to his entourage.

"Come on boys," and they were gone like a tornado down the high street.

Mia whispered into Aiden's ear, "We could go together."

His ear tingled at the closeness of her.

"Definitely," he replied.

27

The Trust meeting was brought to order.

"Firstly gentlemen I would like to apologise for the distractions."

Through the windows, cranes could be seen stretching high into the air. More skyscrapers were being erected all around them.

"Personally," he continued, "I take solace from the knowledge that we own the buildings you see going up."

There were murmurs of approval. The profits were rolling in.

"And I would like to announce our new computer will be functional from tomorrow."

They all looked towards the adjoining office. The giant computer was gone. It had been replaced by something half the size. Technicians were crawling all over it as the board members watched.

"When they have finished, we will be able to further increase operations. We will shortly be conducting takeovers, hostile, if necessary, in the areas of garden centres, funeral parlours, and florists. Many such enterprises are little family affairs. We expect to control all those sectors within two financial cycles. This new computer will help greatly with those endeavours."

"It's much smaller?" a doubtful voice said.

"It's more powerful than the one that put man on the moon." They all marvelled anew.

"Now to business. Jacob, what do you have?"

"We have successfully infiltrated all the groups on the list. I've no doubt the usual punishments will be handed out in due course."

Every time Jacob's department passed dissidents onto the authorities, punishments were severe.

It was important a message was sent loud, clear, and publicly to deter others. Although the best members of each group were discreetly given the option of joining Leetabix. All quietly accepted.

"There are another batch of social clubs we need the police to close down. But dismantling the Unions is working far better than we could have hoped. Many are willing to trade information and passwords for a few measly quid."

The chairman coughed slightly to show his distaste at the vernacular used. He knew this kid was a thug in a smart suit, but he could at least try to speak properly.

"The anti-immigrant work has also been very successful in those places," Jacob added.

"Even union members are gullible it seems," the chairman noted.

"And the other target. Punks living in squats, I believe. Aren't those people high on drugs all the time? How much of a threat can they be?"

"They've been using computers. They are communicating secretly. That's all we know at this stage."

"In your opinion are they going to prove troublesome?"

"They have their capabilities, sir. But they will be no match for our new supercomputer."

All heads pivoted to admire it.

28

A couple of nights later, it was band rehearsal. Except the instruments remained untouched. The room was full with residents from the estate. Something was afoot. The women of the neighbourhood were completely unrepresented. Something big was afoot.

Stevie stood before them.

"Right listen up. As you all know, the National Front have organised a march through our patch."

There were grumblings of discontent. The word *wankers* could be heard over the chatter and people sniggered.

"You all know we can't let that happen," Stevie continued.

The Falcon was the only pub on a housing estate with a high proportion of immigrant residents. The locals did certainly not want such a march.

"However, they've been allowed their little protest. The council have deemed it acceptable. I don't. We are going to counter protest the shit out of it."

Cheers rose to the rafters.

After the meeting, when everyone had gone, Stevie still had an hour to kill so they plugged in their instruments. It was fair to say they had actually improved. Playing tunes from the Bob Dylan songbook was having an effect. They could manage *Maggie's Farm*, sort of.

More a speeded-up version that was so far removed from the original to be completely unrecognisable. But still, that was precisely what they were aiming for.

Finally, if you included *Maggie's Farm*, they had a handful of songs they could play all the way through.

"We're ready," Stevie announced proudly.

"We need an audience," Paulie suggested. "We'll 'ave a party."

"We ain't ready," Spike said.

"Fuck off," replied the other three.

"Let's have it the day of the march."

"That'll be a day to remember."

"Yeah, legendary."

It was agreed. Band practice was over.

Stevie scooped up his tobacco and lighter from the rickety little table and pocketed them. "I gotta meet 'em now," he said.

"So we can tell people about the gig?" Paulie wanted to be sure.

"Yeah, but we need numbers for the protest. Tell 'em that as well," Stevie reminded him as he opened the door.

"Sure."

"Good," and he was gone.

He walked across town to an Irish pub on Duke Street. He slipped quietly in, ordered a pint of Guinness, and went to the end of the bar. His drink had barely settled when a little old guy sat alongside him.

"You can leave that there," he said. "I'll keep an eye on it for ya."

Stevie glanced at a pensioner in a crumpled grey suit, looking completely harmless.

"They're waiting for you outside," he added.

Stevie got up and walked to the door. He stood beneath the pub sign and relit his roll-up.

Across the street in the shadows, the back door of a tatty old car opened slightly.

He pocketed his zippo and went to join the three occupants of the motor. There was the nondescript driver, a large man filling the front passenger seat, and a smaller individual in the back.

The front passenger swivelled round and looked Stevie up and down.

"How ya doin'?" he asked cheerfully.

"I'm good."

"So you're looking after things while Robbie's away are ya?" He smiled slightly. "I guess so."

"Am I amusing ya?" His cheerfulness was gone.

"No. I've just never heard him called Robbie before."

"Are you mocking the way I speak?"

"No. No, not at all. My grandmother's from Derry, I love the way you speak."

"He's OK, Joe," muttered the driver.

"Derry you say?"

He nodded and the man smiled again.

"We hear you like a ruck."

"Sometimes, you know, when it's necessary."

He nodded. "Like when you wanna make sure your enemies never come back. That sort of thing?"

"Yeah," Stevie agreed.

A silence was allowed to settle over the car as it moved through the half empty streets. Stevie knew it was done to unnerve him, but he also knew they wanted a favour. As long as he could cling on to that, he had nothing to worry about.

"Those lads you chased off the market the other week, you think they'll be back to set up again?"

Stevie shrugged. "Not if they got any sense."

"Trouble is, whether they do or not, that's not really the end to it, is it? There's a march coming up soon I believe? Same people."

"We've got plans." Stevie smiled.

"Regardless, they'll still be trying to corrupt our young men, won't they?"

Stevie's smile slipped. He knew that was true, they were selling their rag at the football, outside gigs, all over the bloody place it seemed to him.

"I guess."

"So, what you need to do is cut off the supply. With nothing to sell, they can't attract followers, can they?"

"I guess not," he agreed.

"So tell me, do you know the Ernesettle trading estate?"

He nodded. "Out past the sewage works."

"That's right." He glanced around the car for support. "Isn't it?"

"Yeah," said the driver.

"That's right," said the man pressed up against Stevie.

"And did you know there's a little print shop on that estate?"

Stevie shook his head.

"Well, there is. It's where those skinheads get their filth printed."

"I didn't know that."

"They print all sorts of rubbish there. Even lies about us. It's disgusting."

"Oh," said Stevie. He was waiting for the guy to get to the point. To explain why he'd been summoned late at night.

"Now, we don't want them setting up again at the market, do we? And you can't be down there every weekend, can you?"

Stevie waited. Here it came.

"So how would you feel about putting them out of business permanently?"

"I'd say that's a good idea."

"Good lad, so we understand they keep cash at the printers."
"Really?"
"Yeah. Really."
"How much?"
"Enough to be worth your while."
Stevie nodded.
The passenger gestured with his finger and the car did a U-turn.
"If you do find yourself in there one of these nights, we want you to leave this behind."
He nodded at his companion in the back seat and the man opened the bag on his lap. He said to Stevie, "Now you see this button here?"
Stevie looked and nodded.
"Just press that down and get the hell out, got it?"
He nodded again. The man closed the bag and handed it across.
"OK?' the passenger asked
"No problem," Stevie replied.
"Good lad, now where can we drop you?"
"The Falcon."
At the Falcon, the passenger again turned in his seat. "There's no rush," he said. "Anytime before the march."
"Here you are then, safe and sound," said the driver.
Stevie opened the door.
"I look forward to reading about it," said the passenger.
Stevie took the bag into his lair.

29

When Mia was six years old, she used to talk to her favourite doll.

"One day I'm going to have a baby just like you."

A child of her own was all she dreamed of.

Then, at the age of seven, her parents had proudly waved her off to boarding school. It was time to put away childish things. There would be no more dollies. She was destined to serve the State in an important capacity. One day she might get a medal for some heroic deed of patriotism.

She would forsake her own dreams for the honour of the family.

From the very start, she was being trained to infiltrate the enemy. Once suitably educated, she would be an important cog in the machine. Essential for the smooth running and wellbeing of her country. It was vital valuable work.

Western imperial decadence had to be stopped at all costs, and she could help achieve this.

At the time she had no idea the system she was being indoctrinated to protect was already on its last legs.

She was the best student in her class. She was tested repeatedly, exposed to decadence, and educated in how best to resist.

But a lot changed during her final year of training. One by one the old instructors mysteriously left. Only to be replaced by a new generation.

Such disruption during a critical chapter of her indoctrination was risky. If not handled carefully, there would be chinks in her armour. Her immunity to temptations of the West could not be guaranteed. A half decent interrogator might be able to turn her.

Nonetheless her old instructors disappeared.

The new ones had all been to universities in America or Britain or West Germany. They saw the world very differently to their predecessors. It was confusing for the students. But they kept quiet and did as they were told.

Nobody dared say so out loud, but it seemed as though Communism might actually be failing.

Certainly, the new instructors were thinking and acting more like Westerners.

Smuggling money, gold, and expensive objects out of the country was the new priority. Just as Mia was ready to go into the field.

30

Stevie had called a band meeting for ten o'clock at night. That simple fact was enough for Paulie and Spike to bring their balaclavas.

The seriousness of the meeting was confirmed as soon as Stevie said, "Those skinheads from the market? I know where they print their crap."

He had their attention.

"So we're going to drive over there and bring this." He held up a plastic petrol can. "Any questions?"

His partners in crime shook their heads. They had no questions. His statement couldn't have been clearer. So they piled into the van and Paulie drove slowly around the estate until Stevie said, "Stop here."

He and Spike climbed out and quietly approached Unit 18. Very few businesses had alarms back then and certainly not a low-key print shop.

Spike used bolt cutters on the door, and they were inside in a flash.

Stevie opened his bag. He pulled the petrol can out and handed it to Spike. "Here, sprinkle this around."

Then he took out a crowbar and headed to the safe on the back wall. He forced it open. Inside were some master tapes for something and just about enough cash to make the operation worth their while.

"Light it, and let's go," Spike suggested.

"One second." Stevie pulled a black box about the size of a house brick from his satchel.

"What's that?"

"Nothin'."

He placed the box in the centre of the room and slid back the cover. Pressed the button and said, "Let's go."

They walked back to the van, and Paulie drove away. Nobody spoke. The air was crisp and calm. It was one of those nights when the slightest sound carries for miles. They moved ever further from the scene of the crime with only the engine noise and their own thoughts for company. Suddenly, without warning, there was a mighty explosion. The car actually shook. The noise was so loud it was like it had come from right behind them.

Except when Paulie looked in his rear-view mirror, the giant fireball lighting up the night sky was over the industrial estate.

"What the fuck was that?" he said in awe.

"Who knows," said Spike.

"Could have been anything," said Stevie.

31

Mia knocked excitedly on Nikki's door. It was barely open when she blurted out, "I've got the photos from the shoot."

Nikki screamed in delight.

"Come in, come in."

Mia spread the prints out on the kitchen table.

"Ah, they're really good."

"Thanks. It's because you're such a good designer."

Nikki smiled at her. "Thanks, babe. These will really help me promote my stuff."

"A proper businesswoman."

"I guess, I mean I opened a bank account yesterday."

Mia was hugely impressed. Nikki had said she would but to actually do such a thing.

"A woman with her own bank account?" She said it with wonderment in her tone.

"I know! A few years ago I would have needed permission from my father or my husband."

"I think we still have this in my country."

"Luckily, the world is changing. 'Cos I ain't got a husband, and my father fucked off years ago, so I'd be a bit screwed."

THE KILLSWITCH

They both laughed.

"A woman having her own bank account?" Mia still couldn't quite believe it.

But as she struggled with that particular concept, Nikki hit her with an even bigger bombshell.

"You could start a business. Sell your prints, you know? Everyone wants photos of punks. You could be a businesswoman, too. Open a bank account of your own."

Mia stared at her wide-eyed. She actually looked in shock.

"Are you alright, Mia?"

Mia took a moment to compose herself.

"They'd never let me."

"Who wouldn't?"

Mia looked away. Nikki knew about women too scared to say what they were thinking.

"Don't tell 'em," she advised.

Mia didn't reply and Nikki didn't press the issue.

She spread her photos out on the floor, and they studied them.

"Look at this one. I look like Viv Albertine"

Mia nodded. "Yeah you do."

"Have you read her latest interview?"

"Not yet. I bet its good though."

"She's so cool. Taking charge of her own destiny. That's what I'm going to do."

"Yeah, who knew women could start their own band?"

"Women can do anything!"

32

Stevie hadn't seen Aiden for a while, so was thrilled to spot him walking towards the record shop. He caught up and tapped him on the shoulder.

"Hey."

Aiden stopped and they beamed broadly at each other.

"How you doin'? Ain't seen you around."

"We've been rehearsing a lot." This was his stock response to any questions these days.

"How's it going?"

"Yeah, good."

"How's Nikki?"

"Yeah, good. Mia?"

"Yeah, good."

They walked in silence for a minute before Aiden asked,

"Did you hear about that explosion on the industrial estate?"

"Yeah, yeah, I did. Quite a fire by all accounts."

"What do you think it was?"

"Who knows? Gas explosion maybe. Hey, wanna come hear us play?"

"Course."

"It's the same day as the NF march, so come early."

"We're gonna counter demo?"

"Yep."

"How many's coming?"

"Enough?"

"I'll be there. Put me on the list."

Stevie smiled. "I've already put your name down."

"Been a while since I've had a ruck," he said whilst glancing at a cut above Stevie's chin.

"You?"

Stevie simply smiled. He wasn't getting sucked in that easily. "Your mum's normally got plenty of empties, hasn't she?"

"I'll see what I can find."

Stevie nodded approval.

Aiden was taking in the changes since he'd last seen his pal. There was quite a few. Not just his appearance, he was more guarded, more mature perhaps.

It's like a puppy, he decided. *I haven't seen him for a while so I notice he's growing up.*

"I like your hair."

"Cheers, Nikki did it. She's great. You'll never guess what she did the other night…"

And he was off telling the kind of anecdote that sounded a lot better if you're in love with the person being discussed. Aiden was pleased his mate seemed happy.

"I really love her," Stevie ended by saying.

Aiden smiled. "I know what you mean."

"Mia?"

"Yeah."

"It's great being a grown-up, innit?"

"Yeah, except I don't see you so much."

"At least I'm getting laid," Stevie roared.

They both laughed. They were still laughing when they reached the junction where they had to go their separate ways.

"See you at the Falcon on Saturday?"

"I'll be there."

33

The big day arrived.

Aiden got to the Falcon around nine. It was already surprisingly busy. Residents from the estate and Irish navvies were drinking hard. Upstairs, punks and anarchists mingled with Rock against Racism people, and scattered throughout were a handful of street thugs.

Despite the early hour, the pub was doing a roaring trade in Dutch courage.

The landlord didn't care some of his drinkers were below legal age, and the dealers in the toilet couldn't give a shit as long as they had the cash.

"Whizz or hash? Get in line."

Most who were there for the punch-up opted for whizz, the same drug they filled the squaddies with during World War I before sending them over the top. Most had already started indulging.

Aiden arrived into this madness, carrying two bin liners full of empty bottles.

"Do you wanna take them upstairs?" Stevie suggested.

"Yeah, sure."

Upstairs, a young kid with leopard spot hair took the bottles from him. They were carefully filled with petrol and had a piece of rag stuffed in the top. They were then stacked in a crate which was piled with other crates. Shortly, the whole lot would be taken out and positioned strategically around the estate.

Aiden was taking it all in when Stevie approached him.

"Look, mate."

Aiden followed the point of his finger.

"Like it?"

"It's a stage." He was proud of his buddy. "Your stage."

"Yeah."

He grabbed him round the shoulders. "It'll be brilliant"

"Too right. We can celebrate stopping those bastards marching."

People in his immediate vicinity heard the comment. Cries of 'Yeah' and such like went up. It was only midmorning but already the atmosphere was getting rowdy.

The girls were conspicuous by their absence. They weren't stupid. They were meeting at Nikki's place. Mia arrived at midday.

"Oh, you brought your camera, good. Come in, come in."

By one o'clock there was a roomful of girls. They drank Blue Nun, tried on clothes, and helped each other with hair and makeup. They all wanted photos.

They were pretty tipsy and all talking over each other—

"Are we going to the march?"

"I dunno, what do you reckon?"

"It's gonna kick off innit?"

"Yeah probably."

"I don't want no part of that."

"I ain't getting dressed up for that."

"I should go, show support an' that you know for Stevie and the boys," Nikki finally said.

"I wouldn't mind going. Boo a few fascists," said Karen.

"What about you, Mia?"

"We had fascists in my country. They did terrible things. I want to boo as well."

"Let's do it."

There was one remaining doubter. They all looked towards her.

"Let's not get too close," she said. "I spent a lot of time on this outfit."

So the decision was made. They were just going to have a look. Show a bit of moral support.

Nikki led her little band of punkettes towards the High Street. They saw police vans parked on every corner and crowds of angry people lining the main routes.

The girls could hear chanting. Nikki headed towards it. The other girls followed her.

Just then, a row of flags came round a corner and into view. Shouts on both sides of the street grew louder and angrier.

Mia took off her lens cap and pushed to the front alongside Nikki. She raised the camera to her eye. She saw a Rasta launch a bottle. She shot off a rapid series of frames. Then the marchers were right in front of them and suddenly, all hell broke loose.

Bricks and bottles rained down. Mia snapped away.

The fascists broke rank almost immediately. Pandemonium reigned as they retreated back the way they had come. It was beautiful to behold.

The battle of Union Street went down in history as the day the racists ran away.

That evening, the Falcon was packed. All creeds and colours were there to celebrate their victory. The locals had got organised and won the day. It was precisely the sort of thing that made the government nervous.

But analysis could wait for the morning. Tonight was a party.

The Clash came blasting through the sound system and the excitement ratcheted up a notch. Soon the band would hit the stage.

Aiden shouted in Stevie's ear, "You ready?"

"Born ready."

Paulie leant across and commented to Aiden, "I saw you out there today."

"I saw you too."

"You a musician?"

"Nah."

"Books is his thing," Stevie interrupted.

"Books?" Paulie repeated. "You like readin'?"

Aiden nodded. "Yeah."

"All books?" Paulie seemed curious.

"Pretty much. I'll give it a go. If it's crap, I won't finish it."

"Self-improvement," he nodded approvingly. "I like it! You'll learn more that way than you will from the education system in this country."

Aiden didn't get much approval, so any that came his way was greatly appreciated. He beamed.

"What are your politics?" Paulie asked.

Aiden shrugged. "I dunno really?" Now he was embarrassed. He didn't know why, but it just felt like the wrong answer. "I'm still working that out."

"Writers usually have opinions."

"I'm not a writer."

"Well, somebody's gotta document this shit," Paulie said

"You could be a writer," Stevie interjected. He believed in the *You can do anything* punk spirit. He was caught up in the heady taste of the day's victory, and he'd caught the look on Aiden's face.

"Can't he?" he appealed to Paulie for back up.

"Definitely! Readers make the best writers."

It was a true *eureka* moment.

The realisation that he would be a writer felt so right. Like a coat that fitted perfectly the very first time you put it on. He loved the idea. It completed him like nothing ever had before.

Paulie leaned in closer. "Writers documenting a movement have a responsibility."

He was so intense, so passionate, Aiden felt like starting the first page there and then.

"I agree," he said solemnly nodding his head.

He'd never interacted with Paulie before. His intensity was completely intoxicating.

"I'll tell the truth."

"Our truth," Paulie insisted.

His dark eyes burned into the impressionable teenager. "Are you up to the challenge? Can you document a moment in history? A movement they will still be talking about a hundred years from now?"

His words juxtaposed perfectly with the heady atmosphere of the day. These were Aiden's people. He was in, fully in.

"I was born for it," he replied.

Paulie nodded and flashed an encouraging smile.

"Our truth," Aiden shouted over the music, and Paulie nodded.

"That's right."

Paulie turned to Stevie. "Come on, let's do it!"

They took to the stage and set off at top speed with full volume. The opening track was a stripped back version of that Clash favourite, Tommy Gun.

Everyone in the room knew it, and the pogo-ing started up immediately. The whole room was rocking; God knows what it sounded like in the pub below. But up here, it was youth doing what they are put on earth for. Confirming life.

Mia came to Aiden's side halfway through the first song.

"Hey," she shouted in his ear.

"How you doing?" he shouted back.

She pulled out her little camera and aimed it at him. He pulled a silly face, and she fired off a shot. They both laughed.

"Get one of Stevie," he shouted.

Aiden studied her as she aimed and fired.

He watched her take a few of the band and the individual members. In the time it took her to turn back and smile at him, he knew he was in love.

Her fingers brushed against his hand, and he thought he might die of happiness.

She stopped taking pictures, let the camera hang around her neck, and studied him before asking, "Do you have a girlfriend?"

He shook his head. "No, have you got a boyfriend?"

"No," she said, and they smiled at each other.

"I'm a writer," he said happily.

"Cool," she replied.

Then the camera was hoisted back up and she took a few shots.

Later he walked her home.

"Stand under that streetlight," she said. "Let me take your picture."

He posed for her.

She took a few snaps, moving closer and closer until she was pressing against his chest. He swiped the camera aside, pulled her to him, and they kissed for the very first time. It was a moment that had been building all evening. There were fireworks, and it was the first kiss that had taken his breath away. When it was over, and they looked into each other's eyes they knew that was special. That destiny had thrown them together.

"I want one of those pictures."

"Of course."

She wrapped her arm around his waist, and he threw his

across her shoulder. And neither wanted this feeling to ever stop.

"Maybe I can write some words someday to go with your pictures?"

"Of course," she said in her delightful foreign accent.

He dreamed of them working together forever more.

34

Now that Aiden had been officially sanctioned as the scribe within the tribe, his standing improved.

He began selling hash to the punks as well as Martin's biker customers. For the first time in his life he was in love and had money in his pocket.

He liked it best when Mia sat with him in the evenings as he waited for customers. He would tell her his plans, and she would kiss him passionately.

Other times, he sat alone reading while she went to Nikki's to discuss the sisterhood of feminists.

Nikki would advise her who to read.

"We are the latest wave in a long line going all the way back to the Suffragettes."

One weekend Mia joined Nikki on a women-only coach trip to Greenham Common. There were men on site, but they did the cooking and the child minding whilst the women took care of politics. It was inspiring. Mia took some great photos and promised to send back prints to her new friends.

35

Aiden's mum poked her head around his bedroom door.

"Aiden?" she stage whispered.

He wasn't there. His bed covers were thrown back as though awaiting his return. He'd nipped outside to the toilet, as she well knew. She would have to be quick. There was a book on his bed. She glanced at the cover: *The Sun Also Rises*. She picked it up.

Just then Aiden appeared. He snatched it from her.

"That's mine," he said.

"Alright, no need to take it out on me just 'cos your bird's left ya."

"She hasn't left me. She's gone to visit her family."

"Yeah, right," she said with a sarcastic smile.

She read the title of the book he was clutching between them.

"The sun also rises? What the fuck's that? Of course the sun rises. It also sets. Is there a book called "The Sun also Sets"? You don't 'alf read some rubbish."

"It ain't about the sun," Aiden snapped.

"Anyway," she said, "I need you to go down the corner shop and get me some fags." She attempted a smile.

He held out his hand. "Money."

"I'm a bit skint right now."

"Hasn't he got any money?" He nodded towards the door.

She ignored that idea.

"You must 'ave some money you can lend me. You can't 'ave wasted it all on books."

As she spoke, she picked his trousers from the floor and gave them a shake. They both heard the unmistakable jangle of coins.

"Go on." She smiled again as best she could.

Aiden frowned but was putting his jeans on.

"I'll 'ave some breakfast waiting when you get back," she called.

When he returned, he heard the radio in the kitchen, so he went in.

Only she wasn't there. Martin was.

"Oh, it's you," Aiden's tone was neutral.

Martin was leaning back against the sink holding a knife. He threw it up. It rotated one hundred and eighty degrees. He caught it by the handle.

"Yer mum's getting dressed. I'm doing some toast."

He half slid the tray out from the grill. Gave it a quick glance and slid it back in.

"Nearly there," he said and threw the knife up in the air. Again he caught it cleanly by the handle.

It was only a butter knife, not exactly dangerous, but still Aiden was mildly impressed.

Martin turned to face him.

"Did you get her smokes?"

"Yeah."

"Give us one then."

36

Berlin was bitterly cold. Snow flurries fell from the sky and turned to slush as soon as they hit the ground.

Mia was sitting in an icy classroom. The students in the room knew they were privileged because the heating system was on. Not that it warmed anyone up, but it rattled and hummed so they knew it was on. Knew they were supposed to be grateful. There were thirty in the room. They were all of similar ages but were far from friends. Nobody trusted anybody in the GDR. It paid to be as suspicious of close friends as you were of everybody else.

Mia took notes. They all did.

At the end of the lecture, she was asked to wait behind.

"How is it over there?"

"They are strange people," she replied. "Very strange."

"When are you going back?"

"On Tuesday."

"I hear you have a boyfriend?"

"Yes."

"Don't get close to him."

IAN PARSON

"I won't."
"Stay alert."
"I will."

37

A few days later, Aiden and Stevie's paths crossed outside the record store.

"How's it going?"

"Yeah good."

"I like your hair," Aiden said.

"Cheers."

Stevie modelled a purple Mohican standing half a metre off his head from front to back.

"An' your piercings."

His nose and ears were full of metal.

"Cheers, Nikki dun 'em."

Aiden nodded. He genuinely was impressed. Stevie's response to the fuss his earring had caused was to get five piercings running the length of his left earlobe and a silver stud pushed through his right nostril.

Every single pedestrian that passed stole a glance. In a few short months Stevie had progressed from a nonchalant schoolboy to a fully-fledged preening peacock.

"Wanna go for a smoke?" Stevie suggested.

Aiden nodded. "Yeah, OK."

Behind the record store by the steps for the multi-storey car park, they stopped. Stevie pulled a big fat joint from his pocket and sparked up.

Shoppers passed them in an almost constant stream to and from cars. One or two theatrically sniffed the air or threw unfriendly grimaces at Stevie in particular. Even those that didn't recognise the scent of hashish stared. From disgusted pensioners to extremely impressionable little kids.

The boys paid them no attention whatsoever. Stevie was like the star attraction of the freak show on a break between performances.

"So did you like our gig?"

"Yeah brilliant, I didn't recognise all the songs."

"Some were mine, that's why."

"Yours?"

"Yeah, I'm a songwriter now," he announced between tokes.

"Yeah?" Aiden was sort of impressed yet sort of annoyed. He was the wordsmith around here.

"Go on then," he suggested, "sing something."

Stevie burst into a fast, staccato rhyme,

"Just because it was safe yesterday, doesn't mean it'll be safe today.
Now's the time to have a blast, being young ain't gonna last."

"It's good," Aiden said. *I've got nothing to worry about from him*, he thought

"Thanks."

"How's it goin' with the band?"

Stevie nodded, coughed a bit, and said, "We've got another gig." He passed the joint back.

"Cool!"

"You'll 'ave to come."

"Yeah."

Stevie finished the joint and threw the roach at a passing couple. "Bring Mia if you like." He smirked.

"When is it?"

"Friday, at the Castle."

"She won't be back. She's in Berlin visiting her family."

"Oh."

"We kissed after your last show."

"Yeah, I noticed you left together."

Aiden smirked.

"She took some photos of you on stage."

"Oh, cool. I've gotta see them."

"Yeah, me too. They haven't been developed yet."

"Will Nikki be at the gig?"

"Yeah."

They studied each other. Both a little unsure what the protocols were in this new world, halfway between schoolchild and adult delinquent.

Stevie punched his old pal in the arm. "Kissed her, eh?" But they didn't wrestle like they used to. Back then they didn't care about messing up their hairstyles or looking childish.

"I saw your mum the other day. She wanted to know why'd you left home?"

"Oh. Yeah. What did you say?"

"Why did you though?"

Stevie shrugged. "I'm just sick of all the bullshit. Eat your greens. Did I tell ya about Elvis? Back in my day, blah, blah, blah. I'm fuckin' sick of it."

"I said you was in love."

Stevie smiled like the cat who can't believe he's got the cream.

"Anyway your mum said to tell you to come 'ome whenever you like."

"If you see her again, tell her I'll visit soon. I like living with Nikki."

"I wonder why?"

They both smirked.

"I'll give you a taster of my best lyric," Stevie replied.

"I hear sirens, so I'm hiding.
They're getting closer, now further away...
Darkness is my friend tonight,
Wouldn't 'ave it no other way."

"That's better than the other one."

"Cheeky fucker. Don't forget to tell Mia I wanna see those photos."

"I will."

38

Most punks were outsiders long before hearing their first heavy guitar. Discovering the music just gave them a home. Made them realise it was ok to be a freak.

In the early days, the movement accepted anyone. Gay, straight, black, white, none of that stuff mattered. For the first time in youth culture, all were welcome.

But for punk to appeal, certain ingredients were needed. First a large dose of hopelessness. Kids had to reach the point where they gave up believing. This had to be seasoned with a healthy pinch of cynicism. A refusal to believe the struggle from one year to the next was inevitable.

Then boil up the huge gulf between a generation that accepted authority as the price of security and their kids, who didn't.

But even if these stars all aligned, punk still needed a voice to go global.

Step forward Joe Strummer. He was intelligent, informed, literate, and angry.

His fundamental message was very simple,

"Question Everything."

And they did.

Thousands flocked to the cause for a wide variety of reasons from a vast array of backgrounds from peace-loving art students to violence-loving football hooligans. They were all accepted. Punk was indeed a broad church.

The presence of actual hooligans in the mix made it easy for lazy journalists to brand all punks as vicious thugs.

But to imagine that was all they had in the locker was a huge mistake.

They mainly questioned everything because they were thirsty for knowledge. They were intelligent, open-minded, and they got organised. They had to. Everybody hated them.

As punk developed, as the Sex Pistols fell by the wayside, factions grew; splinter groups formed and broke off. But for a while, in the early days, punks were all singing from the same hymnbook. It made the authorities very nervous.

39

More months passed before the boys got together again.

"I've been saving money."

Stevie stepped back and surveyed his pal from head to toe, clearly impressed. "You what? How the fuck have you been savin' money?"

"You know, selling hash an' just stayin' in."

"What you gonna do with it?"

"I've ordered a passport."

"Wow, that's cool."

"Yeah." Aiden's grin matched his pal's

"Where you gonna go?"

"I dunno. Paris, Berlin, somewhere cool."

"The travelling man."

"That sounds like the title of a book."

"Or a song," Stevie replied and immediately reached inside his jacket. He pulled out a bookie's pen and a little reporter's notebook.

Travel was instantly gone from Aiden's mind.

"You carry a notebook?" He was amazed.

"Course, else I forget my ideas." He looked up. "Don't you?"

Aiden was furious with himself; he shook his head in the negative.

Stevie put it away. "Come on," he said. "Let's get you sorted out"

And they went to Woolworth's to steal a notebook.

After they parted company, Aiden stopped in the park. He pulled his new notebook guiltily from his pocket and glanced around furtively. There were people about, but nobody was paying him a blind bit of attention. He went and sat on a bench beneath a giant oak tree. He pulled out the pen Stevie had also stolen.

Nib poised, he hesitated. This felt like a huge moment, only he was too young to understand why. It was one thing agreeing to document a movement when you're half pissed and caught up in the moment. It was quite another staring at a clean, empty page in the cold, sober light of day.

I'm a writer, he told himself, and his ego laughed and laughed.

Go on then, write something writer boy!

He took a deep breath and wrote the line.

As of now, I'm a writer.

He sat back, exhaled, read it, and smiled.

'As of now' with a comma— that's exactly how a writer would put it, he decided smugly.

I'm a writer, he told himself again, this time it seemed less ridiculous. *This is no game. This is my life. School's finished, and now I'm a writer.*

The satisfaction this simple statement gave him was immense.

Holding this pen was nothing like the hundreds of times he'd held one in a classroom. It was like the clouds had cleared. For the very first time in his life he could see clearly. He prepared to write a list of places he assumed they must employ writers.

THE KILLSWITCH

The first name he put down was *Sounds*.

He sat back and imagined what it must be like working for them. The free gigs, the backstage passes, access to the most hallowed places in music.

He wrote a few more names of places he'd like to work. Crossed some out, added others, then examined it.

Only the music papers had made the cut. *Sounds*, *NME*, *Melody Maker*, even *Smash Hits*, he'd dared to put down *Rolling Stone* as well, although he hurriedly crossed it out before adding it again guiltily. Knowing he was reaching too high.

They would never employ someone like me, he thought.

He expanded the list. *The Sun* and *The Herald*. He crossed them both out and replaced them with the all-encompassing word *newspapers*.

But he was kidding himself. He had no interest in working for a newspaper. He abandoned his list. He didn't want to work for somebody else. He wanted to write books, novels. He had absolutely no idea how that could be made to happen. So he started a new list.

He wrote *Ernest Hemingway*.

He'd read somewhere about the ten-thousand-hour rule. Whereby if you practised hard at something, after ten thousand hours you were accomplished. The article he'd read had cited Mozart as an example. He couldn't recall precisely, but it was something about Mozart achieving his ten thousand piano hours by the age of nine or some ridiculously low number.

Well, if its good enough for Mozart.

And with pen poised he prepared to construct a sentence.

Write about what you know, he'd read somewhere. He looked around the park and autumn stared back at him.

The leaves swayed in the gentle breeze.

He altered a word here, added another there, looked at the trees for a while and put down another sentence. All the time feeling more and more strongly as though this was what he was put here on Earth to do. Nothing else mattered.

A couple of hours later he rose and headed home. He'd written his first original piece. It was naff and would never get published, but it was a start.

40

Jacob didn't go to his old barbers for a haircut anymore. He avoided what used to be his local pub as well. His expensive suits would look out of place. Besides, he had a feeling he wouldn't be particularly welcome these days. He went to the salons and wine bars that were springing up all over town instead. He adjusted pretty quickly.

Officially the Trust set him up as a computer troubleshooter. An expert in this exciting new field. They gave him a budget that would make a government department blush and left him to it.

He was not expected to produce receipts or invoices. He was expected to keep busy.

In the beginning there were plenty of dissident groups. Leetabix infiltrated them one at a time and communications were intercepted. All information was analysed, and viable threats neutralised.

The Leetabix budget included sufficient funds to also clean up his image, his reputation, his past.

Punk rock and fraternising with criminals was wiped away. His record now showed a quiet boy with a master's degree in computer technology. A long list of charitable endeavours was mysteriously made public. Overnight he became a squeaky clean, bona fide celebrity.

He stopped employing activists. Instead he plucked hungry young technical wizards from top universities.

Those willing to disregard all they had been taught about ethics and good business practise. The ones that saw nothing wrong in destroying paper trails or digital footprints when they needed to cover their tracks.

He set them to work familiarising themselves with propaganda and misinformation tactics. As the World Wide Web gained popularity, as more people went online, they were going to be his cyber stormtroopers.

The Trust's very own secret unit operating in areas few were aware even existed. This was the beginning of the digital age.

Nobody questioned what a computer department did, because hardly anyone understood what a computer did.

A year later Jacob had been summoned before the chairman. This was now standard practice whenever a section of society dared question their lot.

"You asked to see me, sir?"

"You heard about that union trouble?"

"Yes, sir. Something about mechanisation forcing their members into the ranks of the unemployed."

"See what you can find out about the leaders." He passed a scrap of paper across the table. "Call our friend when you have something."

"Something he can splash across his front page, tarnish a few reputations, titillate the great British public, that sort of thing you mean?"

"Not just tarnish. I want reputations lying in tatters on the side of the road."

Jacob smiled. This was what he did.

"Yes, sir."

41

It was late at night, and on the wrong side of town a car screeched to a halt. Doors slammed and footsteps ran across the concrete. Stevie reached for his baseball bat, jumped up, and peeked carefully through the gap in the curtain. It was nothing, but he was twitchy all the time these days.

"You alright, hun?" Nikki asked.

"Yeah, I'm fine."

"What's with the bat?"

"It's nothin'. Just being careful." He was already pulling on his clothes. "I'll see you later."

"OK."

The initial excitement she'd felt regarding his secretive exploits had worn off long ago. Now she was worried about him all the time.

42

Mia was in the phone box speaking German.

"They've abandoned political pressure. Stevie is the leader now. He's the one they all look to for orders. He's impatient to instigate guerrilla tactics. Without him they're just another street gang."

Mia could hear typing. Her words would go down on her permanent record.

"And this other boy?"

"He knows everyone. He likes to write so that's useful."

There was a brief pause as though this scenario was being considered.

"You are sleeping together." It was a statement not a question.

"I find it easier to control him."

There was another pause, longer this time. "Call me tomorrow," said the woman in German.

"I will."

After all her training and preparation Mia couldn't believe how easy it had been to infiltrate the group. There was hardly any need for the devious lies she had been tutored to tell. But then punks lived in such abject poverty only the truly committed would put themselves through it. If you wanted to be in, you were!

She walked the short distance back to the squat, slipped into the kitchen, and went to sit by Aiden.

"Busy tonight," she commented.

"Some friends have come over."

"Oh," she replied simply whilst using the fingers of her right hand to draw patterns on the palm of his left. She seemed about to say something else, but a chair was scraped back from the table and now Stevie was on his feet, holding court.

He had truly developed into a force to be reckoned with. That rare breed people are drawn to, a too real firebrand, a natural organiser. He was articulate without being condescending, passionate without being overbearing. Leaders like him were a real thorn in the side of the bourgeois establishment.

Mia took in every word whilst appearing to be interested only in finger wrestling.

Stevie was saying, "There is no point trying to adapt what already exists. We must destroy those things. We waste time and effort trying to adapt and adjust, it's pointless. Any momentum simply withers away. Nothing happens and we turn back to the old ways once again."

He stood to his full height and raised his voice defiantly. "We need to reach the point where turning back is not an option. We need to destroy before we can truly rebuild. Until you are prepared to risk everything, literally all you hold dear, you cannot have a better world."

His eyes were darting across the faces of his audience. He was looking for who was with him, who was concerned, and who didn't belong. As his gaze flitted across Mia, he registered indifference.

When he finished, there was a smattering of applause and whoops.

43

The Trust were holding a meeting for their top clients.

The computer was being upgraded. It no longer took cassettes. It was now equipped for the latest, cutting-edge technology: floppy disks.

"This 'Galactic Network' do we have control yet?"

"I believe they are referring to it as the World Wide Web now, sir."

"What kind of name is that? I've never heard anything so ridiculous."

"It's a game changer, sir. It will change the old 'east/west' divide forever."

"Do we have control?" he asked impatiently.

"That turned out to not be possible, sir. So we have taken a different approach."

"We have?"

Jacob was given the nod. His star was truly rising.

His ability to shut down all dissent as the Trust raped and pillaged their way to the top of the capitalist tree had impressed some very influential people.

He rose to his feet and cleared his throat. "I believe the future is the World Wide Web."

He went on to explain the prospect of connecting offices together via computers.

Not just in the same building, not even in the same city, but anywhere at all on the whole planet.

Naturally, they were intrigued.

He explained how they could oversee everything, have the latest up-to-date analysis at their fingertips, and keep detailed files on all staff members.

"And finally, I cannot stress enough how the law is seriously lacking. The technology is so new it's not mentioned on a single legal document anywhere? We are living in an age, gentlemen, comparable to the gold rush of the 1800s, a real wild west, and we are poised to take maximum advantage."

By the time he sat down, they were convinced that if only half his predictions came true it was going to alter the landscape forever, and they were going to be very, very rich. Thank God they were ahead of the game, ahead of the law.

44

The next morning, Mia gently prodded Aiden awake. He smiled before he opened his eyes. He loved waking up next to her.

When he looked, she was propped up on one elbow inches from his face.

"Mornin'."

She kissed him on the cheek.

"You could write about last night." she said. He loved how her mind worked. The way she was always thinking ahead.

"Really, not much happened."

"But you will make it happen. Who said what to who, the little glances, you know. It's important to practice your art."

"Yeah," he agreed.

She was practically setting him homework, but he didn't see it that way. He saw it as supporting him to create.

She smiled, got up, and ducked under the clothesline.

It spread from a hook above the door to a nail over the window. Clothes were draped across one end whilst Mia's black and white prints were pegged at the other. Aiden's ancient typewriter with the dodgy lower case s sat in the corner on the crate he used as a desk. There was an open box of paper alongside it. All over the floor, crumpled sheets were scattered and forgotten.

On the walls, gig posters ripped from subways masked the damp patches. It was cold and squalid and pure Bohemian, but it was their little love nest.

"We're both artists." He sounded proud.

"Ja," she agreed.

"We're Bohemian," he elaborated.

Of course anyone can claim to be bohemian. To which there is only one response...

Show me the work, the art.

Painting, poetry, writing, sculpture. The medium is unimportant, but a true bohemian creates.

"Like Berlin in the thirties."

"Yeah." He liked the comparison. He liked it a lot.

She stroked his arm and kissed him on the hand. Then she reached for her coat.

"You're going out?"

"You know my grandmother is ill. I should phone."

"Is there anything I can do?"

"You're sweet," she said in her adorable accent.

"Are you coming back?"

"I go to see Nikki. You work."

"OK, I gotta see Martin later. I'll catch you at the pub."

She blew him a kiss.

When she was gone, he brought his typewriter to the bed and pulled the covers over his legs. It was less comfortable but considerably warmer.

Love is Bohemian, he wrote. *It obeys no rules and goes where it likes.*

Before she returned, he had written a thousand words making a strong connection between punks and the original

French Bohemians. To him, they were kindred spirits, *outsiders* asking nothing of conventional society and untroubled by its disapproval.

45

After making her call, Mia went to Nikki's. It fascinated her that such a young woman was so brave. So willing to follow her own path.

She found her flicking through the pages of *Spare Rib* magazine.

"Here look, whaddya think of this?"

She jabbed at the page. It was an article about the stereotyping of women. How they were treated as subordinates to men. Apparently, this was manifested by inequality around pay. It was time for women's voices to be heard. Mia was engrossed. Was the world ready for such a concept?

She was not anti-man but she was beginning to realise she was definitely anti-subordination of women. She loved having a friend like Nikki with whom such topics could be discussed, explored, hoped for.

Mia was reading still when there was a loud rap on the back door. Nikki went to open it, and there stood Paulie.

"Alright, Nik? Is he ready?"

He followed her into the kitchen and saw Mia.

"What you readin'?"
She showed him the cover.
"Women's Lib? They're all hippies ain't they?"
Mia shrugged.
"Leave 'er alone." Nikki leapt to her defence.
"Now you I could see reading that stuff. Not 'er." He nodded towards Mia
"Leave 'er alone," Nikki repeated just as Stevie came into the room.
"Leave who alone?" he asked.
"Your mate is picking on Mia."
Stevie laughed and they left.
Once back at the Falcon, Paulie asked Stevie, "How well do you know that girl?"
"I don't really, why?"
"I don't trust her. There's something about her."
"She's alright."
"How do you know? None of us know 'er, not really. She just turned up."
"We could ask Aiden."
"Nah, he's shagging her. He's too close to see. We should do your mate a favour. Find out what she's about."
"Where does she live?"
Stevie frowned. "They're in a squat down by the canal."
"Except right now he's downstairs and she's at Nikki's. Why don't we go have a look around? Just to be sure."
He shrugged. "OK."
Getting into the room was child's play. Paulie was the more experienced burglar. He cast his eye over the place.
Where would I hide something?
He noticed the bed legs didn't quite match the worn marks on the carpet. They lifted the bed and rolled the rug aside and discovered a secret compartment in the wooden floorboards.

There were films, photos, letters in German. They took the lot and didn't bother replacing the furniture. Let her know someone's on her case. See what she does.

46

Mia had been on her feet all day and knew she and Aiden would be walking home later. By one of those little quirks of fate she decided on a whim to pop home and change her shoes. She stepped through the door, glanced about, turned around, slammed it shut, and left.

She walked to the phone box and dialled the number. She explained what she had discovered.

"Do you have your passport?"

"It's back in the room, unless they took it."

"Get it and call the driver. He will take you to the airport. Go to the Interflug desk. They will be expecting you."

Half an hour later she sidled up to Aiden in the pub. He only needed to take one look at her.

"What's the matter?" he whispered.

She led him outside.

"What's with the bag?" he asked.

"My muti, she is worse."

"You have to go now?"

"Yes."

"Oh," he said, sounding despondent.

She reached inside her coat and pulled out two passports. She was, for the first time in her life, not exactly disobeying an order but certainly putting her own slant on one.

"I brought yours in case you want to come, and your toothbrush." She patted her bag.

He pulled her to him, and they kissed.

"Of course I do."

He considered for a moment, what was there in the room that he needed?

"My typewriter."

"We'll get another."

That was good enough. He wasn't thinking logically. He just wanted to be with her.

"My friend can drive us to the airport. But we have to go now."

He went to go back in the pub, but she grabbed his arm. "There isn't time," she said, "besides—"

"I should go upstairs an' tell Steve."

"—I hate goodbyes," she finished her sentence.

He shrugged. "He'll understand," and got in the car.

They hit the open road in silence. There was a lot to think about. Not, was he doing the right thing, which was a given. He would follow her to the ends of the earth if need be. But somehow, leaving so quickly felt wrong. Aiden decided not to dwell on it. He'd always wanted to leave and now he was, with her, everything else was irrelevant.

"I could write to him."

"Ja," she agreed.

47

Mia was pulled aside at immigration. An officer was waiting in a back room to hear her story. She told them the room had been ransacked, her pictures, her notes were gone. She had no option but to run.

They thought she acted in haste. That months of work had been wasted.

Mia said nothing although she knew Nikki would have stood up for herself.

"I understand, I'm sorry," she said.

Only she didn't understand at all.

"Why did you bring *him*?"

"My notes are gone, but he's a writer. He can document everything that's lost."

"It was not within your remit."

"I had no choice," she lied. "He will be useful in the West. It will be easier to infiltrate with him. Who will suspect him?"

The two officials exchanged a glance. Nobody had told them about the boy therefore they had no specific instructions.

"You must ensure he doesn't write home."

"I will," she promised

"And discourage phone calls."

"I don't think he knows anyone with a phone."

"Good."

"OK, proceed as you suggest and wait for instructions. When a decision is made, we will send a signal. When you see a red flag flying from the guard tower you come immediately."

She nodded.

"Not him, you."

She nodded again. "When will that be?"

That sort of impertinent question was not suited to an insubordinate female who had just messed up. He fixed her a filthy stare.

"You can go."

By the time Aiden cleared customs she was waiting for him.

"They gave me the full search just because I'm a punk," he complained.

"We're here now." She wrapped her arms around his waist.

He kissed her. "Yeah."

The officials watched them through the one-way glass.

"I don't like her attitude. I think exposure to western decadence may be turning her head."

"So what do we do?"

"We watch them."

The official report noted the couple seemed besotted with each other. He stamped *Untrustworthy* across the front page of her file. She would never rise above the position she now held.

The shadowy figure from the Trust nodded his approval.

48

From the window of their little room, they could see a long stretch of the Berlin wall, a little patch of the deadly "no man's land", and right opposite their window a guard tower.

"This is mental." Aiden couldn't believe how close it was, how real. Sunlight reflected off the binoculars of the guard staring back at him.

"I love it," he added for good measure.

"You can write with this?" she queried.

"I just need a typewriter."

"I can get you one."

"Really?"

"Yes, I think there is an old one at muti's."

"Shall I come with you?"

She touched his arm affectionately and kissed his cheek.

"It will be dull for you, and I will be quicker alone. You'll be OK here, won't you?"

"Yeah," he replied, not really meaning it.

"I'll be back in an hour." She was already halfway out. "See you soon."

When the door closed behind her, the room suddenly felt

THE KILLSWITCH

very empty. He moved back into the shadows and tried to spy on the watchtower guards unobserved.

He imagined living under constant surveillance. With hidden cameras and undercover spies taking note of every little thing you said and did. He let his imagination run riot. He quickly came to the conclusion that you wouldn't be able to trust anyone. You would have to take care every time you expressed an opinion. Before long he drew the curtain. It felt like a victory of sorts.

Two hours later Mia returned. She was carrying a bag of food and a box. She placed the box on the bed and the mattress sunk a little.

"What's in the box?"

Mia beamed happily. "Open it my little budding Hemingway. Open it."

Aiden lifted the lid to reveal a beautiful, old-style typewriter. He'd never been given anything that came in its own hand-crafted box before.

"Wow!"

"You can sit here," Mia suggested. She pushed a hard-backed wooden chair towards the window. She pulled open the curtains he had closed.

"Here," she repeated. "You can sit here and work."

Although he had to admit the wide windowsill was perfect, he glanced doubtfully at the guards who had already aimed their binoculars his way. No doubt attracted by the movement of the curtain.

"What about them?"

"If you ignore them, they'll ignore you."

"You think?" he said doubtfully.

"Of course. Watching a man type will soon get boring. It's not as if they can read your words."

He made a face, which suggested that was a reasonable point. Besides the only other place in the room where he could set up was on the bed and that would be inconvenient. He'd be constantly moving piles of paper around.

He made the little facial expression again. It was somewhere between *seems reasonable* and *sod it*. He lifted the typewriter from its box and placed it carefully on the ledge. It was the perfect height. He smiled over his shoulder at her.

"I just need some paper."

Mia opened the door with a theatrical gesture and in the hallway was paper. "Here," she declared, "A4, West German quality."

He was at her side in a flash.

"Oh, wow."

Four boxes. Five hundred sheets a box, that's a lot of writing.

"Where did you get it from?"

She smiled and kissed him. "I get it for you," she replied.

He reached for her, and they had sex right there on the floor. This was perfect. This was how life should be. Aiden completely forgot about the guards.

49

Nobody understands this World Wide Web like Jacob does.

The legitimate computer care and maintenance company he established under the Trust umbrella was going from strength to strength. They were providing technological back-up all over the country.

They include government departments and blue chip companies among their clients.

He had access to the most sought after contacts in the business world.

Jacob was adding a fortune to the coffers of the Trust.

Some customers were nervous about storing all their information in one place. They knew nothing about the subject except the scare stories about hackers they read in the press. They wanted to be reassured that the security was up to the job. Jacob reminded them he has the latest high tech systems on the market, that he is constantly updating and if the need ever arose, he was able to shut down the whole operation instantly. It was extremely unlikely such a measure would ever be needed but if that day ever came, he could do such a thing. He calls it his Killswitch.

50

Aiden lay in bed smoking a cigarette and watching Mia dress.
All too soon she was kissing his forehead.
"I go an' check on muti."
"Want me to come?"
"Not this time." She smiled. "When she meets you, she will have so many questions we will need a whole day."
That seemed like an exaggeration.
"Really?"
She kissed him again. "I will be back soon."
And she was gone. She had a habit of finishing conversations abruptly. Aiden didn't take it personally.
He settled down to work, blissfully unaware he was being manipulated. He had no idea that to all intents and purposes he was now working for the Trust. They were paying for his food and providing his typewriter.
That night they went to a party in a nearby squat. There were a few punks, but how the locals dressed was a mixed bag indeed. Aiden was impressed.
Back home the different tribes followed strict dress codes. Here it didn't matter what you wore.

Your opinions on the big issues of the day were far more important. Politics, poverty, housing, medical care, unions. They had opinions on them all. And if the conversation was sparkling most would rather sit up until dawn discussing the future than get pissed out of their heads. Attitudes were very different where he came from.

But there wasn't a giant foreboding wall back home looming over everything. So there was that.

Over the coming weeks, he wrote by day as she cared for Muti and by night they partied. It was fabulous. Mia knew all the coolest events.

One night he saw a guy wearing tweeds and a bow tie. Nobody cared; he was rocking to the music with the best of them.

Aiden had never been completely sold on the punk look.

I'm gonna get a new image he decided.

To that end they trawled the charity shops. They shunned public transport, walking everywhere holding hands like in the movies. They were so engrossed in each other they barely even noticed when it rained.

They reinvented themselves. Aiden shaved off his punk hairdo and bought a beret. He wanted to look like Che Guvera.

Mia went for a long grey raincoat over men's suits and trilby style hats that she feminised with bows and ribbons.

He told her she looked like a spy, and she laughed and hugged him.

They practically floated around the city. Picking up flyers, chatting to cool people, and always holding hands.

Mia introduced him as the great English literary star. It got them into cool gigs, hip parties, and the most clandestine of meetings.

Aiden had never been happier. Mia never wanted it to end.

Writing was easy because the people they met were so interesting.

The Berlin squatters placed huge importance on keeping up to date on the law. Every action they took was planned with military precision. From spraying anti-government slogans across public buildings to armed robberies on post offices.

Aiden loved it.

Soon he was upgrading his Che Guvera look. He got a buzz haircut, started wearing granddad shirts with waistcoats, and tried to grow a Lenin beard.

Mia encouraged him every step of the way.

He wrote about where they went, who they met, the crimes these people were involved in. He knew he should change the names to protect the guilty, but he'd do that later. Nobody was ever going to see this first draft.

When people asked, he said he was working on a novel. Which was kind of true.

Finally, Mia took him to meet her grandmother. Just the one visit was enough. They were there for nine hours. It was torturous. The old lady made her granddaughter translate every single word he said. Despite no milk or sugar, she kept topping up his teacup and insisted he eat his fill of some kind of tasteless, rock hard biscuits. The flat smelled of illness.

After that, Mia reverted back to visiting Muti alone whilst he filled blank sheets of paper.

Besides, he liked staying home. Every day it seemed to either rain or the cold wind blasted through their very bones. Aiden didn't mind. He was in love with a girl who loved him back.

He would write with the curtains drawn but the guards were still there. Their presence heightened the tension of his words. If truth be told they stressed him out.

In the evenings he craved a release from the pressure. He was far from alone. It seemed the whole city had an urgency to unwind. The bars, the clubs, the whole place came alive after dark. People partied as though it might be their last time. The energy was exhilarating. It was the life he'd always dreamed of.

THE KILLSWITCH

An endless stream of fascinating venues, kick ass music and the most interesting characters imaginable.

Aiden's favourite companions were those who'd come over the wall. He'd buy them a drink and ask his favourite question. *What is it like in the East?*

His fascination with the communist regime, the contrasting lifestyle and the ever present guard tower seeped into his work. He wrote about surveillance, oppression, and prying eyes.

51

"When this World Wide Web goes public I've worked out how we can control it."

Jacob delivered the sentence with the utmost confidence.

Opposite him sat the chairman of the Trust, the deputy chair, and the company's chief lawyer. He had their undivided attention. They liked the sound of this.

"Go on," said the chairman.

"As you know there are multiple servers connecting together that allow the web to operate efficiently. Servers that are able to shut down independently should the need arise. For maintenance perhaps, or if a company is infiltrated. Or if there is something you wish to hide. No big deal, shut down partially, solve the problem, switch back on."

"Continue."

"Most of these servers we already have access to. The rest Leetabix will be able to hack into. Imagine If there were one piece of code able to join all these servers together. Such a scenario would allow the operator to shut down the whole web."

The chairman was no longer smiling.

"Do we want to shut it down? Wouldn't that cost us?"

"There is more than one way to take control. What if we don't actually do anything, just let it be known this code has been written?"

"Is that true? Such code exists?"

"It does. I call it the Killswitch."

"If we breached security our clients would sue for all we have."

The lawyer nodded.

"But if we were hacked and the Killswitch was stolen, could we still be held liable?"

"It's a grey area," said the lawyer.

"Hackers?" The deputy chair sounded agitated.

"Yes, sir, obviously I am restricted in what I can say. Computer hackers are criminals after all and largely untraceable. But imagine if they worked for us."

The deputy chair smiled and the tension around the table faded.

"Wouldn't we get the blame for allowing them to steal sensitive information?"

"That is still a grey area," said the lawyer. "If these people are fanatical, they may well go to lengths you couldn't possibly be expected to foresee."

"Fanatics? You mean terrorists?"

"Cyber terrorists, sir."

"They sound impossible to reason with."

"And if they did negotiate it would only be with one contact."

"Yes, and that would probably be us, sir."

"Do what you have to do."

52

One morning Aiden awoke early. Light from outside was shining across the bed. The room was unusually warm. He jumped up and peeked outside. Not a cloud in sight. It was already a glorious day. He pulled the curtain open.

"Look," he said. "Isn't it lovely?"

Mia smiled and nodded but didn't trust herself to speak. When he'd opened the curtain, the first thing she'd seen was the red flag flapping over the guard tower.

"The sun, at last." He came and kissed her on the cheek.

She grabbed him and hugged him tighter than she'd ever done.

She managed a smile as she slipped from the covers. She dressed quickly and plucked her coat from the hook on the door.

"I won't be long," she said and sort of smiled.

"I'll come with you."

She had unlatched the door and was halfway into the hall.

"You don't have to."

"It's such a nice day." He smiled. "I want to, hold on."

THE KILLSWITCH

Her mind went blank. She stood there unable to think of a reason why he couldn't. All that went through her mind was the absolute certainty this was not what she wanted.

They walked hand in hand down Fredrichstrasse. The wall loomed on their left. For the first time in ages, sunlight played across the colourful graffiti.

"We have good times, eh?" she said as the stark fortifications of Checkpoint Charlie came into view. Her English was better than that, Aiden looked at her puzzled. She was in perfect silhouette. She looked incredible.

"What?" He frowned affectionately.

She looked downwards and let go of his hand.

"Who's that?" Mia answered his question with one of her own, nodding her head towards the checkpoint.

Aiden looked around. There was the usual line of civilians shuffling slowly forward to passport control. He could see half a dozen guards. A handful of random people were scattered between where they stood and the fortifications, but he saw nobody he recognised.

"Who?"

"I'm gonna say 'Hi'."

"Who to?" He attempted to look again, but she raised herself on her tiptoes, twisted his face, and kissed him smack on the lips

"Be kind to me in your novel," she muttered.

Aiden frowned. That didn't make sense either.

"What?" he said, but she was already crossing the road.

Wearing a quizzical expression he watched her hurry towards the checkpoint. His eyes switched to the guards she was approaching. They had fingers on triggers and wore blank expressions. He found them intimidating, even from this distance. What must she be feeling?

Mia kept walking, a half-smile fixed on her face. Every fibre of her being was screaming to turn and run back to him. But the State didn't want it that way, and she never questioned the State.

Aiden's gaze switched back to her. She had covered a surprisingly good distance in what could only have been seconds.

"Mia," he called, loudly enough to be sure she would definitely hear him.

She neither looked back nor slowed down. How could she? To do so would be more than she could bear. If anything, Aiden's voice quickened her pace.

Worry was visibly etched into his face now. She was playing with fire. There was the very real possibility of a bullet slamming into flesh if she took many more steps.

What had started out as a stroll in the sunshine was rapidly evolving into a nightmare. Aiden couldn't believe his eyes. He held his breath waiting for the inevitable sound of a gunshot.

He was helpless, too far away to intervene. His eyes ran across the guards closest to her. He wanted to look but he couldn't bear to watch. One of them must surely raise a rifle to his shoulder.

He started to run. "Mia!" he called as loudly as he could. "Stop!"

No rifles were raised. They stood aside and let her pass. It was as though they were expecting her. But that was ridiculous.

Aiden was nearing those same guards who were now moving towards him. There was no way he was getting through the series of barriers as easily as she had.

He slowed down. He caught little glimpses of the side of her head as she passed along the meshed in walkway. She didn't turn around once. Then he saw her duck into the rear seat of a black car. The vehicle pulled away into east Berlin and turned a corner out of sight.

He stopped beneath the sign declaring he was 'About to leave the American Sector' and watched dumbfounded.

He'd seen enough to reach an obvious conclusion. There could be no denying the facts.

She was returning home, to the East.

He looked again. Four soldiers were blocking his view as best they could.

They weren't coming towards him. They were presenting no real threat. But they clearly didn't like him being this close to their patch of land.

Aiden heard footsteps, then a voice behind him.

"Who was that?"

He turned to see a small, neatly dressed man almost upon him. He looked like an accountant. There were tufts of grey hair flapping at the sides of his head as he moved.

Funny the trivia you notice when you're in shock. I could easily run from him.

But two American marines holding rifles flanked the man. They presented a different proposition altogether.

Aiden decided not to run. He decided to play dumb.

"What?" he said. "Who?"

The man stopped in front of him. He cast his eyes downwards in a sheepish manner as he stroked his chin. He looked about to apologise. Looked the sort of person who always apologised for things, even when he wasn't at fault.

The marines however hadn't stopped. Although they did now, now they were alongside Aiden, practically breathing down his neck.

Aiden glanced nervously from one to the other.

The man before him made a little gesture with his forefinger and Aiden was grabbed from both sides.

"Hey, what you doing?"

He was ignored. The little guy in the glasses turned and

walked back the way he had just come. The marines followed with Aiden between them.

"Where you taking me?"

Crowds watched on but nobody tried to interject on his behalf.

Aiden was beginning to realise this was serious.

They bundled him into a jeep. Although they needn't have bothered. The journey couldn't have been more than twenty-seconds. Then he was hustled out and frogmarched into some nondescript hut.

His pockets were emptied onto a table and he was told to sit. They waited in silence as the guy in the glasses rummaged through his things and collected his thoughts.

"So," he began as he picked up Aiden's notebook and read his name off the first page. "Mr. Aiden Fitzpatrick, tell me about her."

"What do you want to know?"

The interrogator smiled. "Everything."

"I don't really know anything."

The man nodded apologetically. Aiden was hoisted up and marched to a holding cell. He was dumped inside and a big key was turned in the heavy lock behind him.

He had no idea what was happening and could influence nothing. Ten minutes ago his life made sense. He sat and waited and felt sorry for himself.

Finally they came and he was returned to the interrogation room

"We went to your address."

Aiden stared blankly at him. The authorities had questioned him many times. Silence was golden.

"There was nothing in there."

Still Aiden remained quiet.

"I don't mean, you haven't many possessions. I mean, it's been professionally cleared."

Aiden struggled to remain passive at that one.

The man rested his elbows on the table.

"We know you're not involved in any of this. I just need you to fill in a few blanks and you can go."

This got a reaction. Not much of one, but there was a glimmer that flashed across his face. The man saw it, realised he had something to work on.

"We know you flew in together on the 14th of January. We know where you stayed and we know she's been leading you a merry dance."

His last comment elicited another look Aiden couldn't hide.

"All I want to know is what she was doing here. Who you were visiting? You can either tell me and then you can go or we will find out the long, slow, tedious way and you can wait in prison while we do so."

He finished his threat with an apologetic smile.

Aiden was beginning to realise he wasn't half as sorry as he pretended to be. He half nodded and the interrogator took that as a sign they should begin. He turned on a tape recorder and asked, "Where did you meet?"

He told him.

"Where did you live?"

"In a squat."

"You lived together?"

"Yeah."

"Who else lived at this squat?"

He revealed a few of the names of the hangers on.

The hours passed and the interrogator proved himself a reasonable guy. He arranged for sandwiches and coffee to be brought in. He produced a packet of cigarettes and let Aiden help himself. And he extracted information slowly, without making him feel like a snitch.

Aiden was struggling to get beyond: *I really loved her and she used me, the meetings, the good people who wanted to stay anonymous, she played us all.*

He felt terribly guilty.

He hadn't exactly vouched for her, but he had certainly been excellent cover.

I thought she loved me.

53

After two days he was released from custody. He headed back to the room in a daze. He didn't know where else to go.

They were right about it being empty. Everything was gone. Clothes, books, typewriter, his manuscript.

His eyes fell on the tower guards. He hated them now. He aggressively pulled the curtains shut as though that futile gesture were some kind of victory.

He felt completely alone. Destined to travel solo forever. Like a ghost never finding a place to settle, to call home.

He didn't belong here he knew that much, not anymore, not without her. Although where should he go? His head was spinning. But amongst the jumbled thoughts of fear and confusion one idea kept fighting through, demanding to be heard.

This would make a great story.

He knew it would be painful, that he had no typewriter or money or anywhere to actually sit quietly and get to it. But all of that was secondary. He would write the story. It felt like a reason to keep going.

Despite everything, there was one thing he could definitely consider lucky. After photocopying every page the Americans had let him keep his notebook. Tapping his pocket, he took comfort from its familiar feel against his chest.

He moved to the doorway and took one last look. This room had shown him love and happiness did exist. But also that nothing lasts forever. Learning such stark lessons in this painful way would not be easy to shake, Especially for one so young.

He shut the door and descended the stairs.

At first he just walked. It was another beautiful day. As though the world hadn't realised what had happened.

Surely any second now dark clouds would roll in and the inevitable pouring rain would be relentless. Quite possibly that wasn't enough, thunder and lightning was called for. But none of that happened. God didn't care about his insignificant problems.

Eventually he reached a destination. A cafe he'd been to with Mia where some serious activists gathered. Nice people he'd felt an affinity with.

They deserved to know what had happened. He owed them that much at least. He took a deep breath and went inside.

"What's wrong?"

The question came before he'd even opened his mouth. The girl behind the counter had taken one look at him and realised something terrible had happened.

"You've been betrayed," he blurted out. "We all have."

The room fell silent. They believed him.

"Here, take a seat." She came around the counter and helped him into a chair. He barely noticed her hand on his elbow.

"What's happened?" she asked.

Other people moved closer. They wanted to hear this. It may well concern them.

Aiden took in the circle of faces around him. All waiting for him to speak. He didn't know what to say, where to begin.

"What's the problem?" someone asked.

"Mia, my girlfriend?" He struggled over the next words. "She's a spy."

"A spy? From the GDR?"

He nodded so vigorously and looked so sad only a fool would disbelieve him.

"She just walked through Checkpoint Charlie as though they were expecting her. I saw the whole thing. She climbed into a car and it drove off."

"You're sure she wasn't being arrested?"

"I was arrested," he squealed indignantly. "But they let me go," he added in a calmer tone.

Aiden told the story as best he could and the overwhelming opinion of his audience was pity. They felt sorry for him.

He looked broken. He was clearly feeling the blame more powerfully than any of them ever would. They were experienced in the cat and mouse tactics of political agitation and had grown accustomed to infiltrators, betrayal by those closest to home. To them it was all part of the game.

To him it was personal. He had loved her, still did, despite it all. She had offered the companionship he craved. He had dared to dream of growing old together.

That was one dream he wouldn't forget in a hurry.

54

In prison Stevie studied law. On release he got a haircut and some new clothes. He returned to the upstairs room at the Falcon pub.

He set himself up as a social worker of sorts. Somebody who knew the law and worked on behalf of local residents. The upstairs room morphed from a punk hang out to a respectable community centre.

"We're gonna collect rubbish from the estate," he announced one day.

The bin men had been on strike for weeks. Huge piles of household waste were rotting on the pavements. It was stinking. It was unhygienic.

"Kids play round there," he reminded them. "It's fuckin' disgusting. So we're gonna collect the rubbish from the flats and dump it at the council offices."

Paulie read about the incident in the local paper. He was pleased to see his mate in the picture. He was described as the official spokesman. It surprised him to read their old rehearsal venue was now a community centre. He remembered happy times there. He decided to take a walk across town. It would be good to see Stevie again.

As Paulie approached he noticed the Falcon had been freshly painted. In fact the whole area seemed cleaner, brighter, more inviting. Walls that had once been daubed with badly scrawled far right slogans now displayed professional looking multicultural murals. Healthy green flora now grew from plant pots that had once been little more than ashtrays.

He climbed the newly painted staircase smiling. As he saw Stevie sitting behind a desk his smile broke into a huge grin. "Ain't that where the drum kit should be?"

Stevie looked up. "Paulie!" he called in delight.

"Look at you with a desk."

Stevie jumped up and rushed to embrace his former comrade in arms.

"How you doin'?"

"I'm good, all good," he blurted out, his voice teeming with excitement.

"That's brilliant!" And they were hugging again like a pair of teenage schoolgirls.

It wasn't very cool.

They broke apart and Stevie lit two cigarettes. He passed one to his friend. "Let's go outside."

Once they reached the bottom of the staircase where nobody could overhear them, Stevie asked, "And Aiden, any news?"

"Not a word, odd really cos he always loved writing. I thought he might of dropped me a line. You know he did all the time I was away. But I guess he may not know what happened."

"Yeah." Stevie was avoiding eye contact. Paulie could still tell when he was holding something back.

"What is it?"

They were outside now. Stevie glanced around furtively before he answered.

"That German girl, Mia."

"Yeah"

"She was a spy?"

"What?"

"She was spying on us."

"What? Nah."

Stevie nodded so solemnly there was clearly no doubt.

"Wow, but, but Aiden was nothing to do with it, was he?"

"Nah, he got played."

"Oh." He paused, letting the information sink in. "A spy for who? The government?"

"It's really good to see you again."

"A spy for who?"

"Let me know if you hear anything about Aiden will ya?" Stevie slapped him across the shoulders.

He'd always been in the habit of avoiding questions when he was up to his neck in illicit behaviour.

Paulie suddenly wondered if this community based operation was all it seemed. He knew from personal experience that old habits die hard. He also knew Stevie was clever and that clever opponents change tactics when the battlefield alters.

He smiled. "Yeah course," he replied.

"Shall we go back in? I'll show you around."

"Yeah, sounds good."

55

The Berlin counterculture found a room for Aiden until his tears dried up. Then they had a whip round for his ticket. In the wee small hours his plane landed. He was home.

There was a knot the size of a tennis ball lodged firmly between his heart and his stomach. He was desperately pining for Mia. But at least he was unlikely to burst into tears.

Like a wounded animal, he needed to lay low. Nurse his broken heart and avoid painful accusations of failure and betrayal. He was never supposed to come back and he definitely wasn't supposed to come back like this.

Fortunately, this was back in the day, before mobile phones. A time when the welfare state still acted as a safety net. It was the bare minimum but at least it was something.

Falling off the radar was pretty straightforward. All you had to do was move to a different part of town and keep your head down.

Utterly defeated, he found the nearest dole office and signed on. He declared himself homeless and was allocated a berth in a hostel on the far side of town.

At night the moans and groans of the residents kept him

awake. He lay fully clothed with his meagre possessions stuffed into his pillow.

When he did sleep he'd dream about her and keep others awake with his moaning and groaning. But they weren't really dreams because she walked through that checkpoint all over again every single time. They were nightmares in the true sense of the word.

He kept to himself and suffered in silence.

He needed money, a job. But he couldn't face the prospect of looking for one, not yet.

56

Jacob had left the streets far behind. These days he wore five grand Hugo Boss suits. He had been right about computers. They had proven to be more than just a passing fad. These days everybody wanted the newer, faster, shinier version of the latest model. Bill Gates sold so many units he was the richest man the world had ever known.

Home computers could do so much more than just print documents. Nowadays you could produce your own headed notepaper, invoices, even business cards. All in full colour. It was ground breaking stuff. There was however a small problem. The models were updating so fast nobody could keep up. Only people like Jacob really knew how to get the best out of the machines.

He was finally connecting office computers together. Things were turning out as he'd predicted to the board all those years ago. Apparently the computer signal ran through a telephone line. Beyond that it got technical. Who knows, who cares? The bosses loved it.

Head office could oversee everything, from detailed sales figures to intrusive files on staff members. All available instantly and in real time. Having the latest up-to-date analysis at their fingertips was invaluable, essential even. Or so they liked to believe.

The computer care industry was growing at a phenomenal rate.

Jacob could turn up at any business premises and before he left their shiny new investment was doing precisely what it had been purchased for.

He was welcomed with open arms into tech departments on the top floors of the financial district and the inner sanctums of sensitive government departments.

Members of the Trust introduced him and guaranteed his credentials.

"He's a friend of Squidgy. I believe you were up together?"

This was the closing chapter of the twentieth century. The old boys network was still functioning exactly as it was designed to. The codes and contacts system was still granting access to the privileged.

For Jacob it was open house. His pass was approved everywhere he went. And he left a little bit of code in every single computer he worked on.

57

A few years passed. Stevie had given up being a social worker. The delaying tactics employed by those with even a sliver of authority was bad for his blood pressure. He would have ended up killing someone in front of witnesses.

He returned to the street, back to hands on involvement. Back to where he knew he could really make a difference.

He stopped affiliating with the usual left leaning groups. They couldn't be trusted. Certain members would only try and stop his more outrageous stunts or worse, call the police. Instead he switched to flying tactics. This involved starting a fuss, a demonstration. Riling up a crowd with legitimate grievances to the point of boiling over. Then standing back and letting the people dictate.

The trick was recognising the precise moment to get out. Before anyone got a handle on who was instigating proceedings. Before the police could get organised.

He kept to a tight circle of carefully chosen comrades assuming if a crowd was called for one would form organically. He was right, it did.

The trouble was once he'd whipped up a mob there was no controlling them. Things had a habit of ending in violence.

"We need to rein it in." Paulie was trying to impress upon him. "Or the cops will be on our backs."

"What? Would you tell Picasso to stop halfway through a painting?"

"How's that the same?"

"It's all art," Stevie replied. "Pure art."

Art?"

"Yeah," he snapped as though he was being perfectly reasonable. "Art, street art as politics." Stevie was looking off into the middle distance, getting more and more carried away. "We're tearing down the divide between the classes. This time round all must be involved or nothing will be achieved, nothing. We are just there to light the touch paper then the people themselves take whatever action they feel is required."

Paulie said nothing and the rant continued—

"If it's only us manning the barricades while the masses watch without getting involved it'll just be another series of failures, leading to nothing. We will only be able to look back on how we failed."

"If we carry on like this somebody's going to get hurt," Paulie pointed out.

"When the mode of capitalism we are forced to endure is happy to destroy all life on earth, can those complicit be called human? And if they're not human why do I care if they get hurt?"

He spoke with the certainty of the religious zealot. It was pointless trying to persuade him to follow any path other than his chosen one.

Paulie didn't look happy. "What if one of ours gets hurt?" he muttered.

Couldn't we just keep the locality clean and help little old ladies? Can't we just stay out of prison? he thought.

58

More time passed and after a grotty bedsit disaster the council moved Aiden into a nice little flat.

He was writing obituaries and meaningless public interest pieces for the local paper. Earning barely enough to feed himself but still claiming to be a writer. The dream was alive.

He had no social life. Evenings were spent on his real work. His reason for being. The great novel of our times. The book that would finally reveal to the masses how things actually were.

He went over it from start to finish again and again. Like an artist dabbing the finishing touches, he'd add a word here, alter a phrase there. Making it better and better until he could improve it no more.

This morning he awoke early and went straight to his manuscript. He tweaked it here and there unnecessarily for another hour and then he wrote two words,

THE END

. . .

He sat back with a confused look on his face.

It was finished. For the first time in a long time he should be feeling pretty pleased with himself. He waited for fireworks and champagne corks to fly. Nothing happened.

He scanned the room. The second hand on the clock was the only thing moving.

For many months he'd been aiming for this finishing line. Focusing so hard on it that nothing else mattered. Obsessively getting closer and closer to this precise moment without stopping to wonder what that actually meant. Presuming all the while it would make sense, would mean something, that all would be revealed when he got here.

Only on arrival it didn't feel that special.

Not an anti-climax, no definitely not that. But this feeling certainly couldn't be described as a warm glow. If anything, thinking so much about Mia had left him depressed.

A motorbike backfired in the distance and he jumped. That was the most exciting thing about his special moment.

This isn't the end, he realised. All he had really done was put words on the pages. If nobody knew the work existed it was irrelevant. It didn't matter until it was a book.

Even so, it's an achievement, he decided.

He made himself a celebratory cup of tea and pulled out his copy of the Publisher's Yearbook.

He would send his manuscript to all the main ones.

The true tale of a double agent cold war spy. A sexy young female at that, operating out of the punk scene. It was dynamite. They'd be fighting to offer him a deal.

He read carefully through the Yearbook and selected nine lucky publishing houses.

He went to the library made nine copies of the full 244 pages and sent them out.

A month passed. There had been no replies. Nobody it seemed wanted to take a chance on an improbable tale featuring a band of reprobates, half based in Germany. A place many still considered enemy territory. The world didn't care.

But when your lifetime dream is over it's hard to let go. The thought of not being a writer, of being something else, filled him with genuine dread.

Every night he'd lie with his head on the pillow dreaming of being plucked from obscurity and propelled into that magical world he longed to be a part of. A place where he could indulge in long discussions with like-minded people. Feel like he belonged. Like he was home. Like he did in Berlin.

More months passed. He was that child clinging on to hopeless dreams all over again.

A failure to reply isn't a rejection, he told himself every night as sleep refused to come.

Surely not every single door has been slammed shut in my face. Surely I'll get a break soon.

Nothing happened. No one called. Nobody cared.

In his dreams he could see this 'other world' to which he was desperate to belong. But night after night he couldn't find a bridge across. He had thought the book would be his bridge. It turns out life isn't that simple.

A full year had passed since he'd sent out the manuscripts.

Optimism and hope had left the building long ago. He was still producing naff slogans for birthday cards and calling himself a writer. Only now he felt like a fraud. The dream was slowly unravelling one painful thread at a time.

He spent a lot of time drinking and wallowing in self-pity. All the while knowing deep down inside that he needed to pull himself together. Every night the same thoughts crossed his mind.

Maybe I should go down the local pub? I might meet someone nice and get a normal life.

This particular evening he was pretending to consider it whilst eating baked beans straight from the tin. He had no real intention of going anywhere. There were twelve cans of beer in the fridge and two bottles of red wine before him.

It was six o'clock on a Thursday evening in September. Outside it was pouring with rain. The perfect weather to accompany crushed dreams whilst drinking alone. He switched on the television in time for the main headlines of the day.

"This is a historic moment," he heard the news presenter claim.

I'll be the judge of that, he thought argumentatively.

"The Berlin Wall has fallen."

He spat beans across the room. Fucking hell!

"People are pouring through the checkpoints into West Berlin."

"Fucking hell!"

From Thursday evening right through until Sunday he barely moved away from the television.

He devoured CNN and the BBC relentlessly. With each new camera angle a wide kaleidoscope of memories hit him hard. It was like getting pummelled by a heavyweight boxer. Every time a different part of the city appeared on the screen, *Pow*! Have some of that!

Years had passed but as soon as he saw Checkpoint Charlie, *wham*, that psychosomatic lump he'd managed to dislodge was firmly back.

Hello old friend.

He'd already carried it around long enough though. He wasn't sure his mental health could go through that again but neither could he turn of the news channels. He stared at the television, transfixed on live images from Checkpoint Charlie.

He'd stood on that very spot as devastation had battered him. Looking at it now, hurt emanated from the lump in his heart, coming in waves, over and over again.

He remembered every little detail of watching her go. But mostly he recalled how she'd taken love with her.

And you've been alone ever since, his inner voice reminded.

Right there, he thought looking at the ecstatic crowds swarming through the military checkpoint, *is where a childish romantic, looking ridiculous and wearing an extremely confused expression watched love walk right out of his life forever.*

It was a stressful weekend. He drank far too much and swore at the television a lot.

On Monday morning he was lying in bed nursing an almighty hangover when the phone rang.

He reached for it to stop the noise it was making. He cradled it to his ear with his eyes still closed.

"Yeah?" he said sleepily.

"Hello, good morning. Am I speaking to Aiden Fitzpatrick?"

"You are."

He sat up a little. This sounded official. Sounded like the last thing he needed right now.

"The author of *The Punky German Spy?*"

"Yes, That's me."

Aiden was suddenly wide awake.

"My name's Ray. Great story by the way, I loved it."

"You've read it?"

"Of course, of course, and I loved it. Anyway, I represent So and So publishing. We'd love to talk to you about the manuscript. Is that something you might be interested in?"

"Very."

Aiden's hangover had disappeared.

"Great, that's great, but before we go any further let me ask you a question."

"What?" he asked, knowing immediately this was too good to be true after all.

"We feel the work might be better served with a different title. Is that something you'd be willing to discuss?"

"Of course."

Hallelujah. The dream was still alive.

"Great, that's great. Tell me, are you available today?"

"I am."

"I wonder if you'd like to meet for lunch?"

"That would be great."

"Wonderful, my secretary will book a table and call you with the details. Is that ok?"

"That would be great," he repeated in a daze.

"See you at lunch."

"That'll be great."

Aiden sat bolt upright in bed. He was stunned. He replayed the conversation in his head.

Ray from so and so, wow, a new title. He shrugged, he didn't care about that. They can call it whatever they like. It was going to be published, *wow*.

Half an hour later he hadn't moved when the call came through.

At one thirty he was sitting downtown in a mid-priced Italian restaurant wearing his only clean shirt.

There were questions. But nowhere near as many as he'd expected. They placed a contract before him and he read it, but he was wasting everyone's time at that point. He would have signed anything that meant getting his book out there.

They took his last remaining copy of the manuscript. Within a month it was on the shelves.

Seeing it there for the first time gave him the feeling of euphoria he'd expected when writing those loaded words—

THE END

All that time ago.

This is as good as it gets.

THE KILLSWITCH

The publishers had rushed things through in order to take advantage of the massive interest in Berlin.

They booked him onto every radio show that would have him from Land's End to John O'Groats. It was exhausting but there was nowhere he would rather be. The camera loved him. The public couldn't get enough and the tsunami kept on rolling.

Motorway food and cheap hotels seemed a price worth paying for the life of an author.

That summer he was invited to all the prestigious literary fairs.

Aiden loved sitting behind a desk with a pile of pristine books before him. People shuffling to the front of the queue, telling him how marvellous he was, waiting patiently as he signed their book then moving along. Being an author was a million miles away from being a writer. It was wonderful.

Often there were so many people he barely had time to look up. Suddenly everyone was interested in tales from Berlin.

He signed, shook hands, and said, "Thanks" and the next one appeared. Stranger after stranger all singing his praises.

What's not to like?

The book signing tour culminated in his hometown.

Aiden pulled the next copy off the pile. Opened it to the flysheet and brandishing his pen, asked, "Who to?" as he looked at the next customer.

His heart skipped a beat. "Stevie."

"Allo Aiden. 'Ow ya doin'?"

He was older, greyer, and rather scruffy. But it was him alright, no mistake.

"Wow, yeah I'm fine. Its great to see you."

Aiden wrote, *For Stevie, my oldest friend,* signed it with a flourish and passed it across the table.

"This one's on the house."

"Cheers, I'll let you know if it's any good."

"Ha, yeah"

"Got time for a drink when you've finished here?"

"Yeah sure. For old times' sake, eh?"

Stevie nodded and half smiled. "I'll wait in the pub on the corner."

"Yeah great."

"Thanks for the book."

"My pleasure."

Stevie glanced back at the crowd building behind him, fans, members of the public. "They want some of your celebrity to rub off on them."

"They don't care about me. They're just interested in the wall an' Berlin."

"Nah, they wanna stand next to someone famous for a split second."

"Aiden blushed. "See you in the pub."

"I'll be the one reading a book."

There were many more people waiting. By the time he got to the pub, Stevie was gone.

In those days it was normal to leave messages with the bar staff.

Aiden asked. There was no message.

59

The fall of the Berlin wall was humanity's most important event in a generation by far. It was a golden opportunity for global politics to realign in a meaningful way.

But the chance wasn't so much squandered as viciously resisted by shadowy figures with ulterior motives. Huge effort was put into ensuring the fall of the Berlin wall changed nothing and the news cycle kept on turning.

By this time the Trust had fingers in every large news organisation. They were major players in controlling the narrative and they did not want a united Europe.

Divisive headlines began to appear on a daily basis. The editors returned to their favourite winning formula.

The fall of the Soviet Union taught them some valuable lessons about propaganda whilst introducing vast amounts of new money into the markets.

By the time the dust settled the Trust were masters of misinformation.

Cigarettes did not cause cancer and fossil fuels were not as bad as the hippies claimed.

Solar and wind power were unreliable and most importantly of all, 'Socialism' was a dirty word.

Things were under control. The chairman turned his attention to Jacob. "How are you? Any problems?"

"There are too many players on the Net. It's a free for all."

"On the Net?"

"They call the World Wide Web the Internet now sir, or *Net* for short."

"Oh, please continue."

"Now that things are back on an even keel, the time is right for huge financial gain."

"I'm listening."

"Except it's not like the old days. The Net makes it possible for little one-man bands to promote themselves globally. If every Tom, Dick and Sally has their snouts in the troughs, profits will inevitably fall."

"Buy up the small players, everybody has their price."

"It's not like the old days sir. These people don't build up viable companies over time that we can purchase. They have some idea and immediately products are available to buy. You take over one and ten more spring up. The old ways won't work. We need to try something else."

"What do you have in mind?"

"We need to go on the offensive. Smear motives and reputations, muddy the waters, sow a little doubt here and there. But most of all we have to be able to prosecute hackers. These kids are too dangerous to be left to their own devices any longer. It's time to tighten the rules of the game, set a few examples."

"What do you have in mind?"

"Firstly, dissuade others from associating with a target. Often that is enough to drop them from public consciousness. If more is needed, we can discredit our enemies in the court of public opinion. It's much easier for them to be found guilty there."

"And you can do this how soon?"

"I could do it now."

"This writer, the one who won't shut up about spies in Berlin, I believe you knew him?"

"A bit, years ago."

"Are you in his book?"

"I went by a different name back then but yes."

The chairman clasped his fingertips together and nodded.

"Discredit him."

"Consider it done."

I never liked him anyway thought Jacob.

Aiden Fitzpatrick's fifteen minutes of fame lasted for about a year.

Without warning all his promotion work dried up.

There was nothing he could point to. No smoking gun indicating why or what his crime might be. He was simply no longer invited onto television shows or to book fairs. Editors found alternative sources for quotes and material. Nobody could explain why or even if there was an issue. Besides they were busy people, they had their own problems.

Maybe society just found someone else on whom to bestow celebrity status.

This was no gradual decline back to obscurity. It was brutally sudden.

Many years passed. He returned to writing slogans for greetings cards. It was a meaningless waste of his life. He was drinking earlier in the day. His book stopped selling years ago. His confidence as a writer hit rock bottom. Yet it was all he had, he clung to it. Without that he was nothing

A decade later he was still hanging out in late night bars. Places where he could get hammered. He would stagger around, falling off stools, pulling out his notebook whilst loudly claiming to be researching a great book he was going to write.

In the mornings he'd look at his notes. The illegible scrawling barely made sense.

He wasted more years.

It was a midweek night. He was in a dive bar, slumped against the wall watching a group of twenty something's greet their friends.

I don't know why they're so excited, he sneered. *We had The Clash, we had meaning. They've got Covid-19 and a climate emergency.*

But beneath the drunken haze he did know why. They possessed the most valuable commodities known to man. Youth, health, beauty and most importantly of all, hope.

He had hope once. Then one morning it was gone.

He felt sorry for himself but he almost felt more sorry for them. What a clean, sanitised version of a human life they've been reduced to.

Youth needs a meaningful soundtrack, he decided. *To set you up for adulthood.*

Pop these days was barely worthy of the name music. Formulaic, safe, meaningless, nonsensical, bubblegum rubbish. These kids need a leader. Someone to slap them across the face and tell them what's what.

Thank God we had the Clash, we had punk.

He watched the twenty somethings as they took for granted the rights that punks had championed.

The kids these days couldn't care less how others chose to portray themselves.

We did that, he tried to tell them, but nobody listened.

They weren't interested in the pioneers. It was ancient history. They tolerated him sitting around, looking old and taking notes because they'd heard he was famous once.

How can you truly understand unless you were there?

It was a mental leap too far for the average human mind.

The thought depressed him. He took a long slug of whisky.

Once colleges started teaching the formula required to write a pop song it was all over.

He was drunk again.

When punters who all look exactly the same will accept whatever dross they are being spoon fed you might as well pack up and go home.

Aiden harked back to the good old days of small intimate venues. Just you and your friends and a rocking band.

Those places are long gone. You couldn't bring them back no matter how much you wanted to. The insurance premiums alone would be astronomical. Today's overheads and all the staff strictly on the books, every single penny digitally accounted for? Forget it.

All that shadowy money that used to slosh around behind the scenes oiling the wheels that made life bearable was gone. The Trust and corporations like them wanted a cut of everything and they wanted to see the receipts.

Progress— that creeping change moved in such small increments you barely noticed. But when things disappeared they were gone forever. That was what drove him crazy above all else. Losing hard won rights and paying for stuff that used to be free.

Where did all the money go? He took another slug because he knew the answer to that one.

It got hoovered up by ultra efficient digital systems to go and sit on computer screens in the British Virgin Islands where it does nobody any good. That money used to fund roads, schools, society.

If only something could be done.

Aiden scribbled his thoughts down. He was making notes for the next best seller.

60

More years passed.

It was right the government kept cracking down on reprobates, that regular new laws were passed to combat the threat of digital crime. You couldn't be too careful these days.

Jacob's new back-up system was very popular with his clientele. It gave them extra assurance.

Cyber space was a dangerous world. Fortunately one in which the Trust knew what they are doing. Your business was safe with them. They had been leading the pack for years.

Jacob couldn't be more thrilled with the way things were going.

He was in a private meeting with the chairman.

"Data is set to be the currency of the future. There is no doubt. The Net is a total game changer. Directing misinformation, we can easily control public opinion. But the more information we have the easier it is."

"Do what you have to," said the chairman.

One of the services offered to their clients was secure storage of sensitive information. It was sent to a giant server at Trust HQ. Behind the scenes Leetabix were adding this information to what they acquired elsewhere. Obviously this sideline was not mentioned on the official brochures. Faith in security was the cornerstone of their whole business.

These days all crime seemed to be about hackers. Nobody took to the streets anymore. Jacob's team infiltrated or infected the network of every single target they were given. All except one.

A hacker group that went by the name of *Leetabix*. Those people were tricky, clever, a real threat. And incredibly elusive.

As time passed it became necessary to pass ever stricter laws hoping to gain an advantage over them. Whatever Jacob asked for he got. His department grew into a law unto themselves.

After the meeting Jacob was asked to wait behind.

"We've decided to break up the European Union."

The Trust did not like the Union's plans to clamp down on money laundering.

That seemed like a major challenge. The European Union were a powerful body.

"How will we do that?" he asked

"One nation at a time. We need this to happen do you understand?"

Jacob nodded. "Yes sir."

He understood there were to be no limits in pursuit of the Trust achieving their aims. No matter citizens will suffer; there was money to be made. You had to think of the bigger picture.

61

Aiden was on a bus that detoured. He'd been told Stevie lived around here.

I could jump off, he thought. *Go see him.*

It's a funny old thing the human mind. The years go by and people from the past acquire a rose-tinted focus. You only remember the fun times.

You never stop to consider that the only 'good' thing about 'the good old days' was being younger. Aiden finished his thought. *It'd be great to see him again.*

He'd not seen Stevie since the book signing.

That was years ago. I could pass by and say Hi.

Impulsively he jumped off the bus and walked to the address.

Ignoring the feeling that too much water had passed under the bridge, he stepped up and rapped on the front door. He didn't wait long.

"Oh hi, I was just…"

"How you doing? Come in." Stevie spoke as though they'd seen each other yesterday.

He looked a picture of health. His T-shirt was clean. His

cheeks freshly shaved and his eyes bright and clear.
"If you're sure I'm not disturbing you."
Stevie held the door open wider.
"Come on in," he beamed. "It's great to see you."
Aiden sat feeling awkward and watched his old friend rinse a teapot.
Stevie threw a few easy ones over his shoulder to settle them both in.
"Seen your mum lately? Warm today innit?" "How's your health?"
He batted them away. "Nah, Yeah, Good."
Once the tea was poured and the pleasantries all used up, they sat across the table in contemplation. The outrageous clothes of their youth had long gone as had the easy banter.
"This takes me back," Aiden reminisced. "Remember when we were kids sitting in your mum's kitchen."
"Yeah."
"Yeah."
Stevie smiled and the lines around his eyes spoke of difficult years.
"You still into bird watching?"
"Yeah, you know not so much but I keep my eyes peeled. You still writing?"
"Yeah, you know."
There was a pause. They filled it with sipping hot tea. Neither wanting the silence to become too drawn out.
"I read your book," Stevie said.
"Always like hearing that. What did you think?"
He smiled "Not bad, you know how to put a story together. No doubt about that."
"Thanks."
"That Mia eh?" Stevie rolled his eyes.
Aiden nodded sadly. "She made a right dick out of me."

The way he said it made Stevie want to sympathise. "Don't be too hard on yourself. You weren't seeing clearly."

"How do ya mean?"

"Well you were in love weren't ya? But she never fooled us, that's why we searched your room."

Aiden looked surprised. "What? You searched the room?"

"Yeah." He shrugged. "I thought you knew."

"When?"

"Night you left for Berlin."

"Was that why she planned it the way she did?"

"I dunno about that. To me you just left. I always thought it was weird though."

"I'm sorry mate. Of course with hindsight it was weird as fuck. The car straight to the airport especially, I often wonder why I didn't think more of that at the time."

"Like I say, you weren't thinking straight."

"I really loved her."

"Looks like you still do to me."

"Huh," Aiden protested. "Don't be stupid."

"Riiiggghht."

"Did you find anything?"

"What?"

"When you searched our room?"

"It was so long ago. Who cares anymore?"

"Tell me, did you?"

Stevie put his cup down. He weighed up the pros and cons mentally before saying, "There was some photos, rolls of film. The old type you know, that you have to get developed."

"What were the photos?" Aiden asked.

Stevie shook his head. "I dunno."

"I never knew." Aiden said it softly, Hurt clear in his voice.

"Well" Stevie looked down as he spoke "you left and it all got pretty fucked up. People getting nicked for all sorts. I dunno it was chaos."

Aiden was desperately trying to swallow the lump that had reappeared and climbed into his throat. He managed a nod.

"Are you ok?" Stevie felt sorry for his buddy. Nearly as sorry as he was for himself.

Aiden nodded again.

"It was a long time ago," Stevie said, "an' it wasn't just you. A lot of good people got fucked over."

Stevie spoke the last sentence with heavy regret. He sounded halfway down memory lane. "And the rest, those that weren't rounded up, well—" He shook his head wistfully. "—when the going got tough it was incredible how quickly they jumped ship." He shook his head again. "It's not like we didn't know what to expect. We all knew they would come for us eventually."

He looked at Aiden.

"Who knew people you trusted would surrender so quickly? Those that didn't get nicked just sneaked off. Chose marriage, babies, careers, all the things they fucking despised two weeks earlier. All the things we had been fighting against. Conformed like fuckin' sheep." He rolled a cigarette his face the colour of thunder and took a few heavy drags before continuing—

"It might not have hurt so much if we'd got it all out in the open but no, there was no time for any of that."

Stevie looked up. "I got into the gear. I couldn't handle it."

"I get that." Aiden nodded sympathetically.

"It was so frustrating" Stevie continued, "Clearly seeing what was being done to us and not just unable to stop them, no fucker believed us."

Aiden nodded again, "We were too young. Who's gonna take a bunch of kids seriously?"

Stevie's voice softened, "How quickly they all deserted everything we stood for, that felt like real defeat."

He looked at Aiden intently and finished by saying quietly, "I felt completely betrayed."

Aiden was sympathetic. He knew what that was like. "Sorry mate, I didn't know."

"How could you? Forget about it."

"Well, it worked out all right I suppose." Aiden tried to soften the blow. "Look at you now."

"This is just temporary, I'll be back with Nikki soon." Stevie smiled at the thought.

Aiden smiled to, "Like I say, it'll all work out."

But Stevie hadn't got it all off his chest yet. He was off again. "I put all my energy, everything I had into fighting the injustices built into the system. It was my whole life. Then one day you realise you've lost, you're on your own an' you've gotta get a job or kill yourself."

"You chose gear?"

"Yeah," he smirked. "The slow death. When it came down to it I was just as chicken shit as the rest of them. It was the easy way out, avoid reality, you know"

"You're off it now though, eh? Look at you." Aiden was impressed. He knew what a struggle kicking heroin could be.

Stevie smiled sheepishly. "Yeah, I was lucky. Nikki said she'd have me back if I cleaned up."

"I'm glad you did."

He smiled again. "Me too."

"I wonder what happened to her?" Aiden replied.

Stevie shook his head. "Really? After all this time?" He could see the sadness on his friend's face. He wasn't stupid. He put a hand on his shoulder.

"Let it go," he advised.

"My first true love and I haven't even got a picture," Aiden said quietly.

Stevie studied his face. Trying to decide what to say.

"It was so long ago, just forget her."

"Yeah." Aiden nodded agreement but his face told a different story.

The first uncomfortable pause in the conversation dragged on. It was time to leave.

"I gotta go." He rose to his feet.

Stevie followed him to the door.

"Good to see ya."

"You too, I'm sorry it all got fucked up. It was my fault she got close to everyone," Aiden apologised again.

"Don't beat yourself up. They was onto us. If it hadn't been her they would have put someone else in."

"I feel guilty, though."

"Don't, it was so long ago. And it was fantastic for a while, eh?"

Aiden smiled. "Yeah," he agreed. "Yeah, it was."

Stevie let him out and watched through the net curtain. He saw Aiden get to the end of the street and light a cigarette. He was pleased for his old friend. Glad he'd managed to write that book.

It was a matter of public record now. It meant that brief spell, that moment in time when the kids had frightened the life out of the establishment was documented forever.

They all said punk rock wouldn't last. But it was an original idea. You can't kill an idea. All you can do is shatter it into a thousand different pieces. Then all the pieces that survive will still carry the idea with them. Punk kids grew up and took responsible positions in all walks of life. The attitude went with them.

The very essence of punk, the constant search for truth didn't die or grow up. It multiplied and spread.

Music, art, fashion, literature, commerce and of course politics became infected by it and none were ever the same again.

Historians of the future would point to the punk scene as the beginning of something.

62

The Trust were holding a meeting. It started with the good news.

The plan to pull apart the evil, socialist European Union had gone exceptionally well.

Whilst betting heavily against sovereign currencies they had drowned out the cries of 'unpatriotic behaviour' so successfully the accusers were now the accused. All their energy wasted on denying baseless claims.

Well, not entirely baseless. Claims planted by Jacob that went viral.

They had also moved various head offices off the European continent in order to further destabilise it. Besides, Cayman Islands regulations were more tax efficient.

There were developments on the purchase of flood plain land and who needed to be paid in order to acquire the necessary building permits.

There was an update on the various legal cases against them regarding cladding material that had turned out to be flammable. The expectation had been that the incoming American president would quash the proceedings when elected. And this was where the reports started to get decidedly less favourable.

Their candidate, the one whose campaign had cost a small fortune had failed to win. Some hacker group had seen to his chances. And there was more bad news.

The contracts to provide cheap processed meals for schools; hospitals and prisons were also in doubt. Again, the same group had been raising public awareness.

These were projects expected to generate massive returns. Perhaps they had relied a little heavily on the right people being in power. Except that up to now such things had been mere formalities.

It was inconceivable but true. Their man in the American Presidential race had failed to get re-elected.

The gloom had rotated around the table and now it was Jacob's turn.

The chairman glared at him. "Tell us about this group."

"We don't really know much at this stage sir."

"They are bad for business, we know that," the chairman shot back.

This new player had appeared from nowhere and was spreading truth and facts on a wide variety of topics and on an industrial scale. Most of it in direct contradiction to the narratives favoured by the Trust, their paid shrills and useful idiots.

By the time these upstarts had finished decimating his character, the bumbling fool the Trust had lined up for the White House stood no chance.

It was embarrassing. It was extremely costly.

Just as bad, another of their candidates in Europe had been exposed for his willingness to be bribed.

These hackers, or terrorists as they should really be called, kept releasing damaging videos of him on the take.

The stock markets were jittery. The Trust stood to lose billions of dollars.

"We need you to find them and tell the press to refer to them as terrorists at all times from now on."

Jacob attempted to interrupt but the chairman held up a hand of silence and continued. "We will arrange additional resources."

Jacob nodded, his question answered. The chairman continued. "These people are no more than common criminals, terrorists. They need to be stopped."

"Yes sir."

"I have asked the chief superintendent to publicly offer assistance. You will take advantage of this offer."

"Yes sir."

"Any groups you have suspicions about, close them down."

"There aren't any sir."

"Find some."

"Yes sir."

"I want to see computers confiscated and people behind bars."

"Yes sir."

The chairman turned his attention back to the room.

"Does anyone have any good news?"

"Our anti-vaccination message is really cutting through. People don't know what to think. They're blaming Marxists, those Black Lives Matter people, even doctors and nurses. They are squabbling amongst themselves precisely as we predicted they would. We're selling large quantities of placebos."

Across the table the member with a soft spot for flags on his socks spoke up. "Where do radical groups get their finance? Why can't we close their bank accounts? Without money they will be too preoccupied to bother us."

"We should focus on their finances?"

"Financing radical organisations should be a criminal offence."

THE KILLSWITCH

All heads turned to the member of the cabinet. He nodded and took a note.

Jacob spoke up. "And make sure punishments include monitoring of computer usage."

There were nods around the table.

Almost immediately those 'of interest' began to be brought in for questioning. Paulie and Stevie were rounded up. Neither would account for their movements on specific dates. They were detained. The newspapers reacted in fury to the suggestion they were merely scapegoats. It was a preposterous idea. Why on earth would anyone think that?

Leetabix were the only ones to escape the purge unscathed. But everyone knows hardcore terrorists are particularly sneaky.

A month later, in retaliation for the clamp down, Leetabix threatened some major household names with cyber attacks. The Trust were brought in to negotiate on behalf of the companies. Jacob recommended paying the undisclosed ransom demands.

Meanwhile the tabloids kept up their end of the deal, bombarding the populace with more and more reasons to be afraid. Things that might go wrong. Minority groups who might hate you.

The ground became fertile enough to impose even tighter restrictions, ever harsher laws.

Once those on the political left, or the commie traitorous snowflakes as the gutter press preferred to call them had been destroyed as viable opponents, the witch hunt took on broader parameters.

Public protests of any kind were banned outright. Everybody's online activity was monitored and people were not allowed to congregate in public. It became impossible for like-minded individuals to organise. This was essential for the safety of the citizenship. Each mention in the press ended with the phrase, 'The new measures are temporary and have been introduced extremely reluctantly.'

The Trust hurriedly set up moneymaking ventures to take advantage of the new world order. Food and medical deliveries, anti-viral products, security equipment, the list went on. All were brand new companies listed in the Cayman Islands. None paid tax anywhere.

Public services that common people relied on were cut to the bone whilst profits on spreadsheets soared.

The men who sat on the board of the Trust struggled to spend one month's profits before their bank accounts were replenished.

Everything was back on plan. Then Jacob called the chairman.

"That remaining terrorist cell, we think they might be here in the city."

"Do whatever it takes, we need to find them."

63

From her earliest childhood, Mia had been taught the West was the enemy.

She'd been led to believe they wanted to inflict their decadence on decent communist people. Yet her eyes revealed a very different story. Her elders and betters seemed to be doing all the running. The capitalists weren't coming to them. It was the other way round.

Mia didn't understand greed. She understood duty. She was not tempted by wealth and opulence and was losing faith in those who were. The more disillusioned she got, the harder it was for her to live with such cognitive dissonance.

Being sent to the West and meeting Nikki had been life changing. She got it immediately. Men had called the shots for centuries. It was time for change.

Sexual equality was a simple idea, a philosophy she could believe in.

Surely without all that testosterone getting in the way women could do a far better job.

Sitting alone in her room she had plenty of time to dwell on what might have been, on how things ought to be.

She knew her boss' cars had been upgraded again. The blatant corruption sickened her. It had now grown impossible to ignore.

People in the East had eyes. They could see the world was changing. That they were moving away from the status quo into something unknown. It made them nervous so they chose to pretend everything was normal.

They ignored the Mercedes cars and the fast food restaurants that were suddenly everywhere. Acted as though the only way of life they had ever known was solid, destined to last.

But Mia had travelled. One glance was enough for her to see life was no longer any of the things it had once been.

Just like the scared citizens of the technologically developed west, her neighbours longed for a strong leader. Someone to take control, to protect them from the bogeyman.

Fear of the unknown does strange things to people.

She'd been scared that morning in Berlin.

They take advantage of it, she thought. *If I knew then what I know now.*

Memories of what might have been brought a tear to her eye.

All of the old guard were gone now, replaced by a new generation impatient to see what capitalism could offer them.

'Make a deal' was the buzz phrase.

She heard them talking how the Trust would make them all rich. She remained quiet. They weren't ready to hear her political opinions.

Her missions now were less about *the good of the state* and more about ensuring her shadowy superiors grew incredibly wealthy.

And when the dust of time had finally settled it was painfully obvious the old *east* and *west* distinctions were dead and buried.

Disaster capitalism was the only game in town now. A global phenomenon where nothing was of value unless it turned a profit.

If you can't afford a ticket, you're not welcome was the overarching mantra of everything.

Giant corporations had more clout than small countries. And the Trust enjoyed the most clout of all. She worked for them now. She didn't care. Her life was a joke anyway. She just did her duty.

As a reward for a job well done, Mia had been granted an apartment in the suburbs.

It contained a bed, a chair, a fridge and a sofa. In all the years she'd lived there she'd made no attempt to turn the house into a home. Why should she? A home needed children, laughter, companionship. This place offered none of those things. It was just somewhere to sleep and reflect.

She got a copy of Aiden's book as soon as it became available. Reading it wasn't a comfortable experience. After all these years she still missed him.

She felt terrible all over again to learn she'd broken his heart.

Sitting alone with the cruel benefit of hindsight she knew in her heart those were the happiest days of her life. Now she realised a relationship like that is precious and should have been cherished. She had cared for him deeply but she'd been young and foolish.

She wasn't to know there would never be another like him. Someone who would place no restrictions on her, make her feel special and ask nothing in return.

Someone with whom she could have fun on a pittance.

She remembered how they walked everywhere. They didn't even have money for bus fare, yet they were always laughing. She wished it then and she wished it now.

Why couldn't we be a real couple?

She knew why. Because her bosses hadn't allowed it.

There will be others, they'd said. *A nice German boy to give you beautiful children.*

There never was. She knew now they were hypocrites to a man. But it was too late.

She finished *The German Spy* and dabbed at her eyes.

Getting the order to leave him was still her biggest regret. She'd give anything to be able to turn back the clock.

Her buzzer went and shocked her back to reality, to the present. She took a fleeting glance through the window. Enough to take in a black Mercedes. This was official. She blew her nose, smoothed down her skirt and buzzed them in.

"Somebody is threatening our plans."

Mia knew that could never be tolerated.

"We need all hands on deck to locate a terrorist cell," the official announced.

"A terrorist cell?" she asked.

"They might be using a particular cafe, the Zodiac."

"Might be?"

"Yes, we need a closer look."

"So I drink coffee all day?"

"Cafes are always looking for staff. We will provide references and you can get a position there."

64

Like millions of others, Ben Wallace loved Saturdays. He traced it back to being a kid and comics and sweets.

These days he liked a cappuccino at the Zodiac cafe.

He liked the place even more with the new waitress around. He was trying to pluck up the courage to ask her on a date.

He slowly sipped his drink and watched Juanita circle her workspace.

She was wiping tables and collecting cups, blissfully unaware she was brightening up the whole place.

As she came closer Ben tried to think of something clever to say. Nothing came. She smiled at him, he sort of smiled back. She moved on.

On her next lap he caught her eye as she neared his table. He looked about to speak. She paused, waited politely, but he remained silent. She smiled again and moved away just as he felt a tap on his shoulder.

"Hey mate, how you doin'?"

It was Frank. He pulled out the chair opposite and sat down.

Frank wore a black T-shirt beneath a black leather jacket. He was in his mid-forties and unshaven. His long, grey hair was tightly back into a ponytail.

This was a man who rolled his own cigarettes, who knew his way around a protest march.

Ben nodded at him. "Yeah good thanks, you?"

Frank nodded in the affirmative and beamed.

"I just came thru the train station," he whispered. "There was a load of Japanese tourists taking selfies with it."

Ben smiled. It was a genuine expression of happiness.

"They liked it then?"

As Frank nodded, another man in a black leather jacket joined them. He looked about thirty. He was clean shaven. Even his head was shaved.

The Clash, Ben read from his T-shirt. *He's a Clash fan, always a good sign.*

"Meet Bill," Frank introduced them.

Bill put two coffees on the table and sat down.

He reached out to shake Ben's hand. "Saw your piece." He smiled. "Good work, brother."

"Thanks."

Frank leaned forward in a conspiratorial manner. "Bill needs a banner," he said quietly. "Something big. We thought you might be able to help."

"What've you got in mind?"

The Clash fan pulled a folded piece of paper from his pocket, opened it up and spread it across the table.

"Well, I..."

"You finished with these?" The waitress was leaning right across Ben. It was a clear invasion of his private space. He loved her for forcing the close proximity on him. She retrieved an empty cup and saucer from their crowded little table.

Ben smiled at her. "Yeah, thanks."

She smiled back. She looked so sweet he should ask her out

right now. *Wanna come to the cinema on Friday night?* he should have said, or *Can I take you to dinner some time.*

He said neither; he turned red and focused on Bill's sketch.

"She's cute," Bill commented when she'd gone.

"Yeah, yeah she is," he agreed, picking up the paper and practically hiding behind it.

Once composed he returned the sketch to the table. "Its good that you've put the measurements. That makes life easier."

Bill smiled. "How much?" he asked.

"Say eighty quid for materials and a drink for me, call it a ton."

Bill pulled out a roll of notes and peeled off a hundred pounds.

With business completed, they contented themselves with mocking the government until their cups were empty. Then they shook hands and left.

Ben sat alone again.

He watched Juanita bend over to wipe a table. He admired her legs in the tight jeans. He quickly looked away before she caught him.

He imagined them as a couple. The thought appealed to him greatly.

As his girlfriend she would receive nothing but the best.

He would give her the world and all its contents. For the fourth time that morning he stopped short of asking her out.

He caught a glimpse of himself in the windowpane.

I need a haircut. I can't ask her out looking like this.

He rose from his seat and gave her a wave. She smiled. Ben cursed his shyness all the way to the barbers.

Juanita was too old for standing on her feet all day. She certainly wouldn't do it for the pittance wages alone. She'd been casing the cafe for over a month now and nothing had happened. The reports of a hacker group in the area persisted, but she was certain these guys weren't it. She knew the Trust had a hacker department. The best in the business, people said. It was probably best to let them find this threat; they seemed to find all the others.

This is the last job she told herself as she hung her apron in the staff room and headed for the door. *All my experience and they have me doing this. It's demeaning, like they don't value me at all.*

She left the cafe pulling her phone from her pocket. Once around the corner she leant against a wall and tapped in a number. With her phone to her ear, she scanned the crowds for anything out of the ordinary.

"Yeah," a voice answered her call.

"It's me."

"Was he in?"

"Yes."

"And his friend?"

"Yes, him and some other guy, Bill."

"Did they have a laptop?"

"No."

She had seen Ben with a laptop once. She had carried the bug every week since. But to no avail.

"What do you think?"

"They're not hackers, not even particularly militant."

"Ok, It's not them."

"So I'm done?"

"Yes, you're finished there. Go home, we'll be in touch."

"Ok."

There was a series of clicks and the line went dead.

She pocketed her phone and began to walk. She waited at a crossing. When the lights changed she crossed and disappeared into the crowds.

The voice at the other end of the phone crossed Ben and Frank's names off his list. He transcribed her opinion word for word in the comments section and sent his encrypted report to Trust HQ.

His pay grade meant he had no opinion on whether further action was needed.

65

The Trust were ready to make their move. At first they discretely told a handful of valued clients there might be a problem with security.

Later they informed the police that they had been hacked and were looking into it.

Then they emailed all clients informing them there had been a cyber attack on the electronic security system.

A few days later they were forced to go public and admit their computer system had been successfully hacked.

Finally they were forced to acknowledge being the victims of an elaborate sting, perpetrated by the hacker group Leetabix.

Everyone had heard about them. Evil terrorists, hell bent on holding decent folk to ransom. Everyone knew Jacob and the Trust were doing a marvellous job hunting down these enemies of the people. Surely the Leetabix terrorists would soon be behind bars where they belonged. It still didn't occur to anyone that Jacob gave Leetabix their orders.

66

It was late Saturday afternoon and Aiden was on the upper deck of the 38 bus as it headed down a busy road. It pulled into a stop and on the pavement below a waitress caught his eye. She was bent over talking to a customer but seemed familiar. Then she stood tall and wiped her brow with the back of her wrist.

"Mia!"

It was such a shock to see her after all this time, he didn't realise he'd screamed out her name.

He banged frantically on the window just as the bus started to move away. He jumped up, headed for the stairs, pinging bells as he went. He needed to get off as soon as possible.

Mia, how can that be?

His mind was racing frantically as he waited impatiently at the doors. Finally they hissed open. He jumped off and ran back the way he'd just come as fast as the crowded pavements would allow. He hadn't run anywhere in years.

By the time he got to the cafe he was sweating heavily.

The table was empty.

He tried to recall who she'd been talking to. Simultaneously he scanned the area for her, for them.

Men, three men, Good. One looked like an anarchist, had a black hoodie.

That was the only one who's face he'd seen. He scanned the crowds. There was no Mia, no guy in a black hoodie. He consigned what he could remember about the man to memory.

I'd recognise him again, he decided.

He burst through the cafe door on the verge of losing the plot completely. Totally oblivious that he was wild eyed, that he looked like he should only be out in public under strict supervision. He clamoured towards the till scanning frantically as he walked. Customers averted their eyes or moved aside to give him room.

"The waitress, where is she?" he demanded as he reached the counter.

"Can I help you?"

"Not you, the other waitress, where is she?"

"There's only me honey"

"I saw her, I saw her from the bus."

"She gone."

"Where, where's she gone?"

The young waitress was looking at him properly now. She was beginning to realise she was dealing with a crazy man.

"I don't know."

"Where does she live?"

"I ain't gonna tell you that."

"When's she back on?"

"I think you better go mister."

He walked home in a tormented daze. All the memories were back in spades. It was her, he was sure. What the Fuck?

67

Aiden returned to the cafe early the next day to watch it open. He hung around until it closed. She never turned up. He haunted the place for a week. She never showed.

It was Saturday again. Exactly seven days since staking out the cafe had taken over his whole life.

It's now or never, he told himself. *Today's the day.*

He was in position and full of expectation before the cleaners had even arrived. By the time the bulk of the lunch time crowd had been and gone his optimism was waning.

She's not coming. It wasn't even her. Was I really sure, really?

He tried to tell himself it wasn't her. It was a coincidence, a fluke, a waste of his time. He'd been inside the cafe three times already today alone. They'd asked him to leave on his last visit. You can only take up a table with one empty cup for so long.

So he waited on the pavement and ignored the discomfort in his legs. But the hours passed and now his feet were sore as well. Maybe he should just go home, put on the TV, get drunk or something.

He took a deep breath, tried to tell himself he wasn't getting old, but had to admit there was a time when he could have staked the place out for a month solid. Nowadays he felt faint if he missed lunch.

He was on the verge of defeat, after only a week. *I'm getting old,* he admitted. He was set to leave.

Then he saw the customer. The anarchist from last week. He was even wearing the same hoodie. Aiden watched him go in the cafe. He felt a new lease of life. An injection of renewed energy.

Ben was blissfully unaware he'd just been clocked. He strode pleasantly to the counter.

"Hi."

The waitress recognised him. "Hi." She smiled.

"I'll have a cappuccino please."

"Sure."

She reached for a cup.

"Is Juanita here?" he asked innocently.

"No."

"Oh." He frowned. "That's funny. I thought she worked Saturdays?"

The girl shrugged. "Yeah, me to. But they called me in today. She didn't turn up and the manager said they couldn't raise her. Her phone was off apparently." She shrugged in a *who can live with their phone off?* kind of way.

"Oh," he said again.

"Yeah I know, right."

On the pavement across the street Aiden was determined not to frighten the horses this time. He leant against a bus stop and waited.

He's got to come out sooner or later.

With great difficulty he resisted the urge to go in.

When the guy finally emerged and started down the pavement, Aiden fell into step alongside him.

"Hi."

Ben turned and half nodded an acknowledgment. He kept walking.

"You don't know me," Aiden blurted out, "but I think you know Mia."

Ben glanced at him.

"Nah don't think so. Sorry, mate." He kept moving, trying to put some distance between himself and the stranger who bizarrely seemed determined to keep up.

"I saw you talking to her last week."

He glanced at him again. "I don't know no Mia."

"She's a waitress in the cafe you just left."

Ben gave him a look which said nothing at all and attempted to pull away.

"Last Saturday, I saw her serve you, and now she's disappeared."

Ben stopped dead in his tracks. Suddenly the stranger had his full attention. He turned to face him. "Juanita, you mean?"

"Long hair, great legs, killer smile, nose ring?"

"You mean Juanita."

Aiden shrugged. "I knew her a long time ago. She went by the name Mia then."

Ben frowned again. *Who is this guy? What's he talking about?* "What?"

"Do you know her?" Aiden asked.

"Yeah I know her, sort of."

"Do you know where she lives?" Aiden's impatience was surfacing again.

"That's none of your business." Ben felt the need to be defensive.

"Do you?" Aiden asked again with such desperation, such pain in his tone Ben felt obligated to answer truthfully. "No"

"Have you seen her today?"

"No."

"Or this week?"

"No."

"Did you expect to?"

Ben was studying the stranger as they spoke. The guy was desperate for answers to his questions. Not intimidating or aggressive but fucked up for sure. Whatever his problem he was totally serious. The whole thing was weird but he would kind of like to know what had happened to Juanita.

"I dunno."

"What do ya mean?"

"Well, yeah, I did expect to see her today. I asked after her and the girl at the counter said she was supposed to come in but she didn't turn up and her phone's off."

"I know why she's not turned up."

"Why?"

"Because she's a spy and the mission is over."

"What?" Ben actually snorted at the incredulity of such a thing. "Fuck off."

The stranger wasn't smiling. He was deadly serious. "I'm telling ya."

"No way."

"Have you got time for a drink?" the stranger asked.

How could he refuse? He was intrigued.

They went to the nearest pub. Ben listened open-jawed as Aiden recounted his story. It was an incredible tale right enough. Impossible, yet credible. Sort of.

"She just walked through Checkpoint Charlie and you never saw her again?"

"Until last week yeah. With you."

"It just seems so—" Ben was reluctant to use the word 'unbelievable' because he sort of did believe it. "Crazy."

"It's a crazy world."

"But why would she be working in the cafe?"

"Ask yourself this, might she be spying on you?"

"Nah," he dismissed the possibility far too quickly.

Aiden raised an eyebrow. "Really, no reason at all. You're squeaky clean?"

"Well—" he was already reassessing his original answer. "I'm no angel but there are plenty of people out there worse than me. Surely she'd be spying on them first?"

"That's not how it works."

Ben looked him straight in the eye for the first time, his certainty was unnerving. "Really? A spy?"

Aiden nodded. "Yeah."

The colour draining from Ben's face was evidence enough that his initial claim not to be worth spying on was nonsense.

"Shit."

"I know."

They sipped their drinks and let reality sink in.

"I don't suppose you know where she lives?"

"You already asked me that."

"Yeah but you might have been lying then."

"Cheers."

"You know what I mean."

They both smiled. No hard feelings meant, and none taken.

Ben was having trouble digesting the news though. He still couldn't accept that he was worth spying on.

"I thought she liked me."

Aiden smiled wistfully. "Yeah, I get that."

"A spy? Really? The authorities aren't interested in me surely?"

"Well whatever you're up to, I'd give it a rest if I was you."

"I thought she liked me," Ben repeated unnecessarily.

Aiden didn't want to hear it. "Look mate I don't mean to pry but is there anything political attached to what you do?"

Ben shrugged in a way that didn't completely discount such a possibility.

"You know political protest is banned," Aiden reminded him.

"I thought that was just Extinction Rebellion and hacker groups?"

Aiden nodded as though indulging a child. "I'd definitely change plans if I was you."

Ben had a question. "Why was she spying on *you*?"

Aiden smiled. It was a far away, distant expression. Clearly all those yesterdays had come flooding back.

"Eh?" Ben nudged him back to the present.

"Yeah sorry," he paused. "It wasn't me. It was people I could introduce her to."

"She used you?"

"Yeah."

"To get to who?"

Aiden shrugged. "It was a long time ago. Things were different back then. A lot of underground activity was carried out in squats. Me and my mate were punks. She used us to gain access to the scene."

"What happened, did people get arrested?"

"They did. Some did time, some disappeared completely. Who knows what happened to them."

"Shit."

"Yeah."

They sipped in silence for a few moments. Both thinking about the girl as they knew her.

"Then what happened?"

"Then I wrote a book about it."

"Really?"

"Yeah, no need to look so surprised. I am a writer."

"Cool, did you make any money?"

"I did alright for a while."

"And you never saw her again?"

"Until now."

Ben took a sip of his pint and asked casually, "So are you still involved in all that?"

"I still know people but I pretty much keep to myself these days. You know, try not to attract attention." He grinned. "At least until this week."

He smiled ruefully. The glasses were empty now and neither of them could help the other in any meaningful way. The meeting was over. Not because they wanted it to be but because anything of use had already been said.

Now that they had talked, Ben liked the guy. He had a trustworthy quality that was rare indeed. But there was nothing he could do to help.

"Anyway," Aiden rose to leave. "Sorry to put all this on you but I suppose you're better off knowing than not."

Ben nodded. "Yeah I guess so, thanks. So are you gonna continue the search?"

"It's you she was tracking."

Ben raised an eyebrow but said nothing.

Aiden added, "If you do find her I would love to know."

He stood over the table waiting for a response. When none came he said, "I'll give you my address then?"

Ben shrugged. "If you like."

Aiden pulled a pen from his pocket and wrote his address on a scrap of paper.

Ben took it.

"Nice to meet you"

They bumped fists.

"Yeah you too."

Neither of them seriously expected to see the other again.

68

On Monday morning Ben sat upstairs on a bus heading for work.

The city passed him by. It registered but not really. The sirens, the crowds, the hustle and bustle he normally thrived on, offered no release for his troubled mind.

Why would anyone be spying on me?

He'd been running it over and over in his head. Unfortunately, enough reasons came to mind that he was now worried. He scanned the crowds.

Look at those lucky bastards, he thought. *Not a care in the world.*

The bus slowed to stationery. Passengers started to fidget, huff, check their watches. People began to consider if they'd be late for work. A few wondered if something serious had happened.

Ben was miles away, in his own private world.

Why didn't I ask her out? Maybe it's me. Maybe there's something wrong with me. Maybe I am a waste of space, and what I do is meaningless.

Am I worth the authorities poking their noses into?

And he couldn't give a definitive negative answer. That was

what troubled him the most. He'd been around the scene, heard the rumours. Any groups managing to get organised, to actually present a threat to the establishment could expect an almighty series of misfortunes, culminating in prison time more often than not.

That was why he stayed away from organised groups and had as little contact as possible with some of the extremists Frank was friendly with.

Was it Frank? Should I distance myself from him now? Nah, we're no threat to anyone, we're just having a laugh.

The thoughts, the fears, the hypotheticals chased each other around his head.

Finally the bus managed to squeeze past a row of cars and turn right. The driver changed gear. The bus straightened out. They were moving again.

Through the window Ben could see the pedestrian flyover just ahead.

Ten minutes and we'll be there, he told himself as the traffic again closed around them.

What's the point of going to work though? he thought. *Carrying on like everything is normal?*

The bus once more was reduced to a crawl, then a standstill. He wouldn't be at work in ten minutes after all, he'd probably still be sat here.

This world makes no sense.

Ben's melancholy could be traced back to Saturday afternoon. Not finding Juanita at the cafe was bad enough. But being accosted outside like that had shaken him up more than he'd let on. He'd thought for an instant he was being arrested. Something he didn't appreciate having to consider.

Aiden's tale strongly implied the secrecy he prided himself on was a joke, all his precautions pointless. That the authorities were all over him. It had been a real wake up call. He felt dirty.

He glanced around the bus and wondered if any of his fellow

passengers were truly satisfied with their lot. He knew he wasn't.

I was gonna change the world, he told himself for the twentieth time already that day. *I'm not a fuckin' shop assistant. But I can't do it all alone.*

He thought again about Aiden's revelations. He still didn't want to believe it.

A brief glimpse from the top of a bus after God knows how many years? Behave, no one's memory is that good.

I don't believe it, he told himself. *But she had disappeared under strange circumstances. Properly disappeared. Like, vanished off the face of the earth. It was weird. But who's she spying on? Am I worthy of surveillance?*

And there was the conundrum. He knew he was or at the very least was connected to people who might be of interest. Therefore Aiden's tale may actually contain a grain of truth.

Probably is completely true, his inner voice suggested before he could stop it.

He needed a distraction from his troubles.

A pretty blond on a footbridge that crossed above the road caught his eye. He focused on her, trying to change the tack his mind was insisting on taking. If he avoided the subject he wouldn't have to acknowledge it might be true.

He admired the pedestrian. Imagined her long legs wrapped around him. He noted her confident stride.

That's a girl on a mission, he decided. *She knows where she's going in life.*

The female in question looked to be about mid-twenties. She was smartly dressed in Victorian ankle boots, tight blue jeans and a baggy white jumper. She had her head down. The breeze was blowing her hair across her face, hiding her features, but a strong jaw was visible and Ben knew she was a babe.

I want what she's got.

At the top of the ramp where people crossed above the busy

THE KILLSWITCH

main road. Ben watched her pause and flick her hair back from her face.

She's magnificent, he decided.

But appearances can be deceptive; sometimes people are not all they seem to be. She moved with such grace, such confidence, Ben was sure a girl like that was going places.

If I'm wrong, show me a sign, he mused.

The girl flicked her head.

Something was wrong. She looked so sad. He wasn't sure what, but something was definitely out of place. He watched her grip the railing with both hands.

Without a second's hesitation, she flipped herself over, drew her hands back to her sides like a diver and fell face first ten metres onto the solid surface below.

"Shit!" he muttered.

A young woman a few seats in front of him started to scream.

He blocked her out. He hadn't taken his eyes of the girl. Blood was pooling by her head.

The bus was still stuck in traffic. There was nothing any of them could do except point and scream and watch the blood flow away from her lifeless form.

An old woman was on her feet pointing and shouting in horror.

"Go on son," she screamed. "'Elp 'er."

A young man was running down the ramp towards the motionless figure on the road. A car swerved across two lanes of traffic in a futile attempt to protect the already deceased body from danger.

Other people appeared. A commotion was building. But from the bus nobody could hear what was being said. It added to the surreal nature of the situation. It was like watching a television drama with the sound turned down.

Ben made a little expression of distaste without realising he was doing so.

That's not a sign, that's just life in the city, he reasoned dispassionately. Watching it through glass without audio removed him, gave the proceedings a surreal air. *Impending doom is all around. It's a big city, shit happens, people die.*

It would be nice if there was time to properly mourn the passing of each and every precious life, there just wasn't.

Ben put on his headphones and looked away. He refused to acknowledge the feeling of impending doom.

The bus moved and the commotion fell away behind them.

Finally it pulled up on the High Street and he was down the stairs and off, the suicide already forgotten.

69

The following Saturday Ben went to the cafe. There was no sign of Juanita.

He took an outside table where he sulked and wondered 'what if'.

It took a tap on the shoulder to shake him from his self pity.

"Hey Ben, how you doin'?"

"Hey."

"You ok? You don't look ok."

"I was going to ask her out today," he mumbled sulkily.

Frank slid out a chair to sit. "Who? That waitress? The Spanish one?"

"Yeah," he nodded despondently. Then Frank's words hit home.

"How do ya know she's Spanish?"

Did Frank perhaps know her, where she lived, where the fuck she'd disappeared to?

Frank shrugged. "She looks Spanish that's all."

Ben nodded miserably. "Oh."

"Cheer up, there's plenty more fish in the sea."

"Yeah, I know."

Except his expression suggested that he knew no such thing.

"You should have gotten her number ages ago."

Ben shot him a withering glance. "Yeah, thanks for that. Useful advice."

"Have you asked?" Frank tried a more helpful approach.

"What do you mean?"

"Ask her." He pointed at the waitress through the window "She might know where your señorita hangs out."

"You reckon?"

"Yeah sure, why not?"

Ben rose from his chair.

"Get me a coffee while you're there."

He joined the queue.

When he'd ordered he asked as casually as he could, "No Juanita today?"

"Who?" The girl looked at him.

"Juanita," he repeated. "Dark hair, nose ring, works Saturdays?"

The girl shook her head. "She no work here no more."

"Don't suppose you know where I might find her?"

"Sorry, no."

She slid his drinks across the counter.

"Six pound please."

Ben paid and returned to his seat, defeated.

"Waste of time. She knows nothing."

"Bad luck mate."

They sipped their drinks in silence. Frank kept glancing at his pal's troubled expression. He didn't know what to say. *There's plenty more fish in the sea* or *You can't win 'em all* didn't feel like they'd be enough. Then he had a thought.

"Why don't you track her down?"

"I couldn't find her on social media."

"You must know someone who's good at computers."

"I don't."

"You must."

A flit of a smile crossed Ben's face.

"What?" Frank wanted to know. "What are you thinking?"

"Nothin'"

"No what?"

Ben lowered his voice and lent forwards. "There is this guy at work, a computer geek. He might be able to track her down."

"There you go, see? Gotta be worth a try," Frank agreed optimistically.

"He's a bit of a freak though. Not exactly the helpful type."

"I thought only the cool crowd worked at your place," Frank said.

"He ain't cool."

"He doesn't have to be," said Frank.

"I suppose I could ask him," Ben sounded doubtful.

"What harm can it do?" Frank replied cheerfully.

70

It was true Ben worked in a hip and trendy store. The sort of place where all the staff were young and beautiful. All except one, Jonny the IT guy.

Jonny had no fashion sense at all.

In the summer he wore a plain shirt and slacks and in the colder months he added a heavy zip-up brown cardigan. It helped to keep the chill off his chest.

He started each day combing his straight, black hair into a strict side parting. That was pointless. It was sticking out in tufts before the day was even halfway through.

He was born near sighted and had needed thick glasses since he could remember. He still wore the same style frames he'd chosen at age ten. The girls would always be trying to improve his wardrobe, but he wasn't interested in their help.

He was pedantic, humourless, impatient and seemed to think everybody but him was a fool.

Ben came into work and saw him with his head in the back of a PC. One of the shop girls, Beth, passed by. She winked at Ben as she said, "How you doin' Jonny?"

He didn't turn around to speak.

THE KILLSWITCH

"I'm actually concentrating on something here, so please keep your chit chat to yourself until I've completed the task, thank you."

Ben smiled at Beth. She raised an eyebrow and smiled back.

"Like my new tattoo?" she asked, putting her long shapely leg up on the counter.

An artful python curled from her ankle to the bottom of her tiny shorts.

"Yeah." He smirked at her. "Looks great on you."

"Awww thanks babe."

She winked and walked off. Ben could never tell whether girls were flirting or teasing. It always slightly flustered him. Besides, she was too wild for him. He liked quiet girls. He liked waitresses.

"How you doing Jonny?" Ben asked the back of the IT guy's head.

"I'm busy." Again he didn't turn around.

"Can I have a word?"

"I'm busy."

"Maybe later?"

"I'm busy."

"Come and find me when you're less busy"

"Huh."

71

Jacob was reading a report. Leetabix monitors had picked up a signal if not from the Zodiac cafe itself then very close to it. Infuriatingly it had just been one very brief squawk. Too minimal to trace. So the cafe had been put under surveillance. All staff or customers deemed suspect were scrutinised. There were some old punks who fitted the role of suspicious characters. The leader of the group was an activist called Frank. He was known to the police.

However the report concluded this group offered no cyber threat. Frank was never seen with so much as a smart phone. They couldn't be the terrorist cell Leetabix were hunting. Case closed.

Jacob had no reason to doubt the assessment.

The people I'm after would be carrying devices everywhere they went.

He was hunting hackers. Tech savvy young kids had ruined the presidential election, not tired old analogue punks.

One brief squawk in months. These kids were good.

Many years had passed since he'd come across a worthy foe. But he wasn't unduly concerned. They all left a trail in the end.

Leetabix would just have to keep looking. But Frank's crew could be crossed off the list.

He closed the folder and wrote across the front in green pen, NO CYBER THREAT.

Jacob put the report on a pile and picked up the next one.

72

Aiden was eating cereal in bed and listening to the radio. The broadcaster was droning on in the usual manner.

'The country needs to get a grip on the terrorist situation once and for all. Leetabix and those like them were a danger to the very fabric of society. Stricter laws were needed. Government must do whatever it takes and decent, law-abiding people will understand. If they are doing nothing wrong they have nothing to hide.'

What a load of nonsense, Aiden thought.

Somebody phoned the radio show claiming the government should clamp down hard on agitators.

Aiden shook his head sadly. It was the same old story. Like the whole population had been brainwashed. Anything, anything at all and the solution was always 'clamp down hard' on somebody. Agitators, minorities, refugees, even fucking nurses for god's sake. He was old enough to remember when judges became the enemy of the people.

He felt completely detached from the conversation. He could hear the arrogance in one caller after the next—

'Clamp down hard.'

'It was better in the old days.'

'No respect anymore.'

He couldn't listen. He had to take care of his mental health. He went for a walk but fresh air offered no relief.

He was strolling around looking for her in the crowd. Not meaning to, but unable to stop himself. He sat on a bench and tried not to stare at individuals. He couldn't go through that again.

He'd taken a long time accepting he'd never see her again. Never get to ask her *why*?

Fortunately enough time passed and eventually he stopped dreaming about her every single night. But the mind was a fragile thing. It was like all those years never happened.

I'll go look for her down by the river.

73

Ben was waiting for his bus. A discarded newspaper in the gutter caught his eye.

TERRORISTS AT LARGE read the headline.

He looked away.

At least it keeps the cops busy, he mused. *They've got less time for the rest of us if they're all looking for terrorists.*

Down the street he spotted Jonny in the crowd.

He didn't get back to me.

Jonny hopped on a bus. He stood by the door listening to the Clash on his headphones. He never expected a seat at this time of day. Besides, he only had three stops to go.

74

Ben lived in the basement of a big old corner house. His private entrance led straight into his front room.

He was an artist specialising in giant murals that go up all over town.

He was an enigma, one of the city's dirty secrets. His work was famous, yet he was anonymous. Quite a feat in a world obsessed with knowing every little detail about every little thing. He drove the right-wing tabloids crazy.

He did toy with going public a few years ago but in the end decided he was guilty of far too much criminal damage to reveal his true identity.

The idea they knew who he was, had known for God knows how long, bothered him.

All those precautions, all that risk, all pointless.

And the risks were sometimes considerable.

There was the time he'd been on a gantry high above a main road, painting a giant mural and thinking himself badass. When suddenly the noise of a car approaching at high speed had broken through the late night silence.

Ben had watched dumbfounded as it smashed into the front

of a jeweller's shop. Four hooded figures jumped from the vehicle, ran in, loaded up and ran out.

He'd barely taken it all in before the criminals sped off. Suddenly he didn't feel badass. He felt vulnerable.

Sirens were already getting closer and he was now the only person in the vicinity.

He hightailed it from the area and never returned to finish the piece. Eventually it was painted over.

Bad people came out at night, far worse than him.

Another time, he'd been down by the canal when his super-sensitive hearing picked up footsteps.

Instinctively he'd slipped out of sight behind a thick bush. He watched two young men dressed in black from the top of their hoods to the trainers on their feet come into view.

"Here," one whispered to his pal.

Ben saw the unmistakable glint of metal as the guy dropped two items— two handguns into the grateful water.

The pair turned and skulked off without a word.

Ben allowed a good chunk of time to pass before he re-emerged and went the other way. Again he was too shaken to finish the piece.

Unfinished work bugged him. Always had, always will.

He considered the conversation he didn't have with Jonny unfinished.

75

On Monday morning Ben was at Jonny's side as soon as he entered the shop.

"How you doing?"

Jonny looked up from his phone screen. Why was this individual being suspiciously pleasant? They weren't friends, they were barely acquaintances.

"Uh, I'm fine," he replied, his tone dripping with suspicion.

"Do you fancy a coffee?" Ben asked pleasantly.

Jonny's eyebrows furrowed. "What do you want?"

Ben took a step back.

"Woah," he said. "Where did that come from? I'm just being friendly, asking if you want a coffee."

"Why are you being friendly?"

Ben smiled as though innocence personified. "We do work together."

"OK." Jonny dragged both letters out to their fullest extreme. "I'll play along. Cappuccino." He still sounded suspicious.

"Won't be long," Ben turned on his heel.

Jonny returned to his phone. Very soon he was engrossed.

"Here!"

Ben's return made him jump.

"Don't sneak up on me?"

"Sorry, here's your cappuccino." He held it out like a peace offering.

"Still not sure why, but thanks, I guess."

"Smoke?" Ben gestured outside with a tilt of his head.

Jonny glanced at the clock on the wall.

"Ok," he replied. "You obviously have something you want to say."

Outside Ben smiled as warmly as he could. "Do you like working with computers?"

"Yesss," the word was drawn out suspiciously.

"Got a favourite band, 'ave yer?"

"The Clash. They're old school punk."

"I love the Clash, London Calling."

Jonny stared at him.

Ben tried to think of something else to break the ice. "A movie, got a favourite movie?"

"Bladerunner, the original."

The conversation wasn't exactly flowing.

"What do you want?" Jonny asked.

Ben gave up on the small talk. He broached the real issue.

"I wanna try and track someone down," he said, flicking ash on the ground and avoiding eye contact.

He missed the sparkle in Jonny's eye.

"Oh really?" Jonny asked. At last, a subject he could get interested in.

Ben looked up to meet a carefully cultivated neutral expression. A real screensaver face.

"Oh? What does that mean?" Ben asked

"Why are you telling me?" Jonny replied.

"You know about computers."

"What does that mean?" Jonny sounded if not hostile then certainly defensive.

Ben was beginning to feel as though he'd guessed wrong and was wasting both their time.

He shrugged and looked down at his feet.

"Nothing," he said.

They smoked in silence for a while.

"Who are you trying to find?" Jonny asked.

Ben smirked. "This girl."

"Ahh, a girl," Jonny sounded sarcastic.

"It's nothin'. Forget it." Ben was embarrassed now

They fell silent as a train rumbled along somewhere in the distance. When the rhythm of the tracks ceased Jonny flicked his cigarette end into the kerb and made as though to head back inside.

"What's her name?" he asked from the doorway.

Ben looked up hopefully. "Juanita."

"Surname?" Jonny asked.

"Juanita, that's it."

"Where does she work?"

Ben shrugged.

"You must know something about her?" Jonny said.

"Well, she was workin' in the Zodiac café."

"Was?"

"Yeah."

"When did you last see her? What does she look like?"

"Three Saturdays ago at the café. She's cute, Spanish looking, got a pierced nose."

"So no surname and you don't know where she works. Do you at least know where she lives?"

Ben shook his head and looked sheepish.

"Anything you can tell me that might actually be useful?"

Ben considered mentioning that he used the cafe regularly, met people there. But it didn't seem like that would help.

"Nah." He shook his head.
"I can't promise anything."
"Fair enough," Ben said, realising Jonny was no help.

76

At school Jonny hated team games especially sport. Fart jokes and toilet humour didn't amuse him in the slightest. He considered his peers childish. He never really fitted in.

Then one day he got his first computer and a whole new world presented itself.

He took to it like a duck to water, rushing home from class every day to discover what else the machine was capable of. It was as though he'd been waiting his whole life for this. He wasn't a complete human being until he was plugged in.

He was like Peter Parker, mild mannered and invisible by day. But at night he did things that would have amazed them at school, teachers and children alike. And he made his first friends.

Admittedly his tribe were the digital misfits, the outcasts, the cyber punks. But no matter, they shared a passion. Something Jonny could throw himself into wholeheartedly, completely and utterly.

These kids were the future of the human race but at the time nobody took them seriously.

Technicians were forced to acknowledge their existence

occasionally. But they weren't professionals; there was no need for concern. They were regarded as flies in the ointment.

It was inconceivable they should be treated with respect. Besides the World Wide Web was brand new. It was a learning curve for everybody. The mighty would prevail eventually. Then the flies would get squatted as they always do.

So in the early days, when it really mattered, Jonny and his friends were more or less ignored.

Meanwhile they egged each other on to commit web-based mischief on ever grander scales.

They spent their evenings breaking into secure networks, the more official the better. They liked leaving a 'flag' before sneaking back out via a 'wormhole'.

At first it was purely bravado. Just kids breaking into places to earn respect from their peers. It was no different to leaving a tag on a city wall. Juvenile behaviour as old as time adapted for the computer age.

Jonny excelled in wormholes and was leaving trapdoors before it was cool. A secret point of entry, unknown to all except him. A way back in should he ever wish to return in the future. He was dedicated to being the best he could possibly be, like a psychopath.

By the time experts realised they needed these people on their side it was too late.

They'd hacked into Universities, the Formula One system, Coutts Bank and a vast number of offshore tax havens. Jonny even had a wormhole in the Trust's flagship skyscraper. They were Jacob's first target with Leetabix. But by then the friends had grown up and drifted apart. They disappeared into cyber legend.

77

The 2020s were nearly halfway through.

Jacob was adding the best graduates from the top universities to his motley crew of hackers. Money was no object and their equipment was constantly upgraded. They were the scourge of the digital wrongdoer. Since they began, all the major threats had been terminated. Even minor flies in the ointment had been ruthlessly hunted down.

Now their job was mainly damage limitation. No group was allowed to grow into fully-fledged opponents of the regime.

But conditions for common people didn't improve so the same resentments passed on to each generation. New dissident and activist groups were formed constantly.

As soon as they started chatting amongst themselves, Leetabix were able to pinpoint a location.

Once they had that it was fairly straightforward to build up a case before handing over to the authorities.

The country was being run into the ground. Ordinary people were struggling to put food on the table so organised resistance was guaranteed. And this was the digital age, online chatter was inevitable. Every time a group got off the ground they were quickly closed down and the members prosecuted.

Leetabix were truly the masters of the Internet. Outsiders wondered how they never got caught. Insiders wondered how they managed such a phenomenal success rate. There were rumours they had access to encrypted servers but no evidence was ever produced.

People went online to discuss the state of the world and every time they did they were monitored and placed into categories.

Jonny was the exception. He didn't belong to any group because he didn't need anyone. His understanding of the digital world meant he left no traceable footprint.

If by some miracle he were to become a person of interest, his true identity, his birth, his childhood were all files he'd wiped long ago. That person no longer existed.

He was a lone wolf now, a solo operator, society's worst nightmare.

He knew Leetabix were hunting him with all they had. Destroying the presidential nominee's reputation could never be allowed to go unpunished.

78

Jonny resided in a top floor flat in a quiet, respectable street. Most of his neighbours went to bed early. The Neighbourhood Watch notes any late-night shenanigans disapprovingly. Jonny fit in perfectly.

He got home from work around six. He ate sitting in the kitchen window. Then he washed his pans, plate, knife and fork and turned off the kitchen light. Occasionally the flashing of a television played across his darkened walls. Usually he drew the curtains. Thick drapes that make it impossible to tell whether he was up late or has retired early.

He rarely went to bed early. He stayed online keeping tabs on the state of the world and helping out where he could.

It amused him that year after year giant organisations generated billions in profits yet saw no reason to invest in decent security.

It was as though they wanted to get hacked.

Obviously he committed fraud on a regular basis. But he would be offended if anyone called him a thief. He saw himself as a Robin Hood figure working from the shadows.

Jonny only kept one thing. The single commodity with any value in the modern world: information.

He put it down to having an inquisitive mind.

God Bless the internet, that's what I say

He just liked finding stuff out. Unfortunately once you know something, you can't unknow it.

In the early days, very few were adept at covering their tracks. They didn't realise they had to.

He was uncovering secrets on an industrial scale. Finding out things about American billionaires, Russian Oligarchs, Hedge fund bankers. The people who really ran the world and it made him furious.

Inevitably over time his computer joined the dots and made him aware of The Trust. He despised them instantly but put them on the *to do* pile. They were just one amongst many.

All the while Jonny kept on digging.

He uncovered secret documents proving those who benefitted most in this world were least worthy, that the tactics they employed to cheat and swindle fellow human beings were despicable. That just as the planet had been carved up after the Second World War, so it was being again. And just like last time the technology had raced ahead of the laws that are supposed to rein in outrageous behaviour.

These people were a disgrace. They didn't deserve half of what came their way. Somebody had to do something.

He was reading top secret files from the Trust when one marked *Killswitch* caught his eye.

The Killswitch is in case we ever need to switch off the World Wide Web, he read in horror.

Jonny considered the Internet an essential part of his very existance and they wanted to control it? It felt like he was reading that they wanted to control *him*.

He read on.

There is a team of the brightest and best working on this very issue. Using electromagnetic pulse technology they have crossed a Morris Worm with a Solar Flare and created a Solar Worm. This won't fry vital infrastructure, it will take control of the pulse. They refer to it as 'The Killswitch'.

The more Jonny read the more he took offence. How dare they make plans designed to thwart him personally.

The Internet was his toy. He was the main man, and if there was going to be a killswitch, he should control it, nobody else.

He was furious, irrational, unrealistic. Like a child who doesn't want to share. He would rather smash the Internet into a billion useless pieces than allow it to be controlled by somebody else.

He started digging deep, focusing all his attention on the Trust. Wormholes that had lain dormant for years gave him access to files long since deleted. Each morally bankrupt step of the company's growth was presented to him in black and white.

The more he learnt the more he came to regard them as devils. So naturally that put him on the side of the angels. As though that made any difference in the real world.

There was no such thing as too much with these people. They were into everything from grass roots operations to giant government contracts. Each step of the way they employed the cleverest lawyers money could buy. Locked in every time as main beneficiaries. They were using tactics that would put the Italian mafia to shame.

But they wore funky glasses and attended board meetings in open-necked shirts like hippies. So they must be nice guys really.

It's just an act people! Jonny fumed. He was at the end of his tether.

The CEOs were spending a fortune attempting to appear trendy and Eco friendly and the public was falling for it. To Jonny the con was as transparent as the time the emperor took the word of his tailor over a small boy with eyes in his head.

The billionaire's club was competing to see who could be first to fill a solid gold yacht with cash. But that still wasn't going to satisfy them.

All this greed was bad enough but for Jonny the tax avoidance was what really made his blood boil.

How could they be allowed to destroy the very fabric of Western society?

They might as well register their companies on a moon floating around Saturn for tax purposes. They'd end up paying the same amount into the Treasury as they do now.

They were pretending to be hippies but they were as ruthlessly obsessive in pursuit of ever more dollars than Gordon Gecko at the height of the *greed is good* 1980s. They weren't just ruthless; they were a threat to our very existence.

Planet Earth was dying. Yet they saw it as a price worth paying for personal short-term gain.

Jonny had little time for most humans. He had none at all for billionaires.

His anger grew into rage.

Unfortunately having no friends meant he had no one to confide in. There was no calming influence. Eventually, like all young men without a girlfriend, the pressure gauge blew.

His rage became all consuming.

It wasn't just the Trust. It was all of them. He was going to punish them.

Let's see how they can buy a thousand dollar bottle of wine when their credit cards don't work. Let's see how many votes they get when their vices are splashed across the Internet.

He'd had enough. It was time people paid for their crimes.

He was going to make the general public see the light, whether they wanted to or not. Changes were coming, by force if necessary. It was for the greater good.

Unchecked, Jonny had developed the true conviction of a religious zealot.

The way he saw it, if he was willing to make sacrifices for the greater good, others could as well.

It was a shame he had nobody to run his logic by.

But there it was. He worked alone, he slept alone, he had no confidants. If a thought made sense to him, it passed the litmus test and was good to go.

He'd spent many hours plotting how best to ram his message home. How to force the world to listen.

He'd considered going after the corporations but that wouldn't affect enough of the guilty. He pondered shutting down nuclear plants. Or closing oil refineries, or gas pipelines, or even all three.

All tempting options considering humans were prepared to sacrifice the planet and every living creature on it, but none seemed like punishment enough.

Selfish.

He fumed not for the first time. Not even for the first time that day, *selfishness in pursuit of short term gain.*

It will be the death of us all.

And social media? Don't get me started on that. It ain't social, and it ain't media.

Jonny held a special contempt in his heart for that shit. Facebook he considered the worst of all.

Finally a fitting punishment that would affect the guiltiest the most came to him.

He would hack into social media platforms and adjust the settings.

I'll give them all a score.

I'm not a madman, he told himself. *I'm not unreasonable. I'll make it fair.*

Everybody can start with a hundred points. Then algorithms can readjust as we go.

People can earn extra points for being good. Using public transport, recycling, being a member of Greenpeace or Extinction Rebellion, working in something sustainable that benefits humanity, that sort of thing.

And they will lose points for pollution, racism, homophobia, running a giant multinational, that type of thing.

The algorithm will then add and subtract, add their friend's points and that will be their final score.

He briefly considered whether adding you friend's scores was fair, but only briefly.

Good citizens will benefit us all. Bad citizens will find themselves outcasts. It was time the real villains of the piece got punished.

Fail to maintain a high score and you will be blocked from the most popular internet sites. Your credit rating will dive. You'll become a social pariah. Your friends will desert you in droves. Then who will *like* your selfies?

The time for waiting was over. The older generation have responded with the same tired excuses for long enough.

He'd had enough of *It's really awful, Something needs to be done* and *Lessons must be learnt…*

The time to clean up the world whilst it was still worth making the effort had arrived.

If nothing is done we'll all be dead soon anyway. Politicians have dropped the ball, its up to me.

Jonny would be performing a long overdue public service. And it was irrelevant what the price might be.

They'll thank me for it.

He already knew how he'd go down in history. His chosen narrative would forever appear top six hundred positions when his name was typed into a search engine.

He decided it was time for people to get used to the new world order.

He hit a few keys and released a short video clip.

It was an animated robot dog wearing a dinner jacket and a bow tie. It had the largest puppy dog eyes you ever saw and the cutest little face. The dog did a little *yap yap* followed by a backwards flip.

The clip was shared far and wide.

That evening at six o'clock the puppy dog reappeared unexpectedly on people's screens.

It delivered a message.

"*On Monday the 14th your social media scorecard becomes active. Those individuals with low scores will face penalties. It's up to you to be a good citizen.*"

It did the little *yap yap* and the backwards flip again. Then repeated the message.

By the time people realised it was a virus it was too late. Once on your device it could not be stopped from repeating the message every fourteen minutes.

Within a week everybody had seen it, some felt like they'd seen it every fourteen minutes. The newspapers immediately referred to it as a terrorist plot.

'*Terrorists are going to introduce a points-based system on all social media platforms. All users will be categorised, judged with every tap they make. It is outrageous. It is terrorism, pure and simple.*'

It was true, every action people made was logged and their personal scores adjusted accordingly. Just as the Trust had been doing for ages.

Turning your phone off was an option, except not only would you miss out on who was posting what, practically unthinkable. Your score would be heavily downgraded with every hour of continued absence from the web.

And finally, your friend's behaviour affected your score. If they went offline or were deemed offensive, they were dragging you down with them.

Anyone with a low score was denied access to a vast array of things.

79

Jacob was furious. His long-term plan was in danger of collapsing. The fear of what Leetabix might do was weakened somewhat now that there was a hacker group out there actually willing to carry out their threats.

"We need to find these people."

For the first time they were facing something completely unexpected and highly dangerous. How did they manage to get in unseen? Why was there no chatter?

Their very existence was akin to admitting there was a chink in the Trust's mighty armour. It shook the foundations of everything they took for granted.

His people had only ever known total control. Some had excelled at universities specifically so they could come and work here. That the Trust could be shaken by a hacker group nobody had ever heard of was unthinkable.

At least it had been yesterday.

But all was not lost. The social media countdown was terrifying people. If anything it brought the potential closure of the internet into sharp focus.

They were even more terrified of the killswitch being pulled.

Meanwhile the hunt for the hackers, or terrorist group as they must now be called, was top priority.

They set about their usual practices, set their usual traps and waited.

Word got out that they were on the job. Confidence returned, share prices rose.

Nothing happened, nobody was arrested; people ignored the bleeding obvious and went about their business.

80

Ben sat in his front room eating a cheese sandwich. As the streetlights came on he lit another cigarette. Impatiently he wished the hours away until finally there was a tap at his window.
He got up to open the door.
"Alright Frank."
"Alright mate."
Frank came in and perched on the edge of a seat.
"All ready are we?" he asked.
Ben nodded.
"That one's yours." He pointed at a bin liner. It was jammed full of folded stencils.
There was a backpack alongside the bin liner. It held cans of spray paint.
They ran over their plans unnecessarily, just passing time until it was late enough. When the night was at its quietest it was time to move.
They slipped from the basement and took the side streets. Avoiding all cameras, they hit the main road junction. Here they

crossed with their hoods up and heads down. Then continued out of camera range almost immediately.

They passed Jonny's house without realising.

They turned into the target road, took a good look around and set to work.

They worked quickly. Ben planned to get a few hours sleep before starting his shift in the morning.

81

Jonny had tracked down loads of people for all sorts of reasons.

He tapped at his Mac a couple of times and he was into the CCTV outside the Zodiac cafe. He rewound to the relevant Saturday, found her and zoomed in on her face.

He took a screen-grab that he knew would already be printing in his bedroom. Then he zoomed out and slowly span her 360 degrees, studying her from all angles.

He checked her against DWP files and was a little surprised she didn't come up. Even as a foreign national she should be registered to work.

Never mind, he hacked into Border Control instead and ran her through their files, but still she didn't materialise.

This was unusual but he wasn't quite done.

He fed her image into the CIA facial recognition programme.

Immediately his nonchalance evaporated. His face literally turned white. He stared at the screen in disbelief. Frantically he typed a piece of misdirection code into the computer, threw his laptop into his emergency bag and scarpered through the door as fast as his legs would carry him.

Somebody was protecting her. This didn't happen by accident. She was part of the game, a professional. He hadn't expected that. What was Ben mixed up in?

82

Aiden was strolling along half looking for Mia and driving himself crazy. He needed a distraction. Ahead on a lamppost a picture of Joe Strummer stared down at him. His image was encircled by bold type promoting an exhibition in the old railway yard. It was just two streets over.

The History of Protest.

Aiden believed in Joe Strummer and he believed in protest. Question everything. This generation could badly use some of that old punk attitude. If you're never likely to get the house, the pension, or even sick pay for god's sake why the fuck would you go to the office five days a week unless you were already trapped by debt? Why would you pay extortionate prices to commute to a shit job that consumes your whole life? No thanks. Of course the youth should be protesting. It's a no brainer.

But as any good anarchist will tell you before you can protest you have to know your history.

His curiosity was piqued. A little stroll down memory lane might be fun.

There were banners and posters, flyers and fanzines, stickers and badges. He even saw one of the anti-war leaflets he and Mia had handed out all those years ago.

It was disgusting. He felt sick. All that suffering and heartache for what? So it could be fitted with rose tinted nostalgia? So trendy art students could pay a pittance to come and learn a sanitised version of the reality?

There was a whole wall dedicated to the *Battle of Union Street*. It was described as 'Yobs throwing things at each other.'

We were protecting our manor from fascists, he wanted to scream. *I was there.*

Aiden was infuriated.

All our actions, every single one, misinterpreted. History rewritten. It was unbelievable.

He stormed out of the show to the nearest corner shop. He bought the largest permanent marker pen they had in stock. Then he returned to the exhibition and wrote, *CLASS WAR*.

Right across the plexiglass lid of the display he considered most offensive. He circled both A's in classic anarchist style. Then he defaced four more display cabinets.

Pleasantly surprised nobody had grabbed him and ignoring the cameras, he legged it back to the street.

That period, his youth, had been a massive turning point in the history of the country.

Only now, with all the relevance sifted out, it was nothing. His whole life, his history, his suffering, the beatings he took were meaningless. The ruling party had done what the winning side always does. They had made their version of events the official truth.

For years Aiden had tried not to get involved, to not let things bother him but silence just played into their hands. Apathy gave the enemy a massive advantage.

For the first time in a long time he was angry enough to man the barricades. He knew his small victory with the marker pen was barely one notch above insignificant. He wanted to do more. But what?

All the old haunts were abandoned ruins now. The faces he'd known long gone. Even if he wanted to do something, the game had changed.

It was all online now wasn't it?

Aiden dismissed that thought out of hand.

How can it all be online? Revolutions need people, numbers getting together. You can't change the world sitting in your underpants in front of a computer screen. You need a crowd, a mob, something to frighten the horses.

There must be somebody still fighting the good fight?

He roamed through the city like he used to, passing old familiar landmarks. A lot of the places reminded him of Mia, but he was so angry the memories didn't hurt like they should.

But each old squat, cafe and pub had been put out of action. First vacated, by force if necessary, then allowed to deteriorate. Soon they would all be demolished. It was depressing.

He kept walking, barely pausing to look at the boarded up shells. What was the point?

It turned out to be a depressing day. He should never have gone to the exhibition. It had made him feel worse.

He wandered homewards, not quite ready to admit total defeat but pragmatic enough to know the revolution that had once seemed imminent was well and truly dead. There were never going to be major improvements. This was as good as it was ever going to get. Nobody was interested in learning anything from the past.

We're all doomed, he thought.

83

Juanita was in her pyjamas when the doorbell rang.

She glanced suspiciously through the net curtain. To see Pablo standing there was slightly concerning. She pressed the buzzer and let him in.

He had never visited her at home before.

"Evening Sir, is everything alright?"

"Fine, fine," he muttered.

He entered her living room and plonked himself down on the sofa. He gestured for her to sit in her own home. Obediently she did so.

"Are you alright?" he asked.

And there was something in his tone that made her question that she was.

"Why do you ask?"

He sniffed. "I'm sure it's nothing to worry over, but somebody is tracking you."

"Oh," she said, not quite sure what he was telling her.

She pulled her dressing gown tighter. Some kind of subconscious gesture of defence.

"Who is it?"

"We're not sure." He passed over a photograph of her outside the Zodiac cafe.

"But we found this."

"Oh," she said again and pulled her gown tighter still.

"Tell me again, your opinion of the target there."

"I saw them as harmless," she insisted.

Her boss frowned.

"Just graffiti artists you said."

"Yes."

He studied her a moment longer than necessary.

"Is it possible they were onto you? Playing you? Take your time and think. Was there anything, anything at all that you might have missed?"

She cast her mind back. Re-examined every single contact. Ben suspected nothing. If they had been trying to put her off the track she'd have noticed.

"I'm sure," she insisted.

"Ok." He rose to leave.

"Do I go home soon?"

"Sit tight until I get back to you."

She followed him to the door and locked it when he left.

Why would anyone be tracking me? she wondered and a million and one reasons came to mind.

She took a few moments to collect her thoughts. She got up, grabbed her keys and went out.

I'll need to stock up on food if I'm to lay low. I'm getting too old for all this.

84

Jonny's heart was racing. He went to a cafe and found a quiet table at the back. He used their Wi-fi to hack into the council's CCTV system and went to the camera outside his home. He rewound the tape. Five minutes after his hurried exit a figure appeared at his gate. He was moving cautiously, quietly.

Just the way he walked was enough for Jonny.

This guy's a professional.

He watched the stranger slip quietly in, creep around the house, and just as silently back out the gate.

Jonny pressed a few computer keys. Instantly he was watching the stranger get into a Toyota Hybrid. The car moved silently away from the kerb with the lights off.

Jonny's spider senses were tingling like crazy.

He frowned and sipped his coffee as he dwelled over recent events, mentally analysing it all. Despite the irritation they presented he was impressed how quickly they were on to him and the professional discretion.

A brief smile escaped and played swiftly across his lips. He couldn't help it. *This is it, the game is on.*

Hunter or hunted it made no difference. Either way he was in to the bitter end.

He put his cup down and tapped a few keys. Now he was looking through the security camera of a neighbour two doors down. This offered a better view of the car, but still wasn't clear enough for his liking.

He pressed another button and the picture on his screen switched to yet another private security system. That was better. He took a picture of the registration number. He zoomed in closer on the driver. His cap was low, he wasn't smoking nor playing with a phone that might light up his features.

Jonny switched to another camera and tried to zoom in on the driver's face, but he had the sun visor lowered, Jonny was impressed, *irritated* but impressed.

He turned off the cameras, made a false reservation in a dive round the corner and closed his Mac.

He had chosen a place where discretion is still a thing. He booked in with a fake driving license. Then with a sweeping glance around the lobby, stepped into the lift.

He set a micro-camera in the lift ceiling and when he got out, placed another in the hallway. He didn't plan to be here long but while he was a guest he would need surveillance.

Jonny sank down onto the dusty bed and reflected on his bad luck. His mission had been proceeding exactly as planned, now a favour for some random work colleague meant the whole thing could be in jeopardy.

He had come up on the radar. Plans would have to be altered accordingly.

He had just become a person of interest but like a true fanatic had no intention of aborting. There was a way around the problem, he just hadn't figured it out yet. He flicked open his Mac. He had no plan, but simply staring at the screen saver was like having an old friend sitting on his lap quietly awaiting instructions. He felt himself calming down. His mind turned to Ben.

If I hadn't agreed to do him a favour this wouldn't have happened. Why would MI5 be interested in a shop assistant?

He looked him up on the Internet but found nothing that might offer an explanation.

With a few more taps on his keyboard he had Ben's home address. He hacked into all the cameras in the area. He noted a couple of high-end private security systems so hacked into them as well. He didn't have the clearest view of Ben's side steps, but he was fairly confident nobody was getting in or out without him noticing. He set the cameras recording and reduced the page on the screen.

Inside he was stressing out. He was a person who liked routine and now he had none. He tapped away at the keyboard, his comfort blanket, his link with what passed for normality in his world.

He spent the night burying files and bouncing data around the world in a skilful attempt to sever any links between the hacker who had searched for Juanita and himself.

The sun was peeking over the city skyline by the time he got back to the camera outside Ben's flat. He fast-forwarded the recording through to midnight and beyond. Nothing happened on the screen. To most people such a task would be boring. A deserted street in darkness in fast-forward. To Jonny it was fascinating.

Just as he was beginning to think there was nothing to see, a shadow exited the flat and flitted past a shrub, closely followed by another.

Most people would have missed it. Jonny was on it immediately.

He hit pause with lightning-fast reflexes, rewound and watched again in slow motion. The lead character was of a very similar build to Ben. He was all in black, right down to his backpack. He was carrying something large.

Hello, what you up to then?

Jonny felt a certain pride in his co-worker. He liked people with secret lives.

He switched to another camera and rewound to 2.37am. The figure appeared in shot. It was definitely Ben. The second person he didn't know.

In a few minutes he had tracked the secretive ghosts along their whole route. They were sticking to the shadows and clearly aware of CCTV cameras. They were trying their upmost not to be spotted. They needn't have bothered.

Where are you going? Jonny wondered.

85

The following morning Ben went to work in high spirits. He actually had to stop himself whistling on the bus.

Passing under suicide bridge, he spared a thought for the poor girl he'd seen jump. But even her memory couldn't dampen his mood.

He walked in the shop wearing a giant smile. "Mornin' Beth."

The smile dropped from his face as his eye fell across the uniform standing next to Beth.

"Ben Wallace?"

"Yeah." He tried to keep his expression neutral.

Oh shit, they know. I bet there was cameras on us. I should have checked it more thoroughly. This is what happens when you get sloppy.

Ben caught Beth's eye, she offered a sympathetic half smile.

"I'd like to have a word with you," the police officer said. He was holding his cards close to his chest.

Ben nodded focusing on screensaver face.

"Are you alright?" the policeman asked him.

Oh clever, Ben thought. *I ain't falling for that one.*

"Yeah, why?" he snapped suspiciously, then immediately admonished himself. *Not like that. Too much. Reign it in.*

"Yes." his voice trembled slightly. "Yes," he repeated more firmly. "I'm fine."

The copper gave him a funny look. He wasn't suspicious before, this was a routine enquiry. He was getting so with each passing second though.

"This way." He pointed towards the back of the shop.

Ben followed to the rear of the premises and leant nonchalantly against the wall.

"What's up?" he asked.

"How well do you know Jonny Archer?"

Ben could have kissed him.

"What?" he stammered, trying not to appear relieved.

The officer declined the offer to repeat his question. He waited patiently.

"Jonny, I hardly know him. Why, what's he done?"

The policeman hesitated. He'd been sure he was on to something. The guy had guilt written all over him. Now he wasn't so sure.

"Where were you last night?" he asked.

Ben was calm now. This was about Jonny not him.

"I was home officer."

"All night?"

"Yeah."

The realisation that they weren't onto him caused Ben to look downwards momentarily. He couldn't risk showing the smirk that flickered across his face.

"Did you see Jonny Archer last night?"

"No." Ben looked up. From his face it was obvious that was true.

"When did you last see him?"

"Yesterday, here, at work."

Ben looked him in the eye. "Why? What's he done?" he asked again.

"So you didn't see him last night at all?"

Ben pursed his lips and shook his head. "No" he delivered the word with gravitas.

"Have you ever socialised with him outside of work?"

Ben snorted a little. "I don't even socialise with him inside work."

"What do you discuss with him?"

"I hardly ever speak to him."

"When you do?"

"Not much, it's hard to get a single word out of him most of the time."

"I understand you bought him coffee yesterday."

"Yeah."

"Have you ever bought him coffee before?"

"No."

"Has he ever bought you coffee?"

"What does that matter?"

"Just answer the question please."

Ben shook his head.

"So why yesterday?"

"Ben shrugged. "I dunno, I was being friendly."

"And then you went out the back together."

"Yeah"

"What did you talk about?"

"Nothin'"

"Nothing?"

"Yeah."

"You must have talked about something."

Ben relaxed. He knew a fishing expedition when he heard one.

"Look," he said. "I bought him a coffee cos I was getting one for myself. I was just being friendly. We did go out the back at the same time but only for a cigarette." He looked the officer straight in the eye. "You're right, I did try to have a conversation with him. But you don't know the guy, he's difficult to talk to."

Ben shrugged. "Difficult all round actually. There's not much else to say."

"So you exchanged words?"

Ben nodded indulgently.

"What did you say?"

"I asked him what his favourite band was."

"What did he say?"

"I can't remember."

The policeman raised an eyebrow. He clearly didn't believe that.

"I can't remember," Ben repeated.

"So you say," the copper replied dubiously whilst noting something in his little pad. "What else did you discuss?"

"I asked him his favourite film."

"What did he say?"

"Really? You wanna know what his favourite film is? Why?"

"Just answer the question please."

"It was Casablanca."

The officer frowned. "Casablanca? Are you sure?"

"Yeah."

The policeman shook his head and closed his notebook.

"Ok," he said. "Thank you for your time."

He hadn't mentioned Juanita, Ben noted.

Naturally the talk in the store was all about why the police might want to speak to Jonny. Ben doubted it was anything serious and assumed it was a case of mistaken identity whatever it was.

"Did Jonny really look like a lawbreaker?" He asked for the umpteenth time. He couldn't wait for the working day to end.

At last Ben was returning home. He didn't get his usual bus. He wanted to check out his handiwork from the night before. Wanted to cheer himself up a bit.

THE KILLSWITCH

ANTIFA in bright red eight-foot letters adorned the side wall of a pub frequented by Combat 18. It carried the tag *Virmin* below it with a little picture of a rat giving the thumbs up. He smirked looking around the bus. A few seats behind him a Muslim girl was giggling, nudging her friend and pointing.

Ben caught her eye and they shared a smile. She knew who drank there and she knew he knew. They both approved of the graffiti. That was enough for Ben. She didn't need to know his identity.

He wished he'd been able to emblazon the slogan right across the front of the public house but he knew cameras would have definitely picked him up.

Still, he thought, *mustn't grumble. All in all, a good night's work.*

At home he put on *London Calling* and threw pasta into a pan. He expertly sliced an onion and some mushrooms. He grinned as he stirred the contents of the pan. Enjoying the private knowledge that all day people had been loving and hating his work in equal measure.

He knew the fascists would paint over it soon enough but in the meantime it must be driving them crazy. His face actually started to hurt he was grinning so hard.

After wolfing down the meal and half-heartedly washing up, he went through to his front room.

A stencil was taped to his cutting board. He picked up his scalpel and spent the next two hours happily cutting away. Pausing only to grin at how annoyed the fascists must be.

86

Aiden was reading about the terrorist social media scoring system. He nodded approvingly.

He'd never liked social media. Had tried warning people about putting all their information out there, especially when a handful of freaks controlled everything. It amazed him how much folk were willingly revealing about themselves.

Not me, he mused. *It ain't social and it ain't media.*

Information was power. He thought everyone knew that.

He preferred newspapers. Turning pages the old fashioned way. When he'd read it, he just walked away. There was no record of what he'd browsed.

But kids nowadays did everything online. He understood they put great faith in their own ability to cover their tracks. He knew such tricks were beyond him.

Anyway what did it matter? It had been decades since he'd needed to cover his tracks. He sipped his tea still browsing the article about the terrorists. He smiled to himself.

Those guys are really putting the cat amongst the pigeons.

He turned the page.

87

Mia sat alone and wondered who might be taking her picture. She wasn't genuinely trying, the list was too long. She was just passing the time. Outside she could hear people going about their business. She envied them their normal lives. She wanted to be normal.

She crossed the room and looked through the window, hoping for a distraction from her thoughts but it made her feel vulnerable. If someone was out there she should keep away from the windows. She sat down and pulled out her copy of *The Berlin Spy*.

She didn't like the version of herself in the pages but the words, the actual words had been written by Aiden and reading them made her feel closer to him. Besides she was no longer that person. The woman she was today would never leave him like that.

It was ironic, not long after that fateful day the wall had fallen and everything was different.

She wondered where he was now, what he was doing. How many kids he had with his perfect little wife.

She hated her whoever she was. She wanted a life like that.

Like the one she imagined Aiden and his wife enjoyed. She wondered again how many children they had.

She'd never had the chance to be normal. Something always came along.

There was forever *just one more thing* that cropped up unexpectedly and needed to be dealt with immediately. Even when she was officially retired, home alone and out of the game, it wasn't real. Every ring of the phone, every knock on the door, hell even a car in the street and she assumed it was another job. And eventually it always was.

She was sick of pretending to be other people, keeping potential friends at arm's length, never being allowed to have a life. But above all she was sick of her superiors.

She had been trained to protect the integrity of her country from western attacks. Any integrity had disappeared long ago.

Her job had become little more than covering up criminal activities for the Trust.

All pretence of moral superiority had been abandoned. Now everybody travelled in chauffeur driven Mercedes Benz's and wore their ill-gotten wealth as badges of honour. She wanted out.

88

Jonny couldn't stay at the hotel for long. He needed somewhere to lie low. A safe house. Who did he know that he could trust?

Nobody came to mind. He couldn't even think of anyone he trusted in cyberspace, let alone in real life.

Someone with minimal connection to me, that will hide me no questions asked.

He actually smiled. It was preposterous. There was nobody like that.

But he was desperate. There had to be someone.

Only one person ticked enough boxes to be even remotely viable. The lovesick fool who had got him into this mess in the first place.

89

The head of the secret service sat in his study nursing a brandy waiting for the phone to ring.

When it did, he snatched up the receiver. "Well?" he said.

"He doesn't exist sir."

"Excuse me?"

"There are no records of him anywhere."

"Why would he be interested in the girl?"

"She has a long history of infiltration sir. It could be anyone."

"What do the boffins say?"

"They are certain the terrorists we are looking for will have a room full of electronic equipment. We found nothing like that sir, not even a laptop."

"I want him found."

"Yes sir."

"I expect a report first thing in the morning."

"Yes sir."

He dialled the chairman of the Trust and passed on what had been relayed to him. Then he gulped back the last of his brandy and went upstairs to his wife.

90

It was past eleven p.m. when Ben heard a gentle tapping on his window.

Who's that? He wasn't expecting anyone.

He went and pulled the curtain back a tad. A shadowy figure was half visible in the darkness.

"Who is it?"

The shape moved closer. Ben recognised Jonny instantly. He indicated to the side door and went to let him in.

This was a surprise.

Jonny stood in the centre of the room. He made no attempt to explain why he had turned up so unexpectedly. The awkwardness of the situation was palpable.

"So—" Ben felt the need to break the silence. "Can I offer you a beer?"

"I don't drink."

"Coffee then?"

"Do you have any herbal tea?"

"No."

"Water then."

"Yeah, Are you hungry?" Ben asked.

Jonny looked to be weighing up the question.

"What do you have?"

"Er, I dunno, cheese sandwich."

"No thanks."

"Jaffa cakes?"

"No thanks."

"An apple?"

"No thanks."

"I'll get you some water, take a seat." He gestured towards the armchair.

He came back and handed the water to his unexpected visitor. Jonny took it showing no intention to explain his presence.

Ben was tempted to mention the police were looking for him. He didn't bother, it seemed like a moot point.

He left him perched on the edge of the sofa and returned to his cutting.

Eventually Jonny asked, "What's that?"

"A stencil."

"Oh."

Ben worked on, conscious of the stranger over his shoulder.

"You're an artist then?"

Ben glanced up. He smiled trying to be friendly. "Yeah."

A few more minutes passed.

"Street art is it?"

"Yeah." Ben was making a rather delicate cut so didn't look round.

"Careful," Jonny advised.

"Yeah thanks," he replied sarcastically but sarcasm was lost on Jonny.

"Is that two kittens?" he asked suddenly and Ben nearly cut the whiskers of a kitten.

He lifted his scalpel and looked at his guest.

"Yeah." He smiled. "Like 'em?"

"I don't get it," Jonny replied.

"Huh."

Ben returned to his work. He wanted to finish it this evening. Skilfully, he cut out the last of the letters in a circle above the kitten image.

Then he stepped back and read the words out loud, "ANTIFASCIST" above, and "ACTION" below the kittens.

"It's big innit," Jonny said.

Ben was nodding his head in satisfied agreement. "Needs to be. People need to notice it."

"They'll notice that all right."

Silence fell again but it was easier now. There was less tension in the air. They were getting used to each other's presence.

"So what's it for?"

Ben threw him a look that said he had no right to ask.

He studied his work for a moment before asking without looking round. "I guess you need somewhere to stay?"

"Yeah."

A normal person might have found the situation awkward, not Jonny.

In his mind Ben had brought this on himself.

A normal person might have felt the need to explain their predicament; especially to someone they barely knew.

"Can you tell me why?" Ben asked.

"Not really."

Ben shook his head and smiled. He liked to think of himself as a rebel. Assisting a fellow outcast appealed to him. He naively assumed they were in the same league. Minor irritants to the established order.

I've got a secret life; he's got a secret life. We're practically kindred spirits.

"So it's serious," he asked.

Jonny shrugged but didn't reply.

"Not going to get the windows caved in are we?" Ben was making a joke, trying to take the sting out of the situation.

But the way Jonny considered the question carefully gave him the first inkling he might be out of his depth.

"I doubt it," he answered eventually.

Ben could work with that.

"But it's possible," Jonny added.

"Oh, right." Now he was far from easy. "Gangsters, is it?"

"No."

Ben waited for him to expand.

No more was forthcoming. He felt a desire to fill the silence. "What about the door?"

He didn't really want to know, but he asked anyway. "Are we likely to get the door kicked in?"

Again, Jonny took an age to consider. It was an annoying trait already and he'd only done it twice.

"Well?"

"I suppose it's possible," Jonny conceded.

"You know the police are looking for you?"

"Can I stay?"

"You can stay." He didn't feel he could go back on his original hasty decision without losing face.

Jonny immediately pulled out his Mac and started typing away. Like he was home.

He'd seen the giant murals around town. He wasn't stupid, he had eyes. Clearly Ben was *Virmin* the notorious street artist.

"So, you're political?"

Ben looked at him. "Aren't you?"

Jonny shrugged, still typing.

"What you typing?"

"Nothin'"

Ben attempted to look at the screen. "How can…"

Jonny slammed the lid closed.

"Its private!" he snapped.

"Ok, ok."

Ben sat opposite the touchy hacker.

"If you don't trust me what did you come here for?" The question was offered up in amusement rather than offence.

"It's your fault I'm in this mess."

"What? It's my fault?"

"Yes."

"How?"

"Your girlfriend was flagged."

Ben began to worry. This story had a certain familiarity.

"You mean Juanita?"

"Yes."

"She's not my girlfriend".

"Whatever, she's in the game."

"She's a spy?"

Jonny nodded. "Something like that."

"Are you a spy?" Ben asked.

"No," he replied without looking up.

"So if you're not a spy, what are you?"

I'm just someone who likes his privacy, that's all."

"Privacy, really?"

Jonny didn't reply. He wasn't someone who argued facts with ignorant people.

91

Aiden was obsessed with the thought of Mia being back in his city. He tried not to roam the streets looking for her but couldn't stop himself. He knew it was needle in haystack territory. Was never going to get results but he had to do something.

So he walked until his feet hurt then he sat in cafes trying not to get in the way. All around him people complained about the social media scores. They were so busy complaining they were missing the world as it happened around them. It mystified him.

92

Jonny was an infuriating houseguest. He needed everything to be just so and was extremely secretive.

Ben was all for keeping things private but this guy took it to a new level.

He guarded his Mac as though it were the crown jewels.

Ben kept going to work. The time apart allowed them both some space.

But he was rapidly running low on patience.

"Any plans?" he asked casually one evening.

"Not really." Jonny smiled, trying to be nice.

"What have you been doing today while I was out?"

"You wouldn't understand."

"What because I'm thick?" Ben was tired, it had been a long day and he was getting sick and tired of this guy's attitude.

"No, because you're too emotional."

"What the fuck does that mean?"

"And too judgemental."

"I'm neither of those things," Ben protested.

"Ok then," Jonny replied. He drew the words out in that

infuriating manner that meant *You're wrong but I can't be bothered to argue.*

"So who is it you're hiding from? You can at least tell me that."

Ben was beginning to realise first appearances had been deceptive. This guy was much more of a serious rogue than he appeared, than Ben would ever be.

Jonny made no attempt to answer the question. He began to type. The conversation was over.

Ben waited in vain for a whole lot of minutes.

"I'm going to make a cuppa," he said eventually.

Jonny was so engrossed with whatever was on his screen he missed the comment. But he saw him move towards the kitchen, realised he'd said something and answered on autopilot. "No thanks."

Ben headed towards the kettle fuming,

I didn't offer. I purposefully didn't offer.

He stopped in his tracks trying to think of a reply when there was a tap on the window.

"Who's that?" Jonny hissed nervously.

"Calm down."

He padded towards the window blissfully unaware Jonny's finger was hovering over a button, set to release viruses throughout cyberspace.

Ben peeked through the curtain without touching it. "It's ok. Its only Frank."

"Who?"

"Frank, he's a buddy of mine."

Jonny aborted the virus attack. He closed the lid of his Mac and stood up, clearly agitated.

"A friend? What sort of a friend?"

He was pacing the room now.

"Relax," Ben tried to reassure him. "Its fine, he's cool."

Jonny hadn't been expecting company. He hated surprises

and strangers. He needed time to adjust. But things were moving so fast lately that just wasn't possible.

Ben let his friend in. Frank plonked himself down on the couch.

"This is Jonny from work."

"Hi." Frank reached across the room and they bumped fists.

"You sell clothes as well?"

"No, I'm in IT."

"Oh, you're the guy that's going to track down Juanita for him."

Jonny snorted. "Her name's not Juanita." The way he said it made it seem preposterous.

Frank studied the nerdy stranger a little more closely.

"Sorry, if her name's not Juanita, what is it then?"

"Who knows? It might as well be *trouble*."

This was weird. Frank glanced towards Ben. "What the fuck?"

Ben wanted to explain but he couldn't, not really.

"Weird, eh?" he managed instead. "Anyway, do you want a cuppa?"

If in doubt, change the subject, it was an old school distraction, tried and tested.

"Weird?" Frank repeated, his tone strongly suggesting that single word was not an adequate explanation.

Ben was already heading into the kitchen.

"What's he on about?" he heard Frank ask.

Ben left them to it.

He made the tea and walked back into the front room in time to hear Frank's incredulous question. It was delivered with a healthy dose of disbelief.

"She's some kind of secret agent?"

Jonny nodded. "Yep."

"Why was she working at the cafe then?"

"She was probably watching you," Jonny suggested casually.

"What? Nah." Frank looked shocked. He dismissed the possibility much too quickly. "Why?"

Jonny spoke as though he was explaining something basic to a thick child. "You are involved in political law breaking, aren't you?"

Frank was extremely discombobulated by the directness, the matter-of-fact way in which this weirdo delivered questions that for most people would remain unsaid, as all socially awkward comments should be.

He took a moment to answer. "Yeah but the police don't care about a few slogans."

"Today's sloganeers are tomorrows bombers," Jonny replied.

Frank turned to Ben. He was glad of the distraction his arrival with the tea provided.

"Is he for real?" He jabbed a thumb towards Jonny.

"I told him we would never get involved in anything heavy. We're not into violence," Ben said, trying to lighten the atmosphere.

But Jonny's Asperger's ensured he couldn't leave it there. "They don't know that unless they check you out."

Ben plonked the tea down.

"Wanna tell us how you know so much?" Frank asked.

"Not really," replied Jonny. "I hardly know you."

Frank took the offered cup of tea and sat back. It was a lot of information to digest, deeply concerning information.

"So I guess we're cancelling the operation," he said.

Ben nodded. "Maybe for the best."

"What operation?" Jonny asked. "You shouldn't cancel anything. You should carry on as normal." He sounded agitated.

Ben and Frank shared a concerned glance.

93

Jonny was following the chatter. There were a handful of people with enough intelligence to make useful suggestions. But they were the usual, left leaning, liberal luvvies and were easily shouted down.

The mainstream mob blindly followed those right wingers getting the most furious. Fury nearly all generated from servers he traced back to Leetabix.

Jonny wasn't at all surprised. It was a pattern he was more than familiar with.

He could trace these patterns right back to the very beginning, to Brexit and beyond.

From a shady bot farm they generated vast quantities of traffic. Then friendly trolls pitched in and a two-pronged attack was up and running. They could orchestrate campaigns of their own or put all their resources into attacking an opposing point of view. It made no difference which tactic they employed.

The end result was the same. Ordinary members of the public so confused you could have them swearing that black was white or up was down.

Manipulation was taking place on a scale never before seen. And it was as simple as selling tickets for the ghost train.

At the Trust's behest Leetabix further muddied the waters by ensuring a constant stream of headlines flowed from their pals at the gutter press. Inviting people to hate various minorities.

As an added bonus, newspapers were posting website polls with space for comments. Anonymous trolls could spout their vitriol for the whole world to see. They did, in their thousands.

Some readers dared raise a finger of complaint. They became the enemy. Found themselves attacked relentlessly with all guns blazing.

Others read the propaganda, nodded along in mild agreement and absentmindedly clicked *like*. They were bombarded with posts specifically designed for them until they were totally committed to the cause. Any cause, any cause at all as long as confusion and doubt reigned supreme. The game was on.

Other companies, previously respectable household names, began getting into the ocean with the sharks. It was all brand new. Nobody knew the rules anymore. All they knew for certain was normal rules need not apply.

It was a digital free-for-all and there were riches to be had for the lucky few. Riches beyond your wildest dreams. But this moneymaking racket required scapegoats.

First casualties in the war of words were single mothers. How dare they get pregnant and take up all the council houses. Getting angry at them nullified the need to ask why there weren't more houses. Then the unemployed got it in the neck. Sitting around smoking skunk watching flat screen TV's all day. It was disgusting and it was holding the country back.

Next it was the turn of immigrants. Coming over here taking our jobs and stealing our benefits. They'd have difficulty doing both at the same time but no matter, Murdoch's minions printed it anyway. Jacob's sycophants posted the same message and the people who don't like thinking lapped it up.

Eventually teachers, firefighters, even doctors and nurses were accused of disloyalty to the country and her majesty.

That's right, those we trust with our children, with our very lives, the ones getting clapped as heroes during Covid-19 were now classed as enemies of the people.

The politicians went along with it. They had to, they were complicit. Like all who support a liar they were reduced to lying themselves. Then Russia declared war in Europe knowing any claim to any moral high ground was long gone. The authority of State so carefully cultivated that took generations to build, was lost in a few short years.

With the West weakened, countries all over the world fell into line as Leetabix threatened wildly.

The Trust managed to get a few concessions from Leetabix. Naturally there were costs incurred that had to be passed on.

Those CEOs willing to do as they were advised without making a fuss could rely on financial support for themselves and a fair price for their shares. Why risk that against total ruination?

Jonny knew all this. He knew Leetabix were just a subsidiary of the Trust but he wasn't particularly interested in them per se.

He divided big business into two categories, ethical or not. His concern ran no deeper than that. Yes, the Trust were the biggest sharks in the water but they were all sharks.

The Trust's shareholders couldn't be happier. They were making a fortune off the back of all the misery Leetabix caused.

All this greed was a large part of why Jonny had given up on his fellow man (and woman). It no longer surprised or angered him. Just filled him with ever more conviction that the human race deserved to be put out of its misery.

94

Ben and Frank had another bout of criminal damage lined up. The location had been chosen, the stencils and paints prepared, but the possibility they were being observed made them doubt they should go ahead.

Jonny insisted they would attract far more attention by changing their plans. When they seemed reluctant, he offered to help. It was his way of saying, 'Thanks for having me'.

Not that he intended to actually go outside and spray paint onto someone else's property.

No, he could be far more useful than that. He just needed the location.

"Where are you going to put it?"

Ben told him and he pulled up the place on his Mac.

He turned his computer so they could see his screen.

"I'd recognise that location anywhere," said Frank.

He and Ben exchanged a wry smile.

There were two CCTV images on a split screen.

One was the wall they intended to deface and the other was a view of the crossroads where it stood. Both pictures were in glorious, fully loaded, High-Definition technicolour.

THE KILLSWITCH

"Right," Jonny said. "When I see you in position, I'll turn off these cameras here, here and here." He pointed to cameras on the overview image. Two of which Ben couldn't see even when they were pointed at.

"I'll leave this one on and use it to monitor for cops or whatever. Does that work for you?"

Ben was flabbergasted. He was still trying to find the last camera Jonny had pointed at. He nodded.

"Does that work for you?"

"Yeah, yeah, that's fine. Where's the third camera again? I can't see it."

He pointed. Ben still couldn't see it.

"I've set the timer for 1:45am."

Ben nodded in awe.

Of course he'd heard about hackers and how they could conceivably take over the whole world without even putting on clean underpants. But to see how easily Jonny did his thing was sobering.

Frank took the new level of security Jonny offered with a solemn nod of the head.

"Looks good," he agreed. "You're a pro."

Jonny raised his head to acknowledge the compliment.

"Is that why they're after you?" Frank wanted to know.

Jonny ignored him.

"Is it the cops, let it be the cops. It's the cops innit?"

Jonny ignored him.

"I hope it's not gangsters. We're all dead if its gangsters. If you get me killed I'll never forgive you," he joked.

"It won't matter if we're both dead, will it?" As usual Jonny failed to grasp the humour.

"Oh god, he's gonna get us killed."

"No one is gonna get killed," Jonny said.

"See," Ben tried a bit of gentle sarcasm. "No one is going to get killed."

"We don't even know why he's here. It's driving me crazy. Why are you here?"

"I'm here because I agreed to help him find his girlfriend." Jonny nodded towards Ben.

"She's not my girlfriend," Ben protested.

"Lot of effort for someone who's not your girlfriend," Jonny muttered.

"If I'd known she was gonna cause such trouble I would never have asked you to help."

"You should have told me you're an activist."

"I would have if I'd known it mattered, sorry." He didn't sound particularly sorry.

"Hindsight's a wonderful thing, eh?" Jonny sounded sarcastic but he wasn't being.

Frank felt the need to play peacemaker.

"Let's just focus on tonight, shall we? Especially now we've got all this technological backup."

He patted Ben across the shoulders. "Eh?"

Ben nodded, "Ok."

"Do you think we should find her?" Jonny wouldn't let it go.

"What? Why?"

"Well," Jonny asked. "Don't you want to know why she was at the cafe?"

"Hard to say. We don't know what's going on. We may not want to get involved." Frank couldn't resist that one.

"You're already involved," Jonny said.

Frank and Ben exchanged a look.

"What's his problem?" Frank wanted to know.

"I didn't have a problem until she came along," Jonny resisted adding, *thanks to you* but his glance at Ben betrayed the thought.

Again, Frank interjected for the sake of peace. "Yeah it might be good to find her. At least find out who she was spying on."

"And who for," Jonny added.

"If we can find her," Ben pointed out not unreasonably.

"I'll set up facial recognition. If she shows her face in public I'll get an alert. Don't worry we'll find your girlfriend."

"She's not my girlfriend."

"Whatever."

A few hours later it was dark and they were ready to go.

"Here, put these in your ears."

Jonny handed them a tiny gadget each. They slipped in as smoothly as Air Pods.

"If anything happens, if you need to abort, whatever, I'll warn you in plenty of time," he whispered into his pencil mic and they heard him loud and clear.

"Cool," Frank mumbled.

On the way to the job Frank asked Ben, "What do you think his story is?"

"He's hacked into something important," Ben said without a moment's hesitation. "An' the government are after him."

"I can hear you," Jonny's voice came through their earpieces.

95

The mission was a complete success. Technological back-up made life so much easier.

"Wait 'til you see it," Frank purred happily as he slumped down on the sofa.

"I've seen it." Jonny didn't look up from his screen.

"I watched the whole thing. It was very smooth, professional."

Ben raised an eyebrow. "Cheers."

Would you like to see yourselves in action?"

Ben grinned broadly. "Of course."

"Play it," Frank smirked.

They were high with the thrill of getting away with a crime, no matter how minor. It was the rush of owning something that could be termed a 'victory'.

Jonny hit a few keys and turned his Mac around.

They settled down like excited schoolboys.

Ben watched himself extend the ladder, climb up, tape the stencil in place and shake a can. Frank, hood up, head low, but it was definitely Frank, was at the foot of the ladder. He held it while surveying the deserted crossroads and catching empty spray cans as they were discarded by his partner in crime above.

The light from Jonny's head torch danced across the wall as he worked. It was like a firefly deciding where to land. It revealed then hid little patches of colour.

"It's a bit dark to see properly," Frank moaned.

Jonny hit a key and the giant mural was lit up to admire.

"Wow, that's incredible."

96

Now they'd shared an adventure they eased up in each other's company. And eventually like all zealots, Jonny started talking about his beliefs. All of which boiled down to one thing.

His disappointment in the human race.

"Don't let it bother you," Ben suggested.

"People are just stupid," said Frank.

"Yeah but we're going backwards. The human race has got all its young people in the third world where crops are failing and there's no work. While all the old people are in the West wilfully making things worse. It's not like the science is undecided."

"All we can do is keep spreading the word."

"It's not enough," Jonny replied. "People need to get off their devices."

His screen was rarely out of reach.

"Everywhere you look people are just staring at screens." Jonny whined

"Like you." Ben couldn't stop himself

"Yeah, but I'm reading." Jonny snapped

"They're all reading." Ben snorted.

"No, they're not, not really. They're certainly not learning anything. They're just running their eyes over meaningless crap. While the person sat next to them is doing exactly the same."

"Are you suggesting we ban phones?" asked Frank.

"And tablets?" added Ben.

"No need," he replied cryptically.

"What do you mean?"

"Nothin'"

"What do you know about that puppy dog virus?" Frank asked suspiciously.

Jonny ignored the question.

"Oh my God, is that you?" Ben sounded horrified.

"People used to talk," Jonny answered. "Have proper conversations."

"What?" Ben was flabbergasted. This was it, it had to be. The reason why this guy was on the run. But before he could respond, Frank piped up. "It is weird though. I remember when people used to talk to each other, you're right. Tell us more."

Jonny was off, "Humans these days have never been so isolated and lonely. They're little more than robots. Like little puppies."

Was that a reference to the puppy dog virus? Was that an admission? Before Ben could ask, he continued—

"There's no human race anymore. There's just a series of individuals living in their own little bombed out worlds. It's an existence that defies all logic. It goes against everything it means to be human."

"There's nothing anyone can do though," said Frank, but he was fishing. He could tell Jonny was on a roll and thought this might be a good time to shine a light on some of the mystery he carried around.

"Huh," Jonny spat out the word contemptuously.

"There's certainly nothing we can do. They call it progress, don't they?" Frank prodded a little harder.

"We weren't designed to just scroll though complete nonsense day after day." Jonny muttered.

"I agree." Frank raised his voice, pretending to be caught up in the moment. "Someone should do something."

Jonny too the bait, his voice raised as he said, "This system, this capitalism, it's not working. We can all see that?"

Frank glanced at Ben for support.

"Yeah, course we see that." Ben took the cue and piped in.

Jonny warmed to his theme, "The old ways are no longer viable. We need new rules fit for the modern age. We need to mould things into some kind of order. Something people can get on board with."

"We need a revolution," Frank agreed. He was no longer pretending to be on board. He was in. Since he'd been old enough to watch the news he'd known something was wrong.

"Too right," whispered Jonny.

"What do you mean?" asked Ben, momentarily alarmed.

Jonny had an answer for that "I mean these billionaires sucking up every last penny and raping the planet while they do. It's out of control. It's gotta stop."

"Something must be done," Frank agreed.

Jonny's face broke into a guilty smile.

"It is you, isn't it?" Frank sounded as though he already knew the answer.

Jonny couldn't help it. He nodded ever so slightly

"Just you?" Frank was impressed and didn't try to hide it.

Jonny nodded.

Frank clapped him across the shoulders. "That's brilliant. At least my score won't drop with you around."

"Oh, fucking hell," whined Ben. "What have you done? You'll have to leave."

"Why? It's not like he's actually killed someone?" Frank objected. "Have you?"

"No, of course not." Jonny frowned as he denied the accusation.

"An' it's not like he's raped some poor girl. Have you?" Frank elaborated

"Don't be disgusting." Now Jonny was offended.

"See, it's all good. We can't throw him out. We can help." Frank seemed excited

"This is the big one Ben. A chance to make a real difference. We can have genuine input on the direction humanity takes next."

"Eh, I don't think so," Jonny disagreed.

Frank ignored him. "If he wants to stay, he's gotta listen to our ideas," he said, and Ben, seeing the sense of it, ignored the alarm bells ringing in his ears and nodded slightly.

"Good call," Frank patted him across the shoulders.

Ben turned to Jonny. "It sort of feels like we're all in this together now."

"No thanks," Jonny replied.

"No thanks, what does that mean?"

"I prefer working alone."

"This is no longer a one man show. There's three of us involved in this thing now," Frank said. "Like it or not."

Jonny had worked on his own for so long that alternative input was an alien concept. He looked at them both one last time before blurting out, "It's my plan. It's me the authorities are looking for. I'm the terrorists. I should call the shots."

He used the plural of the word so it sounded ridiculous. And he seemed embarrassed by the claim, making him appear young and vulnerable.

"So what are your demands?" Frank asked.

Jonny seemed not to understand.

"What's your ransom, your ultimatum?" Ben said.

"There's no ultimatum. I'm not asking for a ransom."

"Nothing?"

"I'm not a kidnapper who wants payment." He seemed offended at the notion.

"No, not a ransom." Frank was keen not to cause offence. "Of course not. But you'll insist on changes, right?"

"No."

"This is a once in a lifetime opportunity to make the world a better place," Ben pointed out.

"Exactly," Frank noted calmly. "We can re-set the clock, improve things for all."

"Why bother?" Jonny muttered whilst tapping away at his Mac.

There was a moment's stunned silence.

"For the greater good," Frank suggested.

They waited for him to answer. Finally, he looked up and said, "It's pointless. We're all fucked anyway."

Ben threw up his arms in despair. "So why are you bothering with any of this?"

"Because they need to pay. They need to do without, feel a bit of the pain the rest of us have endured for years. I want them to suffer, to realise what they've done and regret at their leisure."

"I don't see why everyone has to suffer," said Frank.

"It's not everyone," replied Jonny. "Only those that deserve it."

"It feels like it's practically everyone," Ben pointed out.

Jonny shrugged.

"You gotta ask for something," Frank whined.

97

Over the following days they kept chipping away.

Jonny hated the thought of altering anything. However at heart he was a computer geek, a numbers guy. He was hard-wired to accept logic over emotion.

In the end he agreed to give the greedy bastards one last shot to see the error of their ways. Humanity would get a final chance to do the right thing before God pulled down the shutters.

"So we should let someone know?" Ben suggested.

Jonny, as usual, had his Mac open on his lap. "I'll do it now." He tapped a few keys. "Done" he declared.

It felt like a bit of an anticlimax.

"Is that it?"

Jonny nodded as he flicked on the television and switched it to a news channel.

They didn't have to wait long. Within minutes the BBC were interrupting programming with the breaking news.

They listened to the presenter say, "After months of silence the hacker gang have released a statement changing their threat."

"Changing?" Ben queried.

Jonny shook his head. "See, you can't even trust the BBC these days, you see why I…"

Ben cut him short, "Listen."

"The terrorists message reads and I quote, 'In two weeks you will experience difficulties. Prepare to receive instructions.'"

Jonny smiled, "Well they got that bit right anyway."

"What instructions?" asked Ben

"I'll release information about what to do if the web goes down."

That evening it was the main item on Newsnight. Ben and Frank watched with extreme interest. Jonny knew it was on in the background but was more concerned with the screen on his lap.

"It's impossible," insisted someone who was then interrupted.

The presenter puffed up his chest to announce a major new development. They had just received a message from the terrorists. "In two weeks the internet will go down."

Chaos broke out in the audience. The producer cut to a close up of the anchor-man.

"These people are a threat to our very existence," he was saying.

"Who are these terrorists?" asked the Tory representative.

"What are we going to do?" asked an audience member.

Nobody had a clue and they kept shouting over each other. It would solve nothing, but it was entertaining television.

Frank glanced towards Jonny who was smiling

Ben could only bear so much. "This is bullshit!" He hit the remote and the channel died.

"This is bad," Ben looked worried.

"Don't worry," Jonny tried to reassure him. "We'll be alright."

Frank had put the television back on. "They're worse than children," he muttered.

"I told you. They don't deserve another chance," Jonny replied.

98

Leetabix had been desperately searching for some kind of lead. No matter how small, there had to be something. But there simply was no chatter. These people were like ghosts. They left no trace anywhere.

They were clever, elusive, seemingly impossible to locate.

The puppy dog virus was bad enough, but pull the killswitch?

This latest development had sent them all into a depression.

99

Ben's alarm kept going off in the mornings. He kept getting up and going to work. The bus kept running and the streets were still busy with people. Nothing changed.

But at the same time everything was different. You could almost taste it in the air.

Keep calm and carry on seemed to be on every second T-shirt.

The government is in control, there is nothing to worry about was the message emblazoned across newspaper boards alongside warnings of the imminent terrorist attack.

Despite the platitudes and false reassurances there was something to worry about and everybody knew it.

As Ben travelled to work the words *Terrorist* and *Terrorising* were everywhere. In print, on screen and on people's lips. He couldn't believe the fuss over the geeky nerd hiding out in his front room. Nor how the words *hacker* and *terrorist* had become so interchangeable.

It made him nervous.

What If they come for us? He wondered not for the first time as he folded T-shirts and piled them onto a shelf.

100

Aiden was sitting in a coffee shop. There were a smattering of youngsters spread around. Most had laptops out and conversations were conducted via headphones.

Aiden kept out of it, just listened. This was their world.

"These guys are good," someone was saying, "Two weeks, fuck."

"Dark Web as well?"

"Yeah."

"Fuck."

"How we gonna manage without the Internet?"

Aiden felt tempted to remind them there was a world before the digital age. It wasn't all living in caves and wearing bearskin clothing. But instead he sipped his coffee and said reassuringly. "You'll think of something."

"Who are you?"

"I'm just a writer."

"A writer?"

"Yeah."

"Written anything good?"

101

Ben got home from work to the sound of the 6 o'clock headlines.

Boing! "One week until the terrorist deadline."

Boing! "Southern Africa enters final stages of severe drought. Millions heading North."

Boing! "Icebergs no longer protecting the Artic shelf."

"Good evening, ladies and gentlemen, this is the news. The terrorist group threatening to bring the world to a standstill is still at large. Police forces from a multitude of countries are working in unison, currently operating the largest manhunt ever known."

Jonny smiled. Ben slumped down and wondered if his nerves would last another week.

"Ain't you worried?" he asked Jonny.

"Why should I be?"

Ben shook his head in amazement. "Because the whole world and his dog are looking for you."

Jonny shrugged. "Not really," he said.

102

Leetabix had threatened to close down the Internet but never had any intention of actually doing so, not in a million years.

That would be crazy. Imagine the money they'd lose.

So it was kind of ironic that the terrorists were willing to do so. Jacob was tearing his hair out.

103

With only six days left until the threats became real, people still weren't panicking as much as Ben thought they should be.

It was bizarre. In the local supermarket he noticed his neighbours putting an extra tin of peaches or carton of long-life milk into their baskets. They were stocking up but in such a relaxed manner they may as well not be bothering.

He wondered how it was playing out in the posh parts of town where they could afford to buy in bulk.

"It's weird," he announced on his return. "Everyone's still going about their business out there." He jerked a thumb towards the front door. "Normally!"

"They've got no vision," Jonny replied.

"What?"

"They got no vision. They can't imagine life changing a little bit, never mind drastically, beyond all recognition."

Ben nodded. That was probably true.

"At least it means they're not panicking and running riot. So there's that."

Jonny said nothing.

"Don't you think?"

"I expect there will be plenty of panicking soon," Jonny prophesied dismissively. "I have warned the authorities to expect unrest."

"I expect they'd worked that one out for themselves."

"Perhaps, but nobody will be able to say they weren't warned."

Ben shook his head in disbelief and lit a cigarette.

Jonny put on his headphones. Joe Strummer sang into his ear,

A lot of people won't get no supper tonight,
A lot of people won't get no justice tonight…

104

It was five days until the shutdown. Until everything changed.

Ben was on the bus heading to work. He was trying to recall what he'd been told about life before the Internet.

He was too young to remember first hand. He'd had a mobile phone since he was eight years old. Had wanted one before that. He vaguely recalled stories of wages being paid in cash and people planning in advance before meeting up, but he couldn't imagine how that worked in practice.

The very thought of life without his phone made him nervous.

How long's temporarily? he wondered.

The bus pulled into his stop and slowly he walked home.

I need my phone he fretted. If he worried about that he could ignore the bigger concerns.

"What are people going to do about their phones?" he wanted to know as soon as he walked in the door.

Jonny shrugged.

"People need their phones."

"They'll manage."

"Will they though?" Ben replied doubtfully.

"They'll be too busy to be looking at the usual crap."

"How will they get stuff done?"

"As you know I've released a tidal wave of information on a wide range of subjects, from growing tomatoes to skinning a rabbit."

"What about money?"

"The UK will lose £15 million an hour, the USA $50 million an hour and China $180 yen every single hour. It's all in the files."

"I don't mean that. I mean normal people, how will they buy stuff?"

"They can't. Hopefully they'll read the information provided instead. It might be a pleasant change for them reading something that will actually matter, actually affect their miserable existence."

"That's not going to work."

"Have you read it? Because I think you should."

Ben had a load more questions but there was clearly no point asking them.

105

It was Saturday. Only three days until what the papers were referring to as *D Day*.

Jonny hadn't left the flat since the day he arrived. He saw no reason to. He had no idea if the authorities had uncovered his true identity and no desire to test out their recognition capabilities.

"You should go to a café," he told Ben.

"Really?"

"Yeah it's Saturday, you know, keep to your routine. Don't arouse suspicion."

"I guess so."

"You can gauge the general mood," Jonny suggested.

"I can tell you that from here, *complacent*, that's the general mood."

"Go anyway. I could use some time away from you."

"Charming."

"I'm sure the feeling's mutual."

That was true, so Ben went to the Zodiac. He took a table near the serving hatch. He wanted to gather as many snippets of conversation as possible.

In very short time he realised nobody was taking the threat seriously. It was winding him up.

Jonny was right. People are stupid. They genuinely couldn't imagine change. Even when the evidence was overwhelming they still thought nothing would happen. What was wrong with them?

Didn't they remember Covid-19? It was only a few years ago the whole world was suddenly turned upside down. Proof indeed that solid, dependable day to day lives can be ripped apart in an instant. That everything is fragile, that nothing lasts forever no matter how solid it appears to be.

Nobody remembered. Not one of them had learned anything from that whole disaster.

Three teenage girls came in and joined the queue. Ben eavesdropped.

"Are you goin' to Tam's on Tuesday?"

"Yeah."

"What you gonna wear?"

You'll be hunting something to eat on Tuesday, he wanted to scream.

Next in line were a couple of elderly pensioners.

"So Bingo Monday night, Elsie?"

"Oh yeah, I can't miss that."

He could feel his blood pressure rising.

What was the matter with these people?

Next in were a couple of hipsters. They stood waiting for their soya milk, low fat lattes. One had his phone ready to pay with a swipe.

"You won't be able to do that on Monday," his pal opined.

At last, somebody gets it. Realises what's going on.

"Don't be daft," came the reply, "That ain't real."

Ben wanted to scream at him, *It is fucking real, I know the guy and he's a fanatic. It's happening, be ready. Get supplies, gather your loved ones, run for the hills!*

Instead he sat in silence, carefully sipping a hot cappuccino, doing his best to look innocent.

It was incredible. Not one single customer seemed prepared for the worst. Ben was very disappointed with his fellow citizens. He was beginning to see Jonny's point. Perhaps the human race wasn't worth saving after all.

106

It was Sunday evening. Ben had gone to the local supermarket to buy more supplies to add to his hoard.

Walking round the aisles he noted concern on people's faces for the first time.

He thought about those around the planet who weren't online. It seemed bizarre that so many lives would hardly be affected.

Those little lost tribes are going to get the last laugh after all, he thought.

The world was due to change beyond all recognition tomorrow morning at 10am Greenwich Mean Time. But looking around Sainsbury's on a Sunday evening you'd never have guessed.

107

Jacob had actually slammed his office door. The minions were in trepidation. Nobody had ever known him so angry. They could see him through the glass partition. He was pacing up and down with a face like thunder.

Tomorrow was supposed to be the big roll out for the cashless society. The silent coup of the stock markets would have been complete. Locked in for at least a hundred years.

He had assured the board repeatedly it was on. They considered it the final piece of a forty-year jigsaw.

They intended to take a cut of every payment everywhere. They'd be able to trace every single transaction on the planet, large or small. Know exactly what people are spending their money on.

The distrust of cash had been working in the background for years. Then with Covid as an excuse, plans had been accelerated.

Don't touch money had been the three-word slogan, *because it's dirty and will infect you*, had been the underlying message.

Jacob had assured the board nothing could stop them now. They had invested heavily in infrastructure and the relevant stock. Only now with literally hours remaining, delay was inevitable. Leetabix had not been able to trace the terrorists. If the cashless system was implemented and the web went down then what? People were going to still need cash. It was infuriating. Who the hell did these terrorists think they were messing with?

Jacob had never come across an opponent able to stay hidden so completely. If his whole career, his extravagant way of life were not at stake he might have even been impressed. His phone rang as he was trying to think,

"Yes."

"Have you made any progress?"

"We're working on it, sir"

"You assured us there would be no delay."

He bit his tongue. He hated having to bite his tongue.

"I know sir."

"This will cost us deeply."

"I know sir."

108

Monday morning rush hour was more tense than usual. By nine a.m. it was as though the country had gone back into lockdown. As 10 o'clock approached, people up and down the land were glancing at their phones and watches even more than usual.

109

Ten o'clock came.

Nothing happened.

Then as ten o'clock passed, as the second hand slipped from due north into the new minute, Jonny flicked the Killswitch. He hadn't shut everything down completely. It was just a warning.

The vast majority of the population would feel some pain but that was a price he was willing to pay.

All around the city, all around the country, traffic stopped. All those cars, buses and lorries were suddenly experiencing malfunctions within their computers.

There were flashing dashboards everywhere and vehicles across the network gliding to a halt.

Afterwards all agreed, the traffic crawling to a stop was the first thing you noticed.

Indoors, things were different. Violently flashing computer monitors were the first indication that something was wrong.

People stared at their screens.

In Selfridges a shop girl smiled nervously at a customer and tried to swipe her credit card again. Nothing happened.

Outside HMV a teenager with a confused expression on his

face was blinking furiously and staring at his phone. It was blank. He couldn't digest the information his brain was receiving. He didn't follow the news. Nobody had told him.

On a bus on a hill a mother stood on the upper deck, pointed her phone at the giant communications mast she could actually see and tried calling her sister again. She was right next to the most powerful telecoms transmitter in the whole of the country. Nothing happened.

Throughout the land, factories ground to a halt. Suddenly defunct workers began pouring out onto the streets. As they passed through the gates some reached for cigarettes and vaping machines. It was unbelievable how many others reached for their phones. Old habits die hard. Instead of scrolling alone, actual conversations started up.

Outside Ben's flat a trendy young black girl was strutting along talking loudly into her phone.

She paused, waiting for a response. Only then did she realise she was having a one-way conversation.

"Maxine? Max? Are you still there?"

She frowned and took the device off speakerphone. She held it to her ear.

"Hello, Max?"

Jonny watched her through the net curtain. He smiled, shook his head and moved back from the window. He sat down, got comfortable and started reading the book he'd been saving for this very moment.

110

Ben sat on a flower box outside the bus station. He smoked a fag and watched a shopkeeper hastily make a CASH ONLY sign to hang above a wall of garish fridge magnets.

They do not miss a trick.

People the length of the High Street were moving from shop to shop.

"Have you got Wi-Fi?"

The traders shook their heads and the shopper moved next door to repeat the question.

Ben shook his head and half smiled.

You have to admire their optimism, he thought.

He watched a group of kids on bikes moving skilfully through the chaos. One of their number rode up the centre of the road pulling a wheelie. His mates were laughing loudly. The youthful exuberance, the sheer joy of life was evident for all to see. They had adapted immediately. The only ones in sight not bothering to check their phones every few seconds.

Ben threw his fag butt into the kerb. All around him a mood that could only be described as community spirited was coursing through the crowds.

Everybody was in this together, and so far it wasn't bad. Actually, it was the opposite of bad, it was good.

It reminded him of carnival. Folk were smiling, upbeat.

But this was a nice part of town.

Ben wondered how things were over on the sprawling estates.

I'll check on Twitter, he thought.

Instinctively he went for his phone. His hand was actually on it before he remembered and felt suitably foolish.

111

Aiden had never bothered much with the internet. It had always seemed like a control mechanism. Like Big Brother collecting data on the machines and categorising them. He justifiably assumed he would fare badly in such a system. So loyalty cards, cashless transaction— he'd maintained a healthy suspicion of all that stuff from the very start.

The consequences of never having embraced the technology meant now that it didn't work he wasn't disadvantaged at all. He had a cupboard full of food, his typewriter and his books and that was enough for him.

112

Across the land the half expected anarchy did not occur.

Folk were checking on elderly neighbours they'd normally cross the street to avoid. Groups and committees were being started up on an industrial scale.

It was beautiful to behold. This was what they meant by the Blitz spirit.

Something vital had been suddenly taken away. It affected indiscriminately. The community spirit was infectious, like when everyone was clapping for carers.

That brief moment when it seemed as though the human race might actually be capable of pulling together, of putting aside selfish ways.

It lasted until Dominick Cummings drove to Barnard Castle and ruined it for all of us. You can't have a *Blitz spirit* in the post Covid world because the poor know they'll get shafted.

Only this was different. A man with the training to butcher an animal or pump water from the ground was suddenly more valued than the bank manager or the CEO.

Jonny had created a crisis that called for human cooperation on an industrial scale. Would humanity be willing and able to step up to the plate?

Nobody knew yet.

This was all happening more or less under a communications blackout. It was difficult to know how others were faring because to all intents and purposes the internet was down.

You just had to suck it up.

Looters did try their luck at a few locations but citizen's justice was so swift, civil unrest had no chance to grow roots.

What was happening went against everything people had been led to believe. A lifetime of being assured we needed old white guys with private educations to steer us through complicated waters was proving to be a long perpetuated downright lie.

Such men were suddenly absent without leave? When it really counted common people were on their own.

As the Grenfell tower disaster proved, it's better to wrap your arms around a situation yourselves than wait for the authorities to provide assistance.

When the need is dire enough everyone chips in and does what they can and together humankind will overcome.

Folk were being respectful of each other. They had to be. There is no telling what that stranger can bring to the situation that you will soon be in desperate need of.

A bulging bank account doesn't cut it anymore.

You might have millions but do you know how to repair a water pipe or start a fire without matches?

However, Ben knew this was the daytime crowd. As any theatre owner will tell you, they are always easier to please. What was going to happen when night fell?

113

The board members of the Trust were furious. An emergency meeting was called. Runners had to be sent on foot to ensure everybody got the memo. To be reduced to such archaic measures so quickly was unfathomable.

"This is a crisis situation, gentlemen."

The chairman addressed Jacob directly. "I thought you were in control of the internet?"

"This is a different situation sir."

"What are you going to do?"

Around the table there was much shuffling of feet and avoidance of eye contact. Not one of them had been able to use a credit card since 10 a.m. Their phones had gone dead and they were effectively cut off from anything not within eyesight. They had been assured it would not come to this. That the *threat* of shutdowns would be as far as it went.

They had lost control of their lives and they were scared. More scared than they had ever been. That fear was in danger of turning to anger.

For the first time in decades Jacob was being made to justify himself.

It was way too late for that. They should have started keeping tabs on him years ago. But the money had been rolling in and not one of them really understood what he actually did.

"I was led to believe Leetabix were the ones threatening to turn off the Internet and they were under our control?"

"That's right, sir."

"Yet it appears this other group have carried out the very thing you were threatening to do."

"Yes sir."

"Did you not see they were a threat?"

"They appeared from nowhere sir."

"What do we actually pay you for?"

"We'll find them sir."

"Good, how long before you have the situation under control?"

"We are working on it right now."

"That is not what I asked."

"We need to locate the terrorists."

"Do we know where they are operating from?"

"No, but we have mobile units going zone by zone. If they're here, we'll catch them in the net."

"Catch them in the net? They're not fucking butterflies!"

"And if the net is not large enough?" asked a calmer voice from the far end of the table.

"We'll expand further. We would be bound to get them eventually."

"This is unbelievable. You led us to believe Leetabix alone could turn off the World Wide Web. Scared us into providing ever larger budgets for you to maintain control and then this mystery outfit turns up out of the blue and does it like it's the easiest trick in the book."

"We're working on it, sir," he managed to say through gritted teeth.

"Work harder. Get your people out there. Find them. We will reconvene here in twelve hours. I expect some progress by then."

114

Aiden was having toast for breakfast when the power went down. He didn't notice straight away because *White Riot* by the Clash was blasting from his battery powered CD player. But when he went to turn on the kettle for a second cuppa, nothing happened.

He tried the light switch, nothing. He looked out the window at the neon sign in the takeaway opposite. It wasn't lit up. He noticed groups of confused looking people scattered along the pavement.

The terrorist threat had begun.

He smiled to himself. A few minutes earlier and he wouldn't be enjoying perfectly toasted morning delight. It felt like a little victory. He looked around the room. What difference was this going to make to him personally? The kettle had just boiled so he could still have another cuppa. Other than that, he wasn't bothered. If there was no power, there was no power. What was he going to do? Start crying or screaming or throwing things around? He'd rather sit here and enjoy a leisurely breakfast and if it didn't come back on, he'd pull out his old typewriter and get to work. It would be good not to have distractions.

He finished breakfast, cleaned his teeth and fetched his typewriter.

The situation reminded him of the early days of Covid-19 when the invisible menace first swept across the world. The human race, well the West at least, well this little island certainly, did not cope well with the sudden upheaval.

At least with the virus they could go online and bitch and moan. This time they can't even do that.

It'll sure put the cat amongst the pigeons, he thought.

Bizarrely he was still smiling to himself, nodding along to the Clash.

White Riot, I wanna riot.

White Riot, a riot in the home…

Aiden wasn't worried, he was excited. Too excited to sit and write, deep down where nobody could see he was on the side of the terrorists.

Still smiling, he grabbed his coat and headed for the door. He told himself he wasn't looking for Mia, he was trying to gauge the mood. It was partly true.

He saw complete strangers chatting together and discovering they weren't mortal enemies after all. Most he encountered seemed remarkably calm about the whole thing.

They look happy enough now, he thought. *But let's see what the night time brings.*

115

Jonny figured it would take him a week to read the novel he'd been saving. That was his plan. Then he would re-assess.

The book was a real page turner. It absorbed him completely until he heard a key in the door and the spell was broken. He scowled at Ben when he entered.

"You're reading a book?" Ben shook his head. *Unbelievable,* he thought. *Unbefuckinlievable.* "Have you been outside?"

"No, I'm reading."

They looked at each other for a moment.

Jonny returned to his book.

Ben watched him in amazement. "Aren't you curious?"

"I'm curious as to what happens in this story." He tapped his book. "If I'm allowed to continue."

Ben went and sat by the window and looked outside.

"So the Internet is down?"

Jonny glanced across at him.

"Yes," he said.

Silence fell across them but it was different. There was no traffic. None of the usual city noises were seeping in.

"No one can turn things back to normal."

Jonny glanced up. "I know."

There was another silent interlude.

"Except you?"

"You can see I'm trying to read."

"Yeah, but, I dunno, this just seems kind of important."

"Ok, I'm aware of what I've done. Happy now?"

Ben let him read another page before replying, "Not really."

Jonny looked up. "I wasn't really asking if you were happy. I was really saying, can I read in peace?"

Ben shook his head. What else could he do? If he tried to engage with Jonny philosophically, he might well end up killing him.

Jonny returned to his book, where he re-read the same page again. He hated doing that.

"You've gotta turn it back on!" Ben barked. He couldn't help himself. "It's killin' 'em."

Jonny sat bolt upright. He calmly shut his book and placed it down on the coffee table. "What is your problem?"

"What is my problem?" Ben repeated, astonished. "What is my problem," he said again, more quietly but clearly struggling with the perspective being offered.

Jonny folded his arms like a defiant toddler. "You knew this would happen."

Ben laughed. It just came out. "No I didn't," he argued. "This is out of control. It's too much, you're mad," he threw in before he could stop himself.

"Life was out of control before this and you're not qualified to judge madness."

Ben bit his lip, took a deep breath and said, "You've got to ask for something. Make a deal. They won't last." He gestured with his arm indicating all those beyond the room.

"They'll be fine." Jonny's tone implied Ben was being ridiculous.

"How can you say that? Based on what we know about humans, what makes you think they'll be fine?"

"They'll pull together. It'll be like the Blitz all over again. They love talking about the Blitz, now they can live like it."

"What about the hospitals?" Ben ventured.

"They have generators."

"Only the big ones, and what happens when the generators run out of fuel?"

Jonny shrugged, "You know what'll happen."

Ben was incredulous. "People will die!"

Jonny shrugged again.

"Don't you care?"

"Care about what? People die all the time. Strangers, people you've never met are dying constantly. What difference does it make?"

"You can't be serious."

Jonny shrugged. Clearly he didn't see what the problem was.

"When the generators pack in, all those hooked up to machines will die."

Jonny waited as though expecting more to come, as though Ben needed to elaborate on his point. "Don't you see that?" he added.

"Of course I see that, I just don't see how it's an issue. Some strangers who are only alive because they're hooked up to a machine will die. So what?"

"They might be strangers to us, but they are loving family members to somebody."

Jonny shrugged. "That's not the way it's supposed to be."

"What the fuck does that mean?"

"When you need a machine to support you, it's time to move on and let the next generation have their turn."

Ben wasn't sure he was hearing correctly. "What?" he asked incredulously. "You can't mean that."

"Of course I mean it. It's only the human race that seems hell bent on dragging out as many extra years as possible, Regardless of quality of life in those years and irrespective of everyone else. And only wealthy humans by the way."

Jonny was on a roll. "You don't see geriatric birds flapping around or ancient rabbits struggling to get by. Why? Because there are limited resources. But we're so arrogant we can't see it. And those that can, just think, *Sod it I don't give a shit.* Why should humans, wealthy western humans drag out their pointless lives at the expense of every other living organism?"

"But, but—" Ben was struggling. How do you appeal to logic in a madman? "It's not just old, rich people. Babies on incubators will die too."

"Why should a baby with a defective heart born in India say, die? Whilst a baby with the same problem born in the West survives. How's that's fair? How is that beneficial to the gene pool of the species?"

Ben stared, not sure how to respond.

"I'll tell you," Jonny continued. "It's not. Now, can I read my book please?"

116

Most people had squandered the warning. Vast swathes of the population who relied on Alexa for everything. People with low scores in Jonny's points-based system suffered like never before, along with all their dependents and associates.

Those with comfortable lives who'd never bothered with politics and had always left everything to the men in charge were panicking now, when it was too late.

They gathered up batteries and candles because that's what people did in the movies.

Neighbours were forced by necessity to communicate as equals. Human instincts kicked in for the first time in years and it transpired they were not all enemies on different sides. They cooperated.

Ex-soldiers arranged security patrols. Logistics specialists turned supermarkets into distribution centres. Middle management pretended they knew what they were doing. People tolerated them and pitched in, things got done.

However, all tasks were accomplished by hand. All messages delivered on foot. It took ages to achieve what until yesterday would have been deemed simple tasks.

Cooperation paid dividends. By nightfall most citizens were more or less fed and watered. Those on high ground looked down on their city and took solace that it was still there.

117

Ben came in the flat actually smiling.

"I can still see the city from the top of the hill. It must be generators and lamps, but it's still lit up. It's still there."

"That's good," Jonny replied dismissively.

Ben's smile dropped away. "How can you be so blasé?"

Jonny shrugged.

Three days later Ben went outside again. He was impressed by what he found.

People had pulled together. For the first time in years many felt like they mattered, were relevant. That they belonged.

An old man was handed a broom and put in charge of sweeping a section of the street. Without him the rats would have a field day, then what? He was suddenly vitally important, and he felt it.

Ben had always loved wandering aimlessly and anonymously. Except now as he walked from one place to the next, he was the conspicuous stranger.

This was how travellers must have felt before the railways.

Anonymity had become impossible. Suspicion of outsiders would surely follow.

Ben wasn't sure the peace could last.

He wondered how things were in towns and villages away from the city.

118

Across the land people adapted as best they could. There is little point doing otherwise when sudden change is thrust upon you.

The vast majority got into the new habit of retiring at sundown and rising at dawn.

Days were filled with laundry, cleaning and preparing meals from scratch.

Bartering took hold as a means of acquiring items you actually needed. Repairmen were valued. Trinkets and baubles were not worth stealing.

Musicians and storytellers entertained and were much in demand.

Cookery lessons were very popular.

Long distance travel was out of the question. People made do with what they had close at hand.

119

The ruling class were running out of ideas. Experts that had been retained at great expense to the taxpayer were desperately trying to justify themselves.

"The terrorists have gone to ground. We are waiting for further demands. They are very unprofessional."

The politician in the room had heard enough.

"Are you implying that terrorists don't play by the rules?"

"I know it sounds ridiculous but yes. At the end of the day this sort of crime is always about money. Like it or not they need to make contact. So we know what their grievances are, what their demands are."

"There's been no contact?"

"No, so then we fall back on the second most successful way of stopping such crimes."

"Which is?"

"Sooner or later someone within the organisation slips up and word gets out."

"And has this happened?"

"Not yet, it's very strange."

"So what else can we do?" the minister asked, not bothering to hide the exasperation in his tone.

"We could flood the streets. More feet on the ground."

"We haven't done that already?"

"Yes, yes of course, but if there were any more bodies we could throw at the situation it might prove fruitful."

The minister turned to his subordinate. "You heard the man. We need more eyes and ears out there."

"Yes sir."

As the room emptied the chairman looked nervously through the window. He was concerned.

"What's next?" he asked his assistant.

"You are scheduled to speak to the Trust, one hour from now."

120

Jonny was typing.

"I don't know how you can just sit and type." Ben definitely sounded on edge.

Jonny glanced up. He didn't bother to reply.

With great difficulty Ben forced himself to remain calm.

"I think you should seriously consider putting the power back on," he said through gritted teeth. "Seriously."

Jonny glanced at him again. "It's a no, I'm afraid." He carried on typing.

"What? Why not? People can't cope without mod cons."

"People coped without mod cons for thousands of years."

"Come on Jonny get real. It's only calm out there now cos everyone is basically still in shock. Once they get pissed off things will get ugly. You know what people are like."

"I disagree."

Ben stared aghast. "You disagree? What the fuck does that mean?"

"I don't think things will get ugly. I think they'll be fine."

"Oh, well if you think so. I'm sure humans don't have violent tendencies. I'm sure two thousand years of history is all wrong then."

Jonny nodded. "Exactly."

It was infuriating.

Ben left the room before he lost the plot. Jonny returned to his Mac. He was glad for the peace and quiet if truth be told. He was able to focus on the page in front of him and forget everything else. He was a good psychopath. Comfortable in his own skin. Unburdened by conscience.

121

Aiden was saving his batteries. He sat quietly trying to spot Mia through the window. Even now, after all these years he'd still catch himself going over and over in his head what he would say to her if she ever turned up.

They say you never forget your first love. He'd certainly never forgotten her.

Current events were making sure he never did.

One man's terrorist is another man's freedom fighter, he mused.

He knew there were those who considered her that way. That was ludicrous. She wasn't a terrorist anymore than this group causing mayhem at the moment were. Sometimes you needed to shake things up, that was all.

It amused him that someone out there was finally taking matters in hand. God knows it was about time. It got him thinking.

He pulled out his notepad. He'd been doing it for so long that note taking was second nature. He did it without realising sometimes.

And what should they demand? He began to make a list.

1. Make Private schools pay taxes. He scribbled that out. Ban them completely.
2. Make all incomes a matter of public record
3. Pay women the same as men
4. Abolish discrimination in all its forms

Aiden looked at his list. He snorted in wry amusement. Everything on it was already law across Scandinavia.

Keep it simple, he thought. *Remember people are morons. They can just about manage a three word catch phrase.*

What do you want, really?

I just want to be happy, he decided, absolutely positive most people would say the same.

He was aware of the United Nations Happiness Index. A yearly chart listing nations in order of their population's happiness.

He knew Sweden had been top or there abouts ever since records began.

He scratched his head and scribbled through his list. He lit a cigarette and replaced the list with a single sentence.

Put the Scandinavians in charge.

122

Stevie was up before first light. He'd always liked the dawn. As a kid he wanted to go out and spot birds, as a young man he liked partying until the sun came up and now he liked getting up early after a good night's sleep.

He walked the short distance to the warehouse and put the kettle on. He liked the solitude. It was a reaction to the lack of privacy he'd endured in prison. He knew it but never analysed it too closely. Why go there?

He topped up the bird feeder, poured himself a cuppa and sat down to enjoy the antics of his feathered friends.

A blackbird landed on top of the roof opposite and let out a burst of song. Immediately it brought those long ago days on the old railway tracks to mind and he smiled.

Everything changes but everything stays the same, he thought.

Many years had passed and he'd travelled full circle.

He was back living in the terraced house he'd grown up in, except his sister lived in Spain now and his parents had passed on. He was the boss of the removal firm his father had founded in the 1970s. He and Nikki were happily married and he was father to five wonderful kids.

He watched the blackbird still thinking about childhood. He wondered what Aiden was doing now.

He'll be muddling along like the rest of us.

A sparrow dropped a mealy worm and lost it to a rival.

We all pay for our mistakes, he thought. *It's just that some of us pay full price.*

123

Jonny presented Ben with a folded sheet of paper. "I've been thinking about what you said."

"Oh."

"I've made a list."

Ben was pleasantly surprised. "You have?"

"Yeah, here."

He took the proffered sheet, unfolded it and read,

1. Less work
2. More play

He turned it over. It was blank on the other side. "Is that it?"

Jonny nodded.

"That's the plan?"

Jonny nodded again, more enthusiastically. "Like it?" he asked.

Ben frowned, "Not really."

"Eh, why not?"

"Well, for starters, it's not really a plan. And secondly, it don't make no sense."

It was Jonny's turn to frown. "What do you mean? It makes perfect sense. It's—" He struggled over which word fitted precisely what he was trying to say. "Concise."

He folded his arms. He seemed to think he'd made a rock solid point.

"It's bullshit is what it is."

"Ok smart ass what should it say?"

"I dunno, it's not my list. I'm not the one holding the world to ransom." Ben took a breath and lowered his tone. "Shouldn't you have thought about this before you started freaking everybody out?"

Jonny was indignant. "I did." His voice increased in volume as he added, "You told me to ask for something. It's your fault! I was quite happy with the plan I had! You make a bloody list!"

With that he slammed an A4 pad down on the table and stormed out.

As silence settled over the room it dawned on Ben that to all intents and purposes he was effectively now the terrorist the whole world was looking for.

He let the enormity of the situation sink in. He was way out of his depth. He should go to the authorities right now, plead coercion, beg for mercy. He could say he had the same thing Patty Hearst had.

A pen rolled away from the pad and caught his eye.

I should tell that twat to leave. This is nothing to do with me.

The pad was right there. He could ask for literally anything. It was practically taunting him.

He pulled the paper and pen towards him and sat down.

Right you bastards, I'm in charge now.

Twenty minutes later he'd still written nothing.

Jeesus, he thought. *This is trickier than I realised. I need some advice.*

He pondered that for a minute.

I don't know anyone in that world, was the undeniable reality.

The only possibility, and it was as remote as they come, was the madman who'd accosted him about Juanita.

He didn't seem half as crazy now. And didn't he have decades of experience in this type of thing?

He mentioned the idea to Frank.

"Do it," he said.

"Don't I get a say?" asked Jonny.

"No."

Ben rummaged in his jacket pocket and retrieved the crumbled address Aiden had given him.

124

The Trust were working flat out. Favours were called in and brown envelopes handed around. It was time for their friends to earn their pay. Suddenly it was a witch hunt. Anyone who knew about the terrorist cell or even worse, assisted the fugitives was a traitor, an enemy of the people. They could expect to feel the full weight of the law. On the other hand, anyone with information who came forward was a hero to the nation.

125

Mia had no radio, nor even any batteries. She was holed up with only her thoughts for company. She actually quite enjoyed this rare opportunity to sit and think.

The prospect of going back to her boring little life filled her with dread. She kept thinking about Aiden. She had intended to Google him but was scared what that might reveal. If she didn't know, she could dream. She assumed he was a famous writer now, married with kids. If that was the case she didn't need to know.

Imagine, just imagine if he still loved me and I could get away once and for all. We could settle down and I'll cook for him and grow roses while he writes best sellers and makes me feel special. That is how I want to spend my twilight years. Not cooped up indoors running low on supplies. It's like being back in the East. Like I haven't moved forward at all.

Her eye ran over the cupboard that contained next to nothing. Even the giant bag of pasta was perilously low. She needed supplies. It really was like the old days. She'd barely progressed in all these years. This game never ended. They didn't want it to end. There was too much money to be made. She wanted out. She needed to stretch her legs. Why had there been no contact?

126

Ben knew the street on the scrap of paper. It wasn't that far away. He walked the short distance wondering what he was going to say.

He rang the doorbell, still unsure.

The noise of the bell made Aiden jump. He definitely hadn't been expecting company.

Who the fuck is that?

He glanced down at himself. Food stains and crumbs stared back at him. He stood up, wiping his top. A trail of crumbs fell around him as he moved to the window.

He leant silently out and glanced down at the top of a head. It was nobody official. It was the guy from the cafe. Concern at who might be ringing his bell was instantly replaced by excitement.

I knew he'd come. I fucking knew it.

That's how life works, he told himself as he descended the stairs.

The years go by and loose threads unravel. Bits of the past that have lain dormant for years are suddenly right back like they never even went away.

He was thinking about Mia.

The past is never really gone, never quite finished with you. Some random act occurs, a thread is pulled and, wham, outta nowhere unfinished business comes back to haunt you all over again.

Ben waited impatiently on the doorstep. Finally he heard footsteps inside, then the door opened and the crazy guy who had accosted him what seemed like eons ago was standing there. He still looked crazy with his wild, unkempt hair, his stained T-shirt, ancient slippers and tatty cardigan.

"Hello." Aiden smiled.

"Yeah, hi." Ben replied, unsure now as to why he had come

"Nice to see you." Aiden sounded like he meant it.

"Yeah," Ben smiled sheepishly. *You ain't heard why I'm here yet,* he thought.

"Ben, isn't it?"

"Yeah, sorry I don't remember your name."

"Aiden."

"Yeah." Ben nodded. "I wondered if you've got a minute?"

"Have you found her?"

"It's not really about her."

Aiden glanced both ways up and down the street. "Come in."

He led the way back to his kitchen, thinking the whole time, *Of course it's about her, finally!*

He could feel it in his bones. This particular loose end was unravelling. The prospect of it leading somewhere excited him immensely. There had never been anyone like her before or since.

"Take a seat." He gestured, and Ben pulled out a chair. He watched the older man put the kettle on a calor stove and take two cups from the cupboard.

"Black coffee ok, instant?"

"Yeah that's fine, cheers."

Ben knew nothing about this guy. Was he really about to tell him everything? Would it be safe?

He looked around the room. Dust coated piles of papers and books everywhere. This guy was a mess.

Perhaps he should just go home and evict Jonny. That would certainly be simpler.

But he was here now and if he was honest, he was desperate. It was far too late to plead ignorance. This scruffy git was his best shot. He had nowhere else to go.

Aiden pulled out a chair and placed the steaming mugs on the table between them. He could see the kid was tormented. He smiled reassuringly.

"So what can I do for you?"

The question was pretty direct and to the point but there was something about the easy way his face settled. As though nothing would shock him. As though he only had your best interests at heart. Somehow he came across as though he would know what to do.

Ben launched in. "There's this guy, he's a friend of mine. Well, sort of," he said hesitantly.

Aiden nodded knowingly and took a sip.

Ben continued. "He tried to find, you know, that girl."

"Mia. Let's refer to her as Mia."

Ben shrugged. "Mia. You really think she's a spy?"

Aiden nodded. "I don't think, I know. She's an undercover operative. She infiltrates activist groups. Has done for years."

"Well, I've sort of been working with some activists and we used to meet at that cafe. And since I've had time to think about it, she was often—" He emphasised the next word, "*Close.* Do you know what I mean?"

Aiden nodded. "She's a professional. It wouldn't have seemed weird at the time."

"Anyway, as you know, then she disappeared. No warning just left and that did seem weird. So I got this guy from work, this computer geek to try and track her down. Not because I was suspicious or nothing, not at that stage. I just wondered what had happened to her." He blushed. "I wanted to ask her out."

Aiden stayed silent allowing him space to continue his story.

"Well I didn't know this guy from work was into some shit of his own an' as soon as he tried to locate her all hell broke loose."

Aiden sipped his coffee. He waited, but no more was forthcoming.

"So why are you telling me?" he gently prodded.

"He needs to talk to someone before he does something stupid." He paused to see the reaction this evoked. Aiden appeared calm so he continued. "An' to be honest, you were the only person I could think of."

"Well I'm flattered."

"You might not be if you knew what it was about."

"Does it involve the terrorists in the news?"

Ben looked panic stricken. "How the fuck did you come to that conclusion from what I just said?"

"Shall I take that as a 'yes'?"

Ben nodded.

"What do you want me to say to him, your friend?"

"I dunno, just stop him being stupid."

"And ask him to find Mia."

Ben shook his head vigorously. "Nah she seems like trouble."

Aiden ignored his last comment. "Because she's the only one there's ever been for me."

"Oh." Suddenly Ben got it. "You still love her. Yeah I bet she's lovely deep down."

Aiden nodded. "She is."

"Right. Although people change. Maybe she's changed after all these years." Ben sounded sceptical.

Aiden shrugged. "Only one way to find out." He said.

"That's a lot of years to hold a flame." Ben commented.

"I know. So this friend of yours, he can find people?" Aiden asked.

"Yeah."

"Will he be able to find her?"

"Probably"

"If he finds her, I'll speak to him for you."

"You'll have to come to him. He's funny about going outside."

"That's fine, I can come now if you like."

"I was thinking this evening, once its dark."

"Sure, what's the address?"

Ben told him and got up to leave. They bumped fists.

"See you about eight?"

"I'll be there." Aiden smiled.

Ben nodded. He had come and unloaded his problems, shared the burden but he didn't feel any better.

Walking home he could feel tension in the air that added to his concerns. There was a divide forming. Some were getting supplies, others not. Jealousy and resentment were starting to make themselves known.

He scurried home as fast as he could.

"How was it?" Frank asked.

"He's coming at eight. I told him we'd be able to find the girl."

"We?" Jonny queried.

"Ok you, you can find her, can't you?"

"I'd have to put the power on." Jonny sounded reluctant.

"Good," said Ben impatiently

"You need to mate. It's for the best" said Frank sympathetically.

Jonny tapped a few keys, "It's done" he said.

127

Mia sat alone. She was always alone.

Imagine if you could go back and do things differently.

She would grow old with Aiden. There was a brief tinge of worry that he would be different. She dismissed it. She wanted to live out her days with him.

Her thoughts were all about what *if's*.

She wondered if Stevie and RobBob were still around. If the films ever got developed. If they still existed. But more worryingly did Aiden forgive her? Could they be happy ever after?

She was lost in thought when the fridge suddenly came to life. It made her jump. Realising what had happened she went to the window and peered outside. Lights were on, People were happily staring at their phones again.

128

Aiden knew the moment he stepped foot in Ben's flat he was legally complicit. Technicalities were irrelevant. He would become involved and could expect the full force of the law to come down on him.

He sniffed, stirred his tea and weighed up the pros and cons.
Pro - See Mia again.
Con - Potentially years behind bars
It was a no brainer. He was in!

The day dragged interminably slowly and the tension grew. When it was so unbearable he couldn't sit around a second longer he left. He walked as slowly as he could but got there far too early. So he waited around the corner. He knocked on the door at eight on the dot.

Ben opened it and he went quietly in.

There was a guy smoking a roll up. Somebody so engrossed in their Mac they didn't even look up and Ben. The room was messy and contained nothing of value. If these were the terrorists holding the whole world to ransom, they were probably doing it for the money.

"Frank, meet Aiden."

The roll up guy nodded.

"Hi," said Aiden.

"How's it going?" replied Frank.

"Jonny."

The computer nerd raised his head from his screen at the mention of his name.

Aiden's first impression was just another geeky kid. Both seemed ridiculously normal. Neither would stand out in a crowd. No wonder the police couldn't find them.

Aiden was unaware Jonny hadn't left this room for weeks thus seriously hampering police operations.

"You came then," Jonny said.

He took a seat opposite him,

"Of course."

Jonny looked him up and down.

"You wrote a book?"

"Yeah, have you read it?"

"No, I googled you."

Aiden smiled.

"Why did you come?" Jonny asked.

"There are a couple of reasons. Firstly to find Mia. Secondly, to help you guys."

"Help us do what?"

"I dunno, what sort of help do you need?"

"None—"

"Advice," Ben interrupted. "More like advice."

"Advice on what?" Aiden asked.

"I'm hoping for change," Jonny said.

"Yeah rip it down and start again," Frank suggested.

"Maybe." Aiden sounded doubtful. "But when you're out to get honey you don't kill all the bees."

Jonny smirked. "Joe Strummer!"

"That's right, you like the Clash?"

"Best band in the world, ever!"

"Well, that's one thing we used to be good at." Aiden said.

Jonny looked puzzled.

"Music, we used to be good at that."

"We did," Jonny agreed, "Nobody around these days that can hold a candle to the Clash.'"

"That's true."

Aiden nodded towards the paperback lying by Jonny's side. "I've read that. It's great."

Quoting Joe Strummer had done the stranger no harm at all. Now he's read *Death in the Afternoon*. Jonny liked him.

"You like to read?" he asked.

"I think all writers like to read." Aiden replied.

"And you like the Clash?"

"Love 'em."

They nodded at each other in a mutually respectful kind of way.

"So..." Aiden smiled around the blank faces staring back at him. "Does somebody want to tell me what's what?"

Ben assumed Jonny would take up the mantle but he seemed reluctant to do so. In the end it was Frank who replied. "The thing is, we were all just quietly living our lives when this girl, Mia is it?"

Aiden nodded.

"Yeah, well then she turned up. Do you wanna shine some light on her?" Frank asked.

"I used to know her a long time ago that's all." Aiden replied.

"I've never met her. What's she like?" Jonny asked.

"It's difficult to say..."

Jonny interrupted, "In your opinion?"

"She's a spy that's one thing we do know. Or at least she was, and I don't think they ever retire do they?"

"What else?" Jonny asked impatiently.

"She's here, we know that, I saw her with my own eyes."

"Yes, Ben mentioned that. You saw her from the upper deck

of a bus and recognised her after hundreds of years?" Jonny didn't hide his scepticism.

"Well not hundreds, but yeah." Aiden seemed offended anyone would doubt him.

"You knew her that well?" Jonny raised a quizzical eyebrow.

He nodded firmly

"Hell of a memory," Jonny persisted

"You wouldn't understand."

"Try me."

Aiden sighed. "When you get old there are certain people so deeply etched onto your memory bank they will always be there. Sometimes in that brief moment before you're fully awake, you hear them or see them like it's real."

"Really?" Jonny replied.

"Yeah really. They carry the taste of unfinished business. They linger like ghosts."

"Like ghosts?"

"Yeah."

"And this Mia is like a ghost."

"Never stopped haunting me."

Frank coughed. He felt uncomfortable. It was like prying on a private moment. Jonny dropped his earlier scepticism. He had no choice, this guy was obviously genuine.

"Ok," he said. "So she's here. And if she's here we can find her."

"So," Frank said softly. "You were an item?"

Aiden smiled. "We were, yeah."

"Huh."

Jonny interrupted the touching moment and gestured impatiently towards Frank and Ben. "Why was she spying on them?"

"I don't know. It depends what they're into I guess." He smiled at Frank to show he meant no offence.

"What sort of people does she go after?"

"Who knows, what difference does it make?"

"Who do you think she works for?"

"Back then it was the Stasi. But everything's changed now. The wall fell years ago so—" he paused, "Whoever pays the most I suppose. It's all about money these days. You should ask my mate."

"What mate?" Jonny asked suspiciously.

"A guy I was at school with. He was more involved than me. I was just an innocent lovesick puppy who blindly fell into that mess. He was right in the thick of it. He was in the band. He knew everybody."

"Was he involved in the darker stuff?"

"He went to prison when it all came on top."

"What band?" Jonny asked.

"Snarling dogs."

Jonny started typing. "What was his name?"

"Stevie, Stevie Williams."

"What was it like back then?" Ben wanted to know.

"It was great."

"Life was easier, yeah?"

"Not really. If I had to sum it up I'd say, easier to get by if you didn't mind livin' in a shithole and eating rubbish. But there was a ridiculous amount of casual violence. People getting beaten up all the time, usually over nothing."

"This RobBob sounds a character," interrupted Jonny.

"He was indeed."

"Who?" Ben asked.

"RobBob. He was an original punk. But he was more than that, much more. Snarling Dogs were his band."

"It says here," Jonny piped up, "That he was an anarchist with connections to the IRA."

Aiden smiled. "He was what you call Antifa nowadays. He liked chasing fascists off the streets."

"He worked with the IRA?" Ben sounded impressed.

"The IRA?" Frank sounded dubious. "Your mates were IRA?"

Aiden smiled. "They were anti-fascist. They'd work with anyone who hated Nazis. And trust me there were a lot of Nazis about in those days."

"It says here that he travelled to Belfast in the 80s to meet known republicans." Jonny interjected helpfully.

"Who cares what some kook on the internet says."

"It's an MI6 file," he replied.

Aiden glanced at the screen. It did indeed show the MI6 logo and had TOP SECRET plastered across the page. He cursed the internet. You couldn't get away with anything these days.

"There were Irish guys around sometimes but I dunno if they were Republicans, probably just drinking pals or something. You know what the authorities are like for exaggerating."

He looked around the room. Nobody was buying it.

"You know what they're like," he insisted.

"It says here he was suspected of planting bombs," Jonny noted.

"I never saw any bombs."

"Never heard any explosions?"

He suddenly had a flashback and smiled reflexively. He had just remembered something. It was time to come clean.

"Actually now you mention it, there was an explosion once. I remember they tried to pin it on him. It was an antisemitic printers that went up. Some people he'd had a run in with. But there was no proof. I remember they tried to blame RobBob and Stevie, but nothing ever stuck. It was just rumours."

"They sound like good people to me," Jonny declared.

Ben and Frank shared a worried look.

This was far more than a bit of late-night graffiti. This was bombs and far right groups and real terrorists. Not the keyboard warrior type sitting opposite them. These people were old school. They planted bombs.

Ben hated fascists as much as the next guy but when he'd

agreed to let Jonny stay for a few nights nobody had mentioned any of this.

But what could he do now?

"Do we need to involve other people?" Ben asked nervously whilst sneaking a glance at Frank, looking for support.

"Yeah," Frank agreed. "He's here now. Why not ask him?"

Jonny stopped typing and directed a question straight at Aiden. "If you were holding the government to ransom, what would you ask for?"

Aiden's face broke into a gentle smile. "It's funny you should ask. I pondered that recently. I even started to make a list."

"I said make a list," Ben interrupted.

"The list was pointless." Aiden continued, "You don't need a list. You only need one sentence."

"Which is?"

"Put the Swedish in charge of the world."

"What?" replied three unconvinced voices in tandem.

"That's ridiculous," said Frank.

"You'd be better off with a list," said Ben.

"Why the Swedish?" asked Jonny.

"What's the one thing everybody wants?"

"Money?"

"A quiet life?"

"Good health?"

Aiden answered his own question. "I think it's happiness. We're only on this little blue planet for a few short decades. Don't we all just wanna be happy?"

"I guess," agreed Ben.

"Yeah, maybe," Frank reluctantly conceded.

"I like the concept," said Jonny.

"Every year," Aiden told them, "the United Nations release a *Happiness index*. It's always the same names at the top of that list: Norway, Finland, Denmark and above all, Sweden. Where are we? Way down, that's where. People here might be a lot of things but happy is not one of them."

"You can't demand people are happy," said Frank.

"It's too simplistic," said Ben.

"I like that you question everything," Jonny said.

"You can't order people to be happy," Frank repeated. "It's absurd. If that's your big plan, I think you've made a wasted journey."

Aiden shrugged. "You asked."

"What would your friend say, the original punk?" asked Jonny.

"I can find out."

Is that necessary?" asked Ben.

"Yes please, find out," said Jonny.

"And in exchange you'll find Mia?"

"It's a deal," Jonny replied.

"Great, I'll see what I can do." Aiden and Jonny shook hands. Ben and Frank exchanged another worried look.

129

RobBob sipped his tea, glanced down at his ankle tag and frowned. With power restored he was at it's mercy once more.

Bloody thing.

Forbidden to leave the house by government order. Lucrative contract to ensure he complied awarded to the Trust.

He'd devoted his whole life to justice and it had all been completely pointless. The realisation was a bitter pill to swallow.

So what if everything he'd prophesied since the 1970s, every single thing, had come true. It was irrelevant. They'd won and he'd lost. They were more powerful now than they'd ever been. There was no way anyone could stop the Trust.

And he, well, he glanced at his tag again. He was a prisoner of war. There was no need to further punish an old soldier.

It was nearly one o'clock. At least with power he could listen to the news. It had come to that. Listening to the news was the biggest act of rebellion left to him. He was riddled with the aches and pains of too many battles. Yet still he struggled to accept his fighting days were behind him.

He sighed as he settled into his comfy old chair. He looked forward to one o'clock these days.

He believed the terrorists were the best thing that had happened to his country for years. He just hoped they were young and when they'd finished with the government, they'd take on the Trust.

He wanted to pass the baton. Rebellion was a young man's game.

His whole life had been late nights and smoky rooms with a diet of takeaways and scraps. It left its mark. Trying to overthrow a corrupt system leaves no time for going to the gym or keeping up with your five a day.

He knew deep down it was hopeless, but the rise of this latest cell offered just enough to keep the embers of hope burning.

Without hope we are nothing. Thank God someone has taken up the mantle and they're running with it. He smiled again.

And who can blame them? What have they got to lose?

Kids today are never going to be property owners. Without the potential to own capital what is the point of capitalism?

I'll tell you, he thought. *There is none. The system is broken and like when the Soviet Union collapsed, people will just have to get used to a different way of doing things.*

He'd been preaching the same old message all his adult life and finally the masses were ready to listen to the kids. It was what he had always hoped for and it was beautiful to behold.

Cut the bullshit and give us some truth, they demanded.

It was a continuation of the old punk message. It was the essence of everything Joe Strummer had stood for.

The revolution that had lain dormant for decades was back with a vengeance. Passed on into the capable hands of dedicated rebels and it filled him with joy.

Can I hear the echoes of the days of '79?

Imagine if they actually manage change? I could die happy.

Although he had to concede there would still be the one regret. Having the talent to make a difference and squandering it. Crossing to the dark side.

Jacob knew what they would do with power once it was in their hands.

The betrayal still hurt after all these years.

He should pay for what he did.

RobBob pushed on the door and a mouse ran behind the fridge. He didn't care, it was one o'clock. He turned on his television.

130

Aiden went to Stevie's parent's house bright and early the very next morning. It felt odd strolling through the streets of his childhood after so long.

He was tempted to approach the house via the back lane for old times' sake.

He recalled Stevie's mum always at the kitchen window. She never missed a trick. Different times. Women don't stay in kitchens like they used to. People don't use back lanes like they used to either.

Neither was he still a kid, so he went to the front and for the first time in his life rang the bell.

Some child opened it.

"Is your Dad in?"

"Oo are you?"

"Is your mum in?"

"Ma," he shouts, hiding his body behind the door.

Aiden heard somebody coming. Back in the day footsteps would have clattered across the wooden floorboards. Old man Stanray would have poked his head out to see who it was. But the hallway was carpeted throughout now. The whole building was a single-family home. Nice people who didn't clatter.

The child disappeared as the door swung open.

"Yes?" she sounded suspicious until she saw who was standing there. "Aiden!" she squealed, throwing the door wide open. "What a lovely surprise. How are you?"

He beamed. It was Nikki. With her headscarf and apron she looked like an old housewife. With her pierced nose and wisps of neon green hair escaping from the scarf she looked about sixteen.

"I'm good, good. You look great."

"Thanks, you too."

"How've you been?"

"Alright, you know."

"I never know who's gonna pop their head round that door, but you, I would never have guessed. Still writing? You look like a writer."

"Yeah, still writing."

"I suppose you're lookin' for him?"

He nodded. "Yeah."

"You're not gonna get him into trouble are ya?"

"No"

"Liar," she laughed.

Aiden laughed along. What else could he do?

"We're all proud of you, writing that book."

"Thanks." He fidgeted uncomfortably. Any second now and she'd want to talk about Mia.

Nikki could see he wanted to get going.

"He'll be at the yard."

"His old man's yard?"

"Yeah."

"Thanks." He turned to leave.

"Good to see you again," she called as he made his way down the street.

He turned and gave her a little wave.

Aiden spotted Stevie filling bird feeders. He crept up on him and in a voice dripping with disappointment said, "Bloody Hell, you reduced to feeding birds like an old man now?"

Stevie turned and squealed in delight, "Look who it is." He rushed to hug his pal.

"Fancy you turning up. I would never have guessed."

He held him at arm's length and studied him, then looked him right in the eye and asked, "Did you bring any sunflower seeds?"

It was a ridiculous question. They burst out laughing.

When the reunion was done, Stevie settled into an old plastic garden chair. He motioned for Aiden to take the other one.

"If we sit quiet, they'll come."

That single sentence took Aiden right back to when they were kids.

They sat in easy silence and stared at the feeders. The companionship had already returned. It was like Aiden had just come back from a bathroom break.

"So this is you now?"

Stevie glanced across frowning. "Shhh."

Aiden nodded an apology.

"Here they come," Stevie whispered, as a pair of sparrows landed on the feeder.

They sat in silence for ten minutes watching the birds and remembering the old days. Only after the sparrows, tits, a robin and a blackbird had taken their fill did Stevie quietly ask, "So what's up?"

"Do you still see RobBob?"

"He's just Rob these days. Yeah, we keep in touch."

"How is he?"

"His health ain't the best. He don't get out much."

"Still fighting the good fight is he?"

"That'll never change."
"But you're a family man?"
"Why?" Stevie asked.
"There are some people that want to meet you both."
"Some people?"
Yeah, it's a long story but they're genuine. They need advice and they came to me. I told them they'd be better off talking to you. Then they googled Snarlin' Dogs and now they wanna meet you both."
"They must be desperate to come to you."
Aiden smiled, "They are."
"An' how do you know 'em?"
"I just know 'em."
"All a bit secretive innit?"
Aiden shrugged.
"Subterfuge." Stevie smiled. "Like the old days."
"Yeah."
A bird Aiden didn't recognise landed on the feeder.
Stevie put his finger to his lips.
When it flew off he spoke again. "As much as I'd love to, I can't get involved. Nikki would kill me." He rose to his feet. "But Rob will love this shit. Let's go an' see him."

131

"Rob it's me," Stevie called through the letterbox.
He stood up and smiled reassuringly at Aiden.
"He takes a while to come to the door. Like I said, his health ain't what it was."
Aiden wondered for the second time what that meant.
Finally a silhouette appeared behind the door. "Stevie?"
"Yeah."
The door opened.
"I got Aiden with me, you remember him?"
"Huh."
"He wants to speak to you. Can we go through?"
Rob huffed something that might have been consent and Stevie passed him in the narrow hallway.
"I've got nothing to drink."
"We ain't thirsty."
Aiden nodded a greeting whilst trying not to appear shocked. RobBob looked at death's door.
With a nod of recognition, he gestured for Aiden to go past him.
The flat smelled of stale air. Aiden walked down the

passageway trying to hold his breath.

In the kitchen RobBob looked him up and down and asked not particularly pleasantly, "So what do you want?"

No preamble? Ok fine, We'll do it your way. Sooner I get out of here the better anyway.

"There's this guy, a friend of mine. He's caught up in some stuff. He needs some advice. I dunno, your name came up an' I agreed to see if you was still around cos maybe you can stop him doing something stupid."

"What is this Piccadilly Circus? I don't want strangers coming round here. I don't like visitors."

"Yeah, don't worry about that. You'd have to go to him."

"Well that's not happening." He lifted his trouser leg high enough to reveal the electronic tag.

Aiden didn't ask why he was tagged,

"Ah," he said. "So you can't leave here?"

"And if I do, they know where I've been. Looks like you made a wasted trip."

Rob turned to Stevie. "Did you bring my biscuits?"

"Of course."

"Put the kettle on then."

They stayed for a cuppa and although he feigned disinterest Rob was clearly flattered that he was being sought out. It had been a long time since anyone had wanted his advice.

"Tell 'em I'd come if I could."

"I will."

They left him and walked to the corner.

"You wanna come back for something to eat? Nikki would be thrilled an' you can meet the kids."

"Another time mate, I should go tell 'em what he said."

They were outside a shop about to go their separate ways. There was a newspaper A-board on the pavement—

Dangerous terrorists still at large.

Stevie nodded towards it. "Crazy eh?"

A smile flitted briefly across Aiden's lips. "Yeah," he agreed. "Be careful, it's a jungle out there."
"I know."
They hugged and headed in different directions.

132

Jacob was explaining himself to the board for the second time in as many weeks. He was feeling a lot better now since power had been restored.

"The terrorists have given our clients a taste of life without the web. They didn't like it. We can exploit that. The House has been able to provide extra resources for us to hunt them down. Even the public accepts harsher measures."

"But we haven't caught them yet and they've warned us. What if they come after us?"

"They won't."

Before, they would have taken him at his word. Now things were different, the public and the clients were not the only ones feeling the pressure.

"What guarantees do you have?"

"None as such."

"None." the chairman let the word hang in the air before he added, "Do we, sorry, do you know who they are? Who they are working for?"

"Not yet sir."

"Not yet." Again he left the words hanging uncomfortably.

"Can they get into our system?"

"I doubt it sir."

"If they gain access to our files, our secrets, I dread to think what would happen."

"We are not under attack sir."

"But if we were, what would be our last resort?"

Jacob umm'ed and ahh'ed as best he could, hoping to move on but the board were not in the mood to be placated. They smelt weakness and they craved reassurance.

"Could you please answer the question."

"The killswitch sir."

The murmurs of discontent grew louder around the table. If any single answer was bad for business, it was that one.

"Shut down the internet completely? Are you mad? This partial shutdown crippled us. Think of the damage to the economy if it was total?"

"I'm sure it won't come to that sir."

"They've already done it!" He sounded exasperated.

"Not completely sir."

"Find them!" he shouted.

"We will sir."

"You better."

Jacob went to rally his troops. They were Leetabix, the best computer experts in the country. He had handpicked them, treated them like royalty and rewarded them handsomely. Now it was time for them to earn those privileges.

Someone must pay for putting Jacob through such humiliation.

When they were finally assembled he addressed them. "I am not pointing fingers of blame but we must have missed something. We need to go over everything again. These terrorists must be on file somewhere. I will be in my office, bring me something useful, people."

Over the next couple of hours Leetabix operatives came into

his office with varying opinions. But nothing really led anywhere until his attention was drawn to the Zodiac cafe operation and a photograph was placed before him.

He snatched it up from the desk. I know this girl," he declared.

"You do?"

He held it to his face as though studying it more closely. He was actually playing for time.

Mia! What the hell?

"Remind me," he said.

"She was watching a cell but they were deemed of no interest." Jacob looked across the desk, the very epitome of composure now. He actually smiled. "Interesting."

"You know her you say?"

"She used to be a photographer, many years ago. I didn't know she was still around."

"Want us to find her?"

"Yes. Ask her again about that cafe cell."

They left and he was alone with his thoughts.

I don't like it.

Then another thought occurred to him, *She might have something on me from back in the day.*

The last thing he needed was his carefully cultivated public image being thrown into question now, when it was imperative to give the appearance of complete control.

Jacob was a wily old fox. HIs instincts were usually reliable and they did not like her turning up unexpectedly. It might just be a coincidence, but he hated coincidences. He felt the pressure turning up a notch.

133

Aiden went back to the flat to give them the bad news.

"That's not a problem," Jonny replied nonchalantly. "I can turn off his tracker."

Nobody bothered to question it. They all knew he was capable of hacking into anything.

"Think he'll come then?" Frank asked.

So, Aiden returned to Rob's.

"If you give me the serial number of your tag, my friend can turn it off."

"What? How?"

"I dunno, he just can."

"Who is this guy?"

"Best he tells you himself."

"Could I guess his identity if I followed the news?"

"Yeah."

On Aiden's next visit they were staring at the flashing green light on his ankle.

It faded then died as they watched.

Rob went to the door. He tentatively dangled his leg beyond the threshold, nothing happened.

"Let's go," he said, barely containing his excitement. He looked better than he had for months.

134

Aiden made the introductions.

Frank acted as though he was meeting a celebrity.

"You actually met Joe Strummer?"

"Yeah here and there, you know back in the day."

"Wow."

Jonny was on his best behaviour, barely argumentative at all.

Ben tried to be enthusiastic but couldn't shake a feeling of impending doom. He expected the doors to get booted in any moment.

He now had a handful of 'undesirables' in his flat. At least one of whom was definitely breaking parole terms.

This was way out of his league. He used to think a bit of graffiti made him a rebel. He was seriously reassessing that.

Still, at least his guests were all reasonably professional, discreet and stood a fighting chance of avoiding detection. And they had a secret weapon. They had Jonny.

He made sure no cameras ever picked any of them up going in or out, but even so, this thing was getting out of control.

"So you lot are the terrorists everyone's looking for?" Rob said. "I'm impressed."

"We're not terrorists," protested Ben.

"He is," said Frank, pointing at Jonny.

"What's your favourite Clash track?" asked Jonny.

"London Calling, every time."

Jonny smiled appreciatively.

"So what's the problem?" Rob asked.

"They don't like my plan." Jonny glanced at Ben and Frank as he spoke.

"What plan?"

"The social media scores."

This rag tag bag of misfits were the terrorists holding the world to ransom. Secretly, deep down inside, Rob was absolutely thrilled.

"I see. So what's next?" he said calmly.

"There is no *next*," Frank blurted out. "That's the problem."

"If you call it a problem," Jonny snapped.

"I do."

Jonny looked as though he might actually be sulking.

"That is so smart," Rob interrupted with a bit of general praise. That got their attention.

"What?"

"Let's say for argument's sake there is no plan." He looked around at their expectant faces. "They don't know that do they?" He beamed. "For all they know we've got it all worked out. We hold all the cards here. Good work guys, seriously. And you've managed to stay out of reach, excellent work."

"We hold all the cards?"

"Yeah, we should go for the kill right now, while we've got the upper hand."

Ben noticed he used the words *we* and *kill*.

Oh shit. He's gonna make a bomb. Now I am a terrorist.

Frank felt the need to chip in. "We could make them stop using fossil fuels. That would be a positive thing."

"Definitely," Rob agreed. "But to really cut the head off the beast we need to go after the Trust."

There he goes with the 'we' again, thought Ben.

"Why them?" Frank asked.

"Because they are making life unbearable for huge swathes of the population. They are using Leetabix to keep everyone in line. They are investing in oil, plastics, fracking— all the things that are killing humanity. They don't give a shit about anything and too much is never enough for those ghouls."

"They control Leetabix?" Ben sounded surprised.

"Yeah."

"The reason they keep making tighter laws against people like us."

"That's right."

"Sneaky bastards," said Ben.

"It's a scam. The Trust wouldn't dare shut down the internet really. It would cost too much financially. But Leetabix can claim they will and governments and businesses all over the world will bend over backward to avoid such a thing."

"Do you want a cuppa?" said Frank.

"Have you got any biscuits?" Rob asked.

They sat around dunking biscuits and listening to Rob. It was his chosen subject. He had years of experience. He was an expert in the Trust and their underhand ways. So naturally up until now, being an expert nobody had been remotely interested in anything he had to say on the subject.

"For years, the Trust have been closing down activist groups and anyone else that threatened the status quo. There's a guy called Jacob in charge of Leetabix."

"I can't believe they bat for the other side."

"How do you think they managed to escape every time there was a purge?"

"I thought they were good."

"Who's this Jacob guy?"

I used to know him. We used to be friends."

"He seems squeaky clean," said Jonny who was already googling the name.

"He's not," Rob insisted. He's just cleaned up his history somehow."

"I'll dig deeper."

"They'll be looking for you," Rob said. "Troublesome cells don't normally last long and you guys are the most trouble they've encountered for years."

"We're not a cell. We only met recently."

Rob nodded approvingly. "Much harder to get caught that way. Stayed apart until the plan was in operation, is that it?"

Jonny half smiled. "Not really. So you know this Jacob?"

"I used to back in the day. A long time ago. Like you just said, he's been squeaky clean for years. His wayward youth has been scratched from the record. If a scumbag like me turns up you don't get anywhere near him. Trust me I've tried. For years I've been trying to bring his past back to haunt him. But it was impossible without proof. I needed photographs or something but the only person with a camera back then was Mia remember, and she's disappeared off the face of the earth."

"Not quite."

"What do you mean?"

"I saw her the other week."

"No."

"Yeah."

"We need to find her."

"I know," agreed Aiden.

Jonny had been searching as he listened. "The Trust are financing candidates for elections all over Europe," he said.

Frank passed the biscuits around.

"We're screwed," Rob moaned. "They've got the newspapers in their pockets. They've got websites chucking out a constant barrage of misinformation. And they come down on any opposition like a ton of bricks. It's impossible to damage an organisation that powerful. You end up broken or in prison, or both."

"What code did you use?" Jonny asked him.

"Code? I don't know about code. What are you on about."

"A little code goes a long way." He tapped a few keys. "They like misinformation do they? It doesn't matter what people think as long as there is doubt, eh? The actual truth is just one of many theories, is it? Whoever shouts the loudest is right are they? Ok, let's play them at their own game." As he ranted so he tapped keys.

Rob was beaming. This was music to his ears. The Trust had always defeated him in the past, but he'd never had an international team of highly skilled terrorists in his corner before.

"If their people win the elections they'll have control of the largest stock markets on the planet."

"It's worse than that," Rob insisted. "They've dusted off the Mussolini handbook and combined it with the internet. In a nutshell, they're gonna put us all into categories. Then when they slip tame puppets into high office, woe betide those in the wrong category."

"The public aren't stupid. They'll see through that."

"Oh really? Have you seen the internet? All they care about is dumb memes and who had what for tea. Fooling them is like taking candy off a baby. No scratch that, like taking candy off a baby with no arms or legs, or eyes."

"Some might bring the average down I'll grant you."

"More than *some*. People on the whole are dumb as fuck. Although it's not completely their fault, forty years of under financing education will do that. The Trust have been quietly playing the long game for years."

"This can't all be down to the Trust," Ben insisted. "One company can't hold that much sway."

"They do," said Rob in a voice weary from decades of defeats at the hands of such a formidable foe.

"They do," said Jonny who was reading up on their wide and varied interests.

"Fuckin' hell," muttered Ben.

"They have a bottomless war chest, they hate being put under the spotlight and they will sue anyone who tries."

"What are the government doing?"

"Fuck all, they don't even realise the country is under attack. They still think the next war will be fought with nuclear submarines."

"There's only really one thing that will solve all our problems," Rob stated matter of factly, and they all stopped to listen.

"We need to run a candidate of our own and make sure they win."

He turned to Jonny. "Can we do that?"

"Of course."

"Have you got anyone in mind?" asked Ben.

"Yeah. *Me*," replied RobBob.

Frank snorted, "You? That's ridiculous."

"Why is that ridiculous?"

"No disrespect but ain't you a bit old?"

"He's younger than he looks," said Jonny, then he turned to Rob. "How old do you wanna be?"

"Is your health up to it?"

"He's a picture of health," said Jonny. "He has an annual check-up, has done for years."

"Aren't you a well-known troublemaker?" said Ben. "They'd never let it happen. This is real life, the good guys never win."

"I like it," said Jonny. "With you in power we could call all the shots."

"Exactly," Rob confirmed.

Jonny started typing. "By the time I've finished you'll be so clean people will wonder why you've never had a medal."

He said it so matter of factly Rob wasn't sure he had heard correctly.

"You'll do what?"

"Clean your history."

"You can do that?"

"Sure, no problem." He typed something into his Mac. "That thing about you having involvement with the IRA." He was tapping away furiously as he spoke. "That has to go, for starters."

He clicked once more and read what was now on the screen. "That's better," he said. "Now you were trying to find peace in Northern Ireland. And the one person who accused you of having Republican ties was sued into bankruptcy. That should make anybody else think twice."

"But you can't alter every single reference on the web."

"I can if I utilise the Killswitch."

"The what? Isn't that what Leetabix are threatening to use?"

"Yeah, but they're doing it wrong."

"What?"

"They are threatening."

"And you're not?"

"No, I'm actually going to do it."

"You can't."

"Nobody will even notice."

"Haven't we talked about this?" exclaimed Frank.

"It's too extreme?" added Ben.

"It's the perfect crime," Jonny said. "Nobody will ever know. I'm not talking about forever. I'm saying just for a nano second. Long enough to get our ducks in a row."

"And that would allow you to rewrite history."

"It would no longer be *his story* it would be *our story*."

That was good enough for Rob. "It's perfect," he said.

"How do you know it'll even work?" asked Frank.

"Will it?" He looked to Jonny, they all did.

"Like a dream." Jonny's enthusiasm knew no bounds.

Rob had waited his whole life for a chance to make a real difference. He wasn't about to pass up an opportunity this promising. He kept his health concerns to himself.

"See!"

"So you'll just turn it off and on again?" Ben asked doubtfully.

"Yep, the briefest of nano seconds and when it comes back on—" he struggled for the correct words to finish the sentence with, "…the world is a better place."

"Rob will make a better Prime Minister than any we've had in my lifetime," Frank sounded genuinely excited.

"The threat of the Killswitch is their golden goose," Aiden reminded them. "You're planning to steal their thunder. They had things neatly wrapped up for years then you come along with your puppy dog virus. Now you're going to steal their last remaining party trick and force changes they don't want. They won't be happy. Aren't you concerned?"

"They'll have enough to deal with," Jonny replied cryptically.

"Do you really think you can pull it off?" Ben asked doubtfully.

Jonny nodded.

135

At Scotland Yard a tense meeting between the country's top police officers was running late.

"You've called in who?" asked the chief superintendent incredulously.

"The Trust."

"The last thing those people need is more access to our files. Why can't you just put our own people on it?"

"Because our budget has been slashed to the bone. They have resources they can utilise immediately."

"I don't like it."

"We don't have much choice."

"And what are they demanding in return?"

"They expect to be considered favourably for any contracts that come up."

"Naturally," the word dripped with distaste. He hated the politics that was deemed essential to the running of the police force these days. In his opinion if the Trust paid their fair share of taxes, the country could afford a proper police force and wouldn't have to rely on corporate handouts.

136

Aiden was still at the flat. He was reluctant to leave until he'd spoken to Jonny.

"Would it be possible to erase Mia's past?"

"Why?"

He didn't want to say, *So we can ride off into the sunset together, complete with new identities.* Instead he said. "I just wondered."

"We haven't found her yet," Frank reminded him. "She may not want to be disappeared."

"She will," he stated confidently under his breath.

"She'll be pardoned," said Rob. "It'll be the first law I pass."

"I'd rather she was clean," he said anxiously.

"That seems a reasonable request," Jonny reassured him.

137

Mia could get to the corner shop and back in a few minutes. It was risky but she had no food left. She put on a baseball cap and pulled up her collar and went for it.

She loaded her basket with basics and went to pay.

The shopkeeper smiled as she approached his till.

"Hi."

"Hi."

She kept her face away from the camera on the wall behind him. She wasn't to know he had another more discrete one positioned for people wearing hats. He knew from bitter experience the public were not to be trusted.

Not her, she seemed sweet. It was the others.

She smiled and handed over cash. The till pinged as he fed it.

Simultaneously alarm bells started ringing, Literally.

Jonny's computer emitted the sound of an old World War II siren. He folded the corner of the page and put down his paperback.

"Gotcha!"

"Is it her?"

Jonny glanced at the screen for a split second. He could see her on the security cameras outside the shop. He pressed a couple of buttons and span the computer around on the table so they could see the picture.

"That's her."

"Corner shop, Ladysmith Road."

"That's just up the hill."

"Let's see where she goes."

He tracked every camera all the way to her front door.

"Let's go," Aiden said impatiently.

"I'll get my car," said Frank.

It was bizarre. She was a fifteen-minute drive away.

Jonny returned to his paperback whilst Aiden tried to smother the adrenaline that was pumping through him.

He was remembering that cruel fateful morning in Berlin. He recalled the crisp winter temperature that sent out little clouds as you spoke. He'd hated cold, frosty mornings ever since.

In his mind's eye he saw her again. It was always her heavy overcoat that came first. The rest of her fell in around the coat. She'd bought it in a charity shop and pinned a purple flower on the lapel. She'd worn it everywhere in those final few days.

She'd ruined purple flowers and crisp winter mornings for him forever. Despite the head fuck, he persevered with his trip down memory lane. He couldn't help it.

The 'normalness' of the whole thing always came through loud and clear. She'd ruined 'normal' for him as well. It was incredible how one bad morning can have so many negative connotations on so many aspects of your life for years and years afterwards.

Even now the mere thought of her churned up his insides.

Despite that, despite everything he would take her back in a heartbeat.

A tap on the window made him jump back to the present. Frank was back with the car. Aiden swallowed hard and tried to appear composed.

138

Mia used her hip to slam the front door closed and went through to the kitchen. She made herself a sandwich and put the shopping away. Then she went upstairs to the loo. She touched up her lipstick and put her phone on the side.

She went downstairs and out through the back door.

139

Frank crawled to a halt a little down the road from her address and gently applied the handbrake. Alongside him Aiden looked like a ghost.

"Are you ok?"

He nodded unconvincingly. "Yeah," he added. He was fooling no one.

"Want me to go?" Ben asked from the back seat.

"No, I'm good, all good," he lied as he opened the door. "Wait here, I won't be long."

The car occupants exchanged a concerned glance as they watched him approach the house. They watched him cross the road.

"Does he look alright to you?"

"Nah, he looks fucked."

"That's what I thought."

Aiden stood on the threshold holding his breath, listening intently for signs of life. There were none. He rang the bell and stood back. He waited a few minutes and rang again. Really held his finger to it this time. He was wasting his time. He already knew there was nobody home. He went to the window and peered through.

"What's he doing?"

They watched him disappear from view.

"He's gone round the back," Frank confirmed whilst checking his wing mirrors for witnesses. The street was deathly quiet. He focused on staying calm and sat tight.

Aiden strolled up the side of the house as though he had every right to be there. He squeezed past a wheelie bin and came to a side gate. He tried the latch but it was locked. He briefly considered jumping it but that was more of a young man's game. Besides he didn't need to. This was the place. She was here. Well, not right now, but he'd found her. He could feel it in his bones. He returned to the car.

"No good?" asked Ben

"Nah," Aiden replied. "She's gone."

"Don't worry mate, we'll find her."

Aiden forced a half smile and a nod of the head. Frank started the engine and prepared to drive away just as his burner began to ring.

It was Jonny.

He put him on loudspeaker.

"She's in a pub. It's not far from your current location. I'll send a map. Call me when you get there."

They drove in silence until Frank stopped the car on a deserted side street. They could see the pub on the corner ahead. He glanced across at Aiden, who looked better than he had a few minutes ago.

"Ok mate?"

"Yeah, Fine."

Frank nodded and dialled Jonny's mobile.

He answered on the first ring. "We're outside the pub."

"Good, she's still inside."

Jonny was watching Mia in real time on the screen on his lap.

"She's sitting on her own at the bar."

"Ok, we're going in."

He ended the call.

"We'll wait here?"

Aiden nodded and climbed out.

Over the years he'd fine-tuned precisely the words he would use if he ever got the chance. Ever saw her again. Now the moment had arrived and he couldn't recall a single one. He'd no idea what he was going to say. He should stop and gather his thoughts. But his legs refused. His feet kept moving until somehow the pub door was closing behind him.

He saw her the moment he entered. Once again the recognition was instant. He would never mistake her. How could he?

He'd barely taken two steps and she looked up. She smiled. It was a weary smile as though nothing surprised her any more. As though she'd seen it all. She sat up straight with her shoulders back and watched him cross the floor.

"Hello, Mia."

"Hallo, Aiden."

He just wanted to sweep her up in his arms and run away.

"Your hair's different?" she said, As though picking up from a conversation they'd had a week ago.

He didn't know how to respond. He laughed; it was more relief than anything,

"It's so good to see you."

"You too," and when she smiled the weariness vanished. She was the same girl he'd fallen head over heels in love with all those years ago.

"What can I get you?" interrupted the barman.

"Pint, pint please."

"Make that two," Mia added.

"Shall we sit over there?" She pointed towards a quiet table in the corner.

He nodded and she moved while he waited for their drinks.

All too soon he was sliding into the seat across from her and the situation was so mundane he felt ridiculous. He'd imagined this moment for years. He'd always thought he'd let her know how she'd made him feel, deep down inside. But when he opened his mouth all that came out was, "I really missed you."

"Same," she said simply, and raised her glass. It was obvious she meant it. "Cheers," she added. He'd always loved that adorable accent.

"Cheers," he replied. And that was it. All the questions, the accusations went right out of his head. He didn't care about any of it.

"I saw you a few weeks ago but I was on a bus," he told her. "I went back and looked for you."

"You recognised me?"

"Straight away."

"How did you find me here?"

He sipped his drink and looked away. That was a tricky one. "What happened that day?" he asked instead and regretted it immediately.

Her eyes filled with sadness. "I was so stupid," she said, refusing to look at him. "I should never have trusted them. I should have told you everything."

She looked up and finished with a killer blow. "I should have stayed with you. We were so happy. That's the happiest I've ever been."

"I used to dream we were still together," he confessed. "Waking up was horrible."

They sat studying each other as the past slipped away like water under a bridge. It didn't matter anymore. They were too old, too tired for recriminations. Let sleeping dogs lie. This was an opportunity at happiness. One they should have grabbed first time around. But when you're young you don't know what you want until it's gone.

They were older now and age brings wisdom. And wisdom tells you if you're fortunate enough to get a second opportunity with the one that got away, grab it with both hands. Hold on tight and let the dice fall where they may.

"I want to be with you," she said simply.

"Good," he replied.

At this point she wrapped him tightly in her arms. It was their first physical contact for many years. Electricity sparked between them. It felt like two halves of the same body coming together. Aiden never wanted to let go again.

He'd had enough of loneliness. He wanted someone to love, someone to love him in return. He wanted her.

They finished their drinks. Then hand in hand walked the short distance to the car.

Ben had moved to the front seat, so they climbed in the back.

Frank started the engine and they pulled away.

"I'm Frank," he said, looking at her in the rear-view mirror, "This is Ben."

"Hallo."

"You can drop us at my place," Aiden suggested.

As far as he was concerned the mission was complete.

"We'll go back to the flat," Frank replied. "Jonny's expecting us."

"Who?" Mia asked.

"Jonny, he's a…" he hesitated. "He's a friend of ours."

She squeezed his hand furtively in the shadows of the back seat and he squeezed back.

140

Jacob was not used to receiving unexpected phone calls in the evening.

"What?" he snapped into the phone.

"We've lost her."

"You said you had her."

"We did but the cameras cut out."

"Cut out?"

"We watched her going into a pub but that's it."

"That's it?" He sounded incredulous.

"She never came out. Only the place is all locked up now, empty. You know what it's like. The cameras were playing up and we missed her. It's really strange."

"How is that strange?" Jacob shot back angrily. "That's not strange. They messed with the cameras. They took her. Get someone over to that pub. Find out where she went, who she left with."

Jacob did not want damaging footage from his youth to surface now. He wanted to speak to Mia.

141

The next day Jonny was up early. Using his wormholes, he entered a variety of networks. With the aid of artificial intelligence, he was breaking encryption, collecting private data in real time and storing it safely away.

When he was good and ready he flicked the Killswitch. Nobody noticed.

From the day the internet was conceived this was the one thing experts had always been afraid of.

Fortunately, most users didn't know enough to be afraid.

Anything Jonny didn't like had just been permanently deleted, altered or infected with malicious malware.

Malware that allowed him to read emails, harvest passwords, record conversations or turn cameras on and off in order to spy on people in real time.

His Mac started flashing so he tapped a key and a live CCTV feed was relayed directly to him.

He watched a car pull up outside a back street boozer.

Oh this is interesting.

Three men got out and headed into the pub.

They're not your average early bird drinkers.

He was already switching to the interior camera and turning up the volume.

Two meatheads hovered menacingly just inside the door. A third man approached the barman. "We're looking for this girl." He produced what was obviously a photograph so Jonny took a screenshot of it for later. "She was in here yesterday."

It was the same barman who had served Aiden and Mia. They were strangers to him. He owed them no favours. Jonny watched. Expecting him to give them up without hesitation.

"What are you then, police?" the barman asked.

"Do you remember her?"

Jonny thought the question too abrupt. His attitude was not one you'd immediately warm to. He was the sort who relied on intimidation more than a sparkling personality.

"I wouldn't tell you anything," he said to the screen. "You wanna brush up on your people skills."

This was a rough pub on the seedy side of town. The barman was not easily intimidated. "Show me the picture again," he said.

He gave it a cursory glance.

"Nah, 'fraid I can't help you. You're sure she was here?"

"I am. It was early evening. You must remember her, who she met, who she left with?"

"Nah sorry, never seen her before."

Jonny watched in deep appreciation. The barman would have no idea why his social media score was sky high the next time he checked it.

There was a sullen standoff. The barman cleaned a glass and smiled. He was toying with his visitors.

"Do you boys want a drink?" he asked.

The men returned to their car.

Jonny invalidated their tax and insurance and registered their MOT as failed. He also hacked into the police computer and registered the car as stolen. Then he returned to his work.

. . .

It was mid-morning before Mia joined them in the front room. She went and sat next to Aiden.

"Remember me?" asked Stevie.

She nodded. "You were the singer."

He sort of smiled. "Yeah, That was a long time ago."

"Yeah."

"You're not a punk anymore?"

"I'll die a punk."

She nodded.

"So what goes on here?" she asked.

"Who do you work for?" Jonny shot back.

She had met enough people like these in her time. She was fairly certain they were activists. The stroppy one with the Mac looked like a hacker. She assumed he had tracked her down as a favour to Aiden. His question confirmed things in her mind.

She turned to Aiden. "What does he want to know that for?"

"Best tell him. It's important" he said.

"You work for the Trust right?" Rob asked directly.

"Who are you guys? Aiden?"

"When was the last time you saw Jacob?"

"Who?"

"Why is he looking for you?"

"I don't know a Jacob."

142

In Jacob's department the elation at the web returning in full quickly turned to despair as they frantically searched for files that no longer existed. Something was horribly wrong.

They were Leetabix, they were the hunters. They were hand-picked, the best of the best. They could manipulate cyberspace and stop others doing the same.

Only whatever had happened here was beyond their comprehension. It had to be the terrorists. It was unnerving. As the morning wore on concern grew. Then just as mid-morning coffee was on the horizon they were suddenly under attack themselves.

Computer screens all froze in the same instant. Concern turned to blind panic. There was much frantic tapping of keys. It made no difference. They were locked out and couldn't understand why or how. It was a lot to get their conceited heads around.

Then just as suddenly, the computers jumped back into life. Three words played in a loop horizontally across the screens:

YOU WERE WARNED

All they could do was watch helplessly as one by one, every single file emptied.

Jacob was horrified. Things had gone his way without a hitch for so many years he genuinely couldn't grasp what was happening.

"It's impossible," he whispered, watching it happen. "Impossible."

143

In an ideal world the hacking of Leetabix would have remained strictly *need to know only* for many years. Except Jonny was setting the agenda now.

He gave up the location of the Leetabix farm on all constabulary social media sites. Everyone could see the posts. Leetabix had been ruining lives for years. They were in danger of being physically ripped apart. The police were forced to attend. With blue lights wailing they arrived just after the press. It was a great shot for the evening news.

A small crowd was already in attendance but they were just getting started, still at the chanting abuse stage. They hadn't yet formed a mob or started throwing things.

The police fanned out with military precision. One section formed a barricade to keep the public at bay whilst another entered the premises. Television cameras relayed it all into millions of homes.

Jacob was brought out in handcuffs loudly proclaiming his innocence. He was drowned out by angry chants. He could protest as much as he liked. His guilt was a foregone conclusion.

It was all there in black and white. Detailed files proving that he'd been a criminal his whole life. A teenage street thug who went on to defraud a nation. The evidence was overwhelming.

144

At Ben's there was a real party atmosphere. They were avidly devouring Sky news. The cameras had caught everything. The members of Leetabix being led away, the interior of their lair with all its electronic equipment, reams and reams of documents.

There was no need for press speculation as to what the files contained. Jonny had released everything. There were Trust archives going back decades. They revealed a clear strategy from austerity to Brexit and beyond, implemented purely to further enrich the super wealthy. They could never spend the money they already had. That was cynical enough. But the plan involved many, many poor souls suffering to satisfy the greed of those arrogant few.

People had long suspected as much but to have the incontrovertible truth laid out bare was infuriating. Soon the mob was baying for blood.

All files were available online to peruse at your leisure.

The same day, twenty million quid appeared in Aiden's bank account. He and Mia were going to grow old gracefully somewhere quiet where he could write and she could grow roses.

145

With the government guilty by association a snap election is called.

RobBob won by a landslide. His long history as a champion of the common people is there for all to see.

The online revelations about his opponents damaged them greatly. They got less than half Rob's votes between them.

On his first day in office he introduced a Basic Income and pumped billions of pounds into the National Health Service.

By the end of his first month a law was passed banning politicians from taking jobs in the private sector for twenty years after stepping down.

The public are ecstatic. They have a guaranteed monthly income and the doctor can see you at your earliest convenience. It's a great start for the new regime.

On the first anniversary of his coming to power, excitement was palpable. Rob was to appear in public for the first time in a year. A giant rally was to be televised live. When the time finally came the crowd welcomed him on stage as though the Kardashians were coming to town.

For the past twelve months he had been working round the

clock. Passing laws onto the statute books at a phenomenal rate. All of them based on the Swedish principle of what was best for the majority. Common people were seeing major improvements in their day-to-day lives and without the racist tabloids inviting them to get furious, they relaxed. Discovered they had more in common with a plumber from Poland than they did with an Eton toff. Public anger was redirected where it belonged and they wanted to thank Rob for showing them the light.

He raised his hands and the crowd fell silent. Rob began to speak. "As a nation we lost our way in recent years. The press forgot one guiding principle. To question what authority tells them."

The crowd cheered and whooped its agreement.

"Those in power forgot they are expected to provide answers. They opted instead to deny, delay, kick things into the long grass and even hide in fridges to avoid awkward questions. No more!"

The cheering went on so long Rob began to feel embarrassed. He raised his voice and soldiered on. The crowd quietened.

"Our beliefs are wide and varied but we can live in harmony if those in power remember one vital thing, GIVE US THE TRUTH!"

Rob sipped his water and waited for the pandemonium to abate. When they settled he continued his monologue.

"Since I was young this country's been a mess. The establishment's hypocrisy knew no bounds. Common people struggling to survive and never getting a chance to thrive, to actually live. Few were happy. And if there's one thing a wealthy economy should deliver, it's the right to be happy."

The crowd cheered.

"In one of the richest countries on the planet, day to day existence should not be a struggle. We did it because they said there were no other options. But it felt wrong. Like we knew we were being deceived and it left a bad taste. Now with the Leetabix files we finally have the truth."

They cheered so loudly he had to pause again. When the volume died down enough to continue, he shouted, "The truth, that is what I am promising you from here on in!"

Again, he was forced to pause for the cheers and hollers.

"The old ways must never be allowed to return!" he shouted, and the decibel level raised the roof.

He actually had another two pages prepared but he ended there because the cheering was so loud carrying on was pointless.

He waved at an assistant and music boomed through the speakers. The dancing that would carry on long into the next day exploded across the space below the stage.

It was a time for celebration.

Rob went back to his desk and left them to it.

He'd started with the important stuff, the NHS, a Basic Income. Then non-resident tax avoiding billionaires had their newspapers confiscated and handed over to proper journalists. Private schools were abolished. Every child from the royal family down would receive the same education. He knew ambitious parents would insist on a high bar and the whole country would benefit. Then he'd privatised the industries a country relies on.

There was much more to do but giving the speech had cost him a lot. Sitting at his desk he threw a handful of painkillers down his neck and forced himself to carry on reading. His pain was so bad he could barely move after exerting all that energy. Few were aware because the populace only ever saw him on a screen from the waist up.

He knew his body was failing, that he was dying. But he took enormous comfort from the knowledge his vision would reach fruition, come what may.

Jonny had developed RobBob02. A clone powered by artificial intelligence. So lifelike it had already appeared in his place at numerous zoom meetings and no one had been any the wiser.

His bones may be shovelled into the ground any day now, but he would live on. His manifesto would be implemented in full. What people really wanted was sex and drugs and rock and roll and Rob would give them exactly that. The first two were covered in the new public health act; details courtesy of the NHS and to ensure the third Joe Strummer's birthday would become a national holiday. His music would blast from sound systems across the land and rock and roll would never die.

Then Rob will pass away peacefully in his sleep, surrounded by his loved ones. The obituary had already been written, he'd approved it.

146

People needed a hero but with Aiden and Mia somewhere off in the sunset. With Jonny and RobBob busy taking care of the admin backlog and with Ben badly shaken by the whole experience and just wanting a quiet life, only Frank was left to soak up the focus, the thanks, the adulation.

The Internet proved conclusively that he risked life and limb to lead a crack team of punks, hackers and misfits to save the human race. Frank embraced his newfound celebrity status. He liked to sit in pubs and cafes impressing youngsters with elaborate tales of how he and his friends saved the world.

A young wide-eyed girl stared at him. "You're so brave," she said. "Were you ever scared?"

"I never considered my own safety. It just got so corrupt somebody had to do something. There comes a point when change has to happen. Like revolution is the only answer, you know?"

She smiled seductively at him and nodded.

"Besides, deep down we were just artists. Creating art is to embrace change. And nothing changes unless we make it change."

She nodded again. "Yeah," she said. "Can we do a selfie?"

147

Stevie and Nikki lay curled up together watching the news.

Nikki kissed him gently on the cheek. "I'm proud of you babe," she said.

He grinned, pointed at his cheek for another peck.

"Me? Why what did I do?"

"You did the right thing."

"Yeah, I suppose I did."

She kissed him again and her lips lingered for longer.

They headed into the bedroom with crossed wires. To him, 'doing the right thing' meant putting RobBob in the mix. To Nikki it meant putting her and the kids first and not getting involved.

But who cares? What difference does it make when you love someone?

148

Aiden had just written a real purple patch. He practically floated back into his chair and realised he was ravenous.

He started to read what he'd written but his stomach refused to be ignored a second longer. He hit *save* and headed to the kitchen.

Mia was at the table with dozens of red roses before her. She was pruning stems and arranging them in a giant glass vase.

"Crimson Glories if I'm not mistaken," he said.

They smiled at each other and he went to kiss her.

"Hungry?" she asked, sliding a plate towards him.

"Thanks babe."

She waited until he finished his first mouthful.

"How do you know about Crimson Glories?"

"I read it in a book."

"Ha!" she mocked, "You an' your books. Nobody reads books anymore."

"I do," he said. He winked at her and took a bite of his delicious sandwich.

ABOUT THE AUTHOR

Ian Parson, the Author of 'A Secret Step', 'The East End Beckons', 'The Grind' and 'Make or Break in Marrakesh' has written numerous articles and been published many times in a variety of magazines both in the UK and abroad. He is an active member of The Whitechapel Society and the Orwell Society, and currently divides his time between the South West & London.

To learn more about Ian Parson and discover more Next Chapter authors, visit our website at www.nextchapter.pub.

The Killswitch
ISBN: 978-4-82415-286-2

Published by
Next Chapter
2-5-6 SANNO
SANNO BRIDGE
143-0023 Ota-Ku, Tokyo
+818035793528

4th October 2022

Lightning Source UK Ltd.
Milton Keynes UK
UKHW031538221022
410927UK00006B/101